The Murder Makers

Suddenly, taking me by surprise, he pressed the sharp edge of his iron-bound shoe heel on to my instep. My foot was jammed immovably against the leg of the chair on which I sat.

He bared his teeth and blew cigar smoke in my face, increasing the pressure and screwing the flesh sideways until I sweated with the pain.

I smiled back and reached over, grabbing his thick wrist and straining his arm down on to the table cloth. I held it there as if we were friends shaking hands on a deal. Then I took my cigarette and pressed the red coal of it sizzling on to the soft flesh of the back of his hand.

He blinked, not admitting the pain by more than a slight involuntary jerk of his burning hand, but the pressure on my instep slackened as he took back his foot.

I released him and he gazed for a moment at the red blister. Then he raised his eyes to mine and smiled with his thick lips.

JOHN
ROSSITER
The
Murder
Makers

WALKER AND COMPANY · NEW YORK

First published in the United States of America in 1977 by the
Walker Publishing Company, Inc.

This paperback edition first published in 1985.

ISBN: 0-8027-3124-4

Library of Congress Catalog Card Number: 76-57854

Printed in the United States of America

10 9 8 7 6 5 4 3 2 1

To Willow, Judy and Nefertiti

Other titles in the Walker British Mystery Series

1

The sunlight ricocheted off the blue Mediterranean in sharp splinters, making me screw my eyes against its intolerable brightness.

Below me lay my hotel, a dazzling white block of masonry and, above me, a jet plane with swept-back wings climbed steeply into the clear sky, bleeding a twin trail of burnt kerosene from its straining engines.

There was an inner excitement thumping my chest as I waited for the slim woman in the green silk tunic walking slowly up the earth path towards me, her eyes anonymous behind tinted glasses.

I wasn't in Malaga for the running of the bulls. Nor to *sauté* my flesh in the brazen sun. I was bait, carefully chosen to snare this woman.

That I *was* bait didn't necessarily make it easy. Even a worm on a hook has to wriggle a bit. So she was still a challenge. Both to the ancestral goatishness I thought still lingered in my veins and the expertise I brought to the job.

I had seen her in the hotel, sitting alone at her table and in the bar, an expression of elegant self-assurance fixed on her attractive mouth. If she disliked eating or drinking alone, she wasn't going to admit it to the *hoi polloi*. But it was there for a perceptive male to recognize. As I had.

When she was near to me she smiled. Anything else would have been difficult. Apart from the lizards, the bees and a browsing goat with wrinkled udders, we were alone on the baking hillside.

I showed my teeth in return, made a token gesture at rising and sank back gratefully on my warm rock when she said, 'No, please do not.'

She nodded at the binoculars I held and paused. Her teeth were very white in her brown face. 'You are spying on the Spanish Navy?' she asked. Her voice was precise, the ghost of a foreign accent flattening its vowels.

Sliding to one side, I made room for her on my rock. 'Nothing more serious than the skiers.' There were several cutting frothy wakes in the flat water. It would have been difficult to explain I had been watching her since she left the hotel.

Sitting near me, smoothing the tan skirt over her bare thighs, she was near enough for me to smell the perfume she wore. Schiaparelli, I guessed, having slept with it before and knowing it cheaper to buy a yacht. The mouth was happily naked of paint and totally desirable. Her almost-black hair had the glossiness of a crow's wing and was flicked up round her cheeks. She was very, very sure of herself and should, I thought, have had two Afghan hounds on gold-studded leashes. She possessed that sort of a presence.

When she removed her spectacles, I saw that the sherry-brown eyes were bold, ready to minimize a man's ego should he deserve it. She fanned herself with an open hand. 'I am not disturbing you? It seems the only place.'

Indeed, it was. The outcropping of rock on which we sat was the centre of a natural amphitheatre of Corsican pines and Spanish broom facing the panorama of the sparkling sea. 'I was getting bored anyway,' I admitted, rehousing the binoculars.

'You ski yourself?' She was more polite than interested.

I pulled out my cigarette case and opened it. She produced a long black holder from her handbag and twisted a cigarette into the end of it, gripping the stem between her teeth as a man would a pipe. I snapped my lighter at it, staring at her over the flame while she costed its gold plating and lizard's skin trim.

After I had lit my own and blown smoke to mix with the warm afternoon's air, I said, 'Yes. When I'm satisfied the water's warm enough and the jellyfish aren't hostile. It passes the time . . .'

'You have plenty?' She was still being polite, making conversation.

'I'm virtually unemployable.'

She looked down the slope to the rear of the hotel where my Porsche glittered quietly to itself while it awaited my pleasure. An industrious youth had earned himself some pesetas a few evenings before by swilling from her the yellow dust and macerated flies of the long journey through France and across the Pyrenees.

'It is a lovely car,' she said. Like most women she called things 'it'.

'A clapped-out old reject I picked up in Warren Street.'

Her wrists were thin and the blue veins showed through the smooth tan. She pulled at the gold watch on one of them. 'I beg your pardon . . . Warren Street?'

'You don't know London?'

She shook her head 'Not well. You live there?' The un-English intonation of her voice was more marked. As if she wanted to make a point of her foreignness.

'As little as I can. I hop about chasing the sun.' My face showed dissatisfaction. 'I've to cut short my holiday in a day or so and return.'

'I am sorry,' she said conventionally.

I flicked my cigarette stub inaccurately at a metallic blue beetle walking in slow motion on a patch of baked earth. 'It has its compensations. I'm to brief myself for a trip to Phoenix. A torture of sun and hot sand.' I was joking. 'You know it?'

'It is in America?' Her eyes swivelled to mine were alight with sudden interest.

'Arizona. Full of Gila monsters, black widow spiders and Apache Indians.'

She laughed, abruptly warming to me, her tongue pointed and pink between the glistening white teeth. 'More holidays for an unemployable gentleman?'

'No,' I said regretfully. She had put one of her espadrilles on her finished cigarette and I offered her another. She shook her head so I lit one for myself. 'I'm a sort of junior tea-boy for a caucus of tough property developers. I've to get things ready for them: dust the pending baskets and fill the ink pots.'

She took feminine note of my Hardy Amies trousers and John Stevens's tailored shirt and remembered the cigarette case and lighter. She wrinkled her brow. 'You are joking?'

I showed my teeth. 'Not altogether. I'm a relative of a relative, if you understand, who has strong views on nepotism. However, I've no head for financial quackery so I'm used as a . . .' I stopped suddenly, remembering my manners. 'I'm so sorry. It's unpardonable of me to bore you.'

She made a gesture of denial with one hand. 'No. I am sorry. It was my fault for asking you.' She smiled and stood. 'It has been pleasant, Mr. . . . .'

I stood with her. 'Tallis. Roger Tallis.'

She bowed her head in acknowledgement. 'Mr Tallis. We shall speak again?'

I watched her for a minute or so, picking her way carefully along the path. Then I relaxed against the rock behind me, closing my eyelids and working out the score.

She probably didn't know it but she was the type of woman who could use me any time she wished for face-powder. Which could make the future very difficult for both of us.

*

The following day, matters were better ordered. I was permitted to knead Ambre Solaire into her shoulders while she lay face down on a blue airbed on the beach. Under the burning sun, the smell of it on her was heady.

She told me her name was Ingrid Hansson, that she was Swedish from the far pine forests—Norrkoping I think she said—and that she knew more first-class hotels in Berlin and Barcelona than in Stockholm.

She lay on the airbed, a slim golden seal fresh out of the water, her swim suit two strips of material barely sufficient to make me a bright pink necktie. Her disturbing eyes were shuttered behind white-rimmed sunglasses.

A straw-thatched sun shelter threw a round shadow ready for the occasion we chose to use it and two cane chaises-longues waited our needs.

In between rubbing oil, I relaxed and drank Campari and tonic water with her; long ice-cooled glasses of the blood-red stuff.

Someone had, before breakfast, scrubbed and clipped the palms and combed the sand to a civilized tidiness. There were other people comatose around us, oiling and being oiled, frying in the rising sun and drinking expensive drinks. None intruded in the small sandy oasis of our privacy. It was that kind of an hotel.

She screwed the base of her empty glass into the sand and turned over, pulling herself to a sitting position. 'I will oil you now,' she said, reaching for the Ambre Solaire.

She made love to me with her hands then and there in the

4

blue and golden morning. What she did wasn't the soft rubbing of familiar fingers and the neutral patting of greasy palms but the sinewy and languorous smoothing of an urgent sexuality, promising an unbearably exciting intoxication of physical intimacy. It was an accomplished performance, meaning only what I chose to read into it. When her arms looped over my shoulders and her hands massaged the amber liquid into the blond wool of my chest, I felt her soft breath on the back of my neck and I grunted like a fondled bear.

'You have a very big chest,' she said softly.

'I tear up menu cards with my bare hands,' I boasted.

She stopped her rubbing and pushed me away, drying her hands of oil on a towel. 'When are you leaving, Roger?' she asked, wriggling herself back into the voluptuousness of the airbed, making the movements of her body an allurement.

I lay prone on my matting of woven straw and the sun prickled my shoulders. The smoke from our cigarettes threaded invisibly into the bright sky. 'Tomorrow morning.' I flicked thumb and finger at the white-coated waiter standing attentive on the terrace above us. When he arrived, I ordered two more Camparis.

'I'm sorry,' she murmured. It was a politeness. One or other of us was always saying it.

'High finance calls,' I said. 'I might make a dollar or two out of it.'

There was a long silence until she remarked, 'I will be in London myself in two or three days.' She said it offhandedly. Like her hand-smoothing, I could take it or leave it.

Not looking at her, I took the drinks from the *mozo* and gave him a hundred-peseta note from my cigarette case and a 'muchas gracias.' To her, I said, 'When you have a free hour or so . . .'

She took the drink from me and dabbed her tongue in it, bobbing the lemon slice up and down. 'There might be many Roger Tallises in the telephone book . . .'

'Look for one with an address in Lancaster Gate.'

'Tea-boys are highly paid in London?'

'A tiny attic,' I said apologetically, 'and on an expense account.'

'I will telephone. You really are going to America?'

5

'I really am.'

'You fly?' A tanned leg slipped from the airbed and rested intimately against mine. I didn't do anything about it and it stayed there. My breath made hard work of pumping my lungs and I shivered.

'T.W.A. leaving Heathrow in about ten days' time,' I replied. 'The only doubt I have is whether to go via New York or direct to Los Angeles.'

She looked surprised. 'Why New York?'

'I usually have fun there. You know? Footloose and un-attached with the firm's credit card in my wallet.'

She moved her leg back on to the airbed. 'You have been before?'

'To Arizona?'

'Yes.'

'Yes. It's a wonderful State now they've stopped shooting horse rustlers.'

Her hands reached over and brushed sand grains from my back and the flesh crepitated its pleasure. 'You live an interest-ing life,' she said.

'And yours?' I was careful not to appear too curious.

'Um,' she said and pulled a face into her Campari. 'Not so very. I move around between disappointments.' She did not elaborate on this. 'Could I have a cigarette, please?'

When she was biting thoughtfully on her long holder, I returned to the digging. 'How was the flight?'

'I'm sorry . . .?'

'You flew here?'

'I flew,' she said, 'from Wiesbaden.' Her manner dis-couraged further questions and I didn't push. She hadn't been given time to prepare her homework but it would come. In the meantime, she was telling me to shut up.

While she drew in smoke through her holder, her brain almost ticking its activity, I studied her face. The nose was gently and attractively curved above a wide mouth. The dark eyes had the merest suggestion of a slant and were beautifully clear. Her throat was slender and long and made for the wearing of heavy gold necklaces. Under the edging of the abbreviated swimsuit, I saw her untanned flesh was a milk-coffee duskiness.

She reminded me vividly of the tomb painting of a Coptic high priestess I had seen at the site of Thebes.

Perhaps nostalgia for a lost Thebes prompted an invitation against my better judgement. 'About London,' I said diffidently. 'There's room in the old barouche if you haven't more than two or three travelling cases.'

She unhooked the sunglasses from her face and stared at me with a curious and calculating expression. 'I really *am* sorry,' she said and looked as if she meant it.

'You won't?'

'I cannot. I have things to do. Many people to see.' For a moment she licked her lips at me as if I was a rhum baba, letting me see her doing it. 'It would have been lovely.'

'Some other time,' I said easily. 'I'd settle for dinner tonight. Say, at the Tropicana?'

Her leg was back against mine when she said, yes, there was nothing she would like better.

I ordered more Camparis to celebrate while we chatted each other up about the relative merits of smörgåsbord and paella à la valenciana. It was as if the two of us were actually on holiday and hadn't a more serious worry than what was on the menu for lunch.

*

I took more than the usual trouble over my grooming that evening, emerging a scrubbed and swarthy Nordic; browned and bleached by too much sun. I wore a white jacket with dark trousers and a maroon bow tie.

She was dressed in white and wore the heavy gold necklace I had envisaged around her throat.

We sat at a table on a balcony looking down on to the small islands of shaded light that were white-naperied tables glittering with silver and glass. From the diners came a subdued hum of unimportant conversation and the non-stop clinking of cutlery. Chunks of deep shadow had been pushed to the corners of the room for those preferring anonymity. Moving deftly between the tables were the dim forms of the waiters, sweat shining on their faces.

Above us, the roof had been pushed back and stars pulsated in the exposed patch of plushy blue. From outside, adding a cadenza to the flamenco music inside, came the clicking stridulations of cicadas.

At one end of the room was a bar bathed in enough purple glow to identify and serve the liquor and no more. Standing at it and drinking steadily was a big lean man. He was savaging a cigar with strong teeth and staring moodily up at Ingrid. He had THIS MAN IS DANGEROUS written all over his face and in the way he carried himself. Even from the distance separating us I could detect the promise of violence built into him.

I said to Ingrid, making it light, 'Wiesbaden did me well once. I stayed at the Schwarzer Bock. The lifts were as big as gymnasia . . .'

She had eaten well and refused none of the wine or liqueurs but it hadn't loosened her tongue. 'I do not know it,' she said. 'I only used Wiesbaden to come from. May I have a cigarette, please?'

Leaning across and lighting it, I smelt her. She was Princess Nefertiti's boudoir and all the myrrh and incense of a costly perfume. 'You get around,' I commented.

'Yes, I do.' Torn between being nice enough to keep me amiable and interested and telling me to mind my own bloody business wasn't so easy as she might have imagined. 'I am sorry, Roger. Perhaps some other time. It is painful . . .'

I patted her on the back of one hand. 'Of course,' I said understandingly. 'I shouldn't be nosy.'

She had seen the big man and tried to hide the fact by dropping her eyelids and scrubbing out the cigarette I had only just given her. 'I would like . . . would you mind if we went, Roger? I am a little tired.'

It was too late. He stood over her, a glass of whisky in one fist, his cigar wet and frayed between his teeth. 'Ingrid!' he said as if he hadn't seen her before that evening. 'Baby! Am I glad to see you.' He wasn't a good actor and his gladness not very convincing.

I had risen to my feet and she gestured towards me. 'Paul, this is Roger Tallis. Roger, Paul Gost.'

Gost looked at me as if I had stolen his wallet and turned his broad back on me. He was rough, impatient with her. 'I wanna speak to you, baby.'

8

The look on her face was of anxious indecision and I intervened, poking his shoulderblade with a forefinger, smiling as I did so. 'No you don't,' I said. 'At least, not now you don't. The lady is with me.'

He swivelled around at that, looking even less friendly. He was big enough to do without explanations, but he gave one. 'She's an old friend, bud, so suppose you fall over.' He pulled a chair from an adjacent table towards him and sat. Then he lifted one of his thick sausage fingers and waggled it at a waiter. 'Boy!' he shouted. He was Simon Legree summoning a slave. 'Lemme have some drinks at this table.'

I sat too and lit a fresh cigarette. Apart from kicking his head in, there seemed no alternative. And kicking his head in was the quickest way I knew of not being able to leave for London the next day. I had seen the two shiny-hatted Civil Guards with their carbines in the foyer when we arrived. They were friendly, but not that friendly.

For the first time I was able to fill in on Gost's details. Beneath the sharp tan suit he wore he had a powerful body. His fists were hairy and as big as mallets. His hair was grey-white but didn't fool me for a minute. Some of it dropped over his forehead. I thought—wrongly as it turned out—because he was drunk. He was ugly-handsome and pockmarked. His mean yellow eyes were watchful and intent on what moved and he was ready to do something about it when it did. His mouth was wide, his lips everted and he had not yet taken the cigar from between the big square teeth.

Apart from his manners, which seemed non-existent, everything about him was twice as large as life. Even the waterproof, airtight, black-dialled diver's watch he wore so conspicuously on his wrist was jumbo-sized.

Despite the mode of his speech and the classless accent most Americans enjoy, I pegged him as articulate and intelligent.

I said to Ingrid, 'Would you like to go?' leaving the insults for later.

Before she could answer, he swivelled on me again. 'I thought I told you to blow, blondie,' he said, his face hard and the cigar waggling his irritation. 'Go and curl your whiskers.'

'*Please*, Roger,' she said. 'I am sorry . . .' She was apologizing again and my presence was being excused.

'No,' I said mildly enough. 'I don't know who this uncouth oaf is but I don't like him. Is there any reason why I should go on being polite to him?' I suspected I was beginning to lose some of my colour.

She put her hand on his arm. 'Paul,' she coaxed. 'Please, Paul. May I speak to you later?'

It made me cold inside to hear a Coptic priestess use that tone of voice with a savage like Gost.

The waiter had arrived with his card. He would have arrived sooner had not Gost spoken to him as no sensible man speaks to a Spaniard. 'Whisky,' Gost said. 'What about you, baby?' he asked Ingrid.

She shook her head impatiently. 'Please, Paul,' she repeated.

Suddenly, taking me by surprise, he pressed the sharp edge of his iron-bound shoe heel on to my instep. My foot was jammed immovably against the leg of the chair on which I sat.

He bared his teeth and blew cigar smoke in my face, increasing the pressure and screwing the flesh sideways until I sweated with the pain.

I smiled back and reached over, grabbing his thick wrist and straining his arm down on to the table cloth. I held it there as if we were friends shaking hands on a deal. Then I took my cigarette and pressed the red coal of it sizzling on to the soft flesh of the back of his hand.

He blinked, not admitting the pain by more than a slight involuntary jerk of his burning hand, but the pressure on my instep slackened as he took back his foot.

I released him and he gazed for a moment at the red blister. Then he raised his eyes to mine and smiled with his thick lips.

It was a childish conflict of wills on both our parts and it had frightened Ingrid.

He rose, ignoring the waiter who stood behind him with his whisky on a tray. He was too dangerous a man to shout at me and what he said was spoken conversationally, the smile still on his face. 'O.K., blondie. This isn't the place. When I decide what is, you'll know.'

He put his fist in his trousers pocket and took out and dropped a handful of pesetas on to the tablecloth. He did not speak to Ingrid but turned and left, his cigar smoke hanging between us until it slowly drifted skywards.

There was a reflective silence. 'You have some cuddly friends,' I said at last.

She reached across the table and held my fingers. 'Thank you, Roger,' she whispered. 'I am so glad you did not.'

'If there'd been four of me, I'd have tried.' I smiled at her. 'You're upset. Who is he?'

She looked at nothing at all while she thought and I held her fingers. Then she said, 'Paul? . . . he married Karin, my sister. It all went wrong and she left him.'

It wasn't bad really for an off-the-cuff explanation and I looked interested. 'He used to beat her?'

'Worse.' She shuddered.

I wondered what could be worse. 'You mean . . .?'

She nodded. 'Horrible things.'

'Not other women?' I regretted the flippancies I allowed myself when my purpose was so serious.

'Those as well. She could not stand it and left him.'

'Where was all this?'

She didn't hesitate. 'Frankfurt.'

'And now he wants you?'

'No,' she said shortly. 'He thinks I will lead him to Karin.'

'Your brother-in-law's a persistent man.'

She looked blank for a second. 'My bro . . .? Oh, yes, Paul. Why do you say that?'

I drew invisible lines on the palm of her hand with my fingernail. 'Frankfurt—Wiesbaden—Malaga. It's a long haul after the wrong woman.'

'Karin is in America although he does not know it. I am the only link he has with her.'

'You can sometimes hide just as effectively in your own back yard.' I changed the subject. 'There's a lot of time yet to *mañana* and my departure at dawn.'

Her dismay appeared genuine. 'As early as that?'

The foil-wrapped bottle in the silver pail of ice was empty. 'We'll have another bottle of wine to help us forget.'

It wasn't any good. Although she acted as if I had become the centre of her universe, there was no fire in it. The remainder of the evening was an expended electric light bulb. Gost had left more behind him than my bruised instep and his cigar smoke.

She spoke little and was withdrawn and pre-occupied as I wrestled the Porsche along the switchback coast road to the hotel. It was late enough for the cicadas to have called it a day and the night air was pleasantly cool. She had put a chiffon scarf over her hair to trammel it against the buffeting wind of our progress.

I walked her to the door of her room, unlocked it and waited. With the insurance of an open door behind her, she lifted herself on to tip-toes and kissed me on the cheek. It wasn't much after what she had promised with her hands. She would have let me make physical love had I pressed it but her response would have been a pale spiritless thing with no satisfaction in it for either of us. Even as a guarantee of the success of my plans, I didn't want it that way.

I said, 'It's been wonderful, Ingrid. I shall miss you,' and left her there.

Unlocking the door to my room and opening it, I dodged sideways and waited. Gost wasn't a man to be put off by a mere cigarette burn. And in the inflicting of it I had noticed he carried a gun in a shoulder holster.

I felt a little foolish as I locked the door behind me and went to bed. I did not see Ingrid again before I left.

2

The London I returned to was a crouching grey beast drifting dirty smoke into a weeping sky. Tyres hissed wetly over the shiny asphalt of the streets and everywhere there was the musty smell of soaked clothing.

I telephoned the offices of T.W.A. in Piccadilly and provisionally booked two seats on Flight 771 to leave for Los Angeles on the following Wednesday. It seemed worth the gambling of the extra fare. I planned to pay it from my own account because I suspected it might not be passed as reasonable expenditure by the nameless auditors curbing Charles's more generous instincts.

Charles, a man with the most daunting blue eyes I have ever flinched from, was the arbiter of my destiny. He had bumped into me a year or so previously; accidently, I had thought. There had been lots of handshaking, buying of pink gins and glad cries of 'long-time-no-see-old-chap.' In between gins, he did a bit of cleverly-casual probing into the state of my discontent.

Although a long-retired Detective Inspector with too much money to stay with the Flying Squad, I had retained more than a vestigial interest in the clobbering of *homo sapiens criminalis*. And I suppose it showed. Like canine teeth in a sheep. I'd been blooded on some of the most dangerously ruthless men of all: the gang bosses of London and their cohorts of mindless thugs.

My brother's death had given me an unexpected, unrefusable share in the comparative wealth of Tallis Properties and access to his unimpressed widow. What I hadn't counted on was the virus of the old job remaining in my bloodstream. I saw villainy rampant with no power to do anything about it. I was a nobody. A civilian. Writing letters to *The Times* wasn't a palliative. I itched to scythe their sneering disregard for decency from under them.

There was little about me that Charles didn't know before he approached me. Although we were friends from the same school, I discovered much later he had done a frighteningly detailed intelligence rundown on me. It had started with a matey, slap-up dinner for my former Housemaster, finishing with an interview and a scrutiny of my service record in the Commissioner's office.

I became, on paper, a Grade II (Administrative) Executive attached to a Ministry that would never demand from me the duties this undoubtedly exalted appointment entailed. Or ask me to wear a bowler hat.

I later said to Charles, 'What if somebody sporting a larger carpet than your own has grounds for asking what I do for my salary cheque?'

'No danger of that, Roger,' he said. 'It'll be referred to me by Minute, Memorandum and the Lord knows what. Safely in my pending tray it will die of inanition. I have,' he smiled, 'discovered a Way of Life. If you refuse to acknowledge Government papers, they cease to exist.'

I came to know that Charles had a fairly large carpet of his own. He also possessed a document shredder, four telephones fitted with scrambling devices and a reproduction oil-painting of the Queen. This put him solidly in the second tier of the executive structure, answerable only to a Minister who would choose not to admit, if ever pressed, that the office existed.

It *was* an office and not a department. A department connotes official recognition. Ministers cannot disown departments but they can happily deny the existence of an office.

Charles's office was in a Ministry block situated discreetly off Whitehall. To the casual visitor, nothing above the first floor was navigable, being cleverly sealed off with no door or stairs existing. Access was by an ordinary-looking lift that never by any chance took you anywhere unless you were known personally to the operator. And *he* was a plain-clothes warrant officer from the Army S.I.B. A man you instinctively wanted to call 'sir'.

The Directorate of Special Services sounded too stuffed shirt for its use in serious conversation. To the members it was known as 'Charlie's Bar'.

I had been there only once. Contacts with Charles were in civilized places like bars and restaurants. I had met none of my fellow operatives. We were an ungregarious lot.

Charles recruited men who, fifty years ago, would have been eaten by piranhas in fording the Orinoco, emasculated by

Tuareg women while harrying slave-traders in the Sudan or died clapped out with unmentionable diseases from forays into the seraglios of Basra.

Now, *Homo sapiens criminalis* was their target and Charles demanded a total involvement in fighting him. If you felt unable to give that, you could go back to selling old Bentleys or collecting butterflies or whatever you were doing before he put the finger on you. As a corollary, he widened a man's horizons from the parochial to the international.

Charlie's Bar used none of the refinements of civilized detection techniques. Nor was there any hierarchy of command. Only Charles and 'us'. We used no scientific aids, possessed no gadget-equipped fast cars and carried no conventional weapons or aids to recognition.

The words 'Charlie's Bar' said in the proper ear were alleged to be more effective than an open cheque on a Swiss bank.

If we had money (and most of us had), so much the better. The salary of a Grade II (Administrative) Executive may well provide a cupboard full of hard liquor and a motorized lawn mower in the stockbroker belt. For even subsidized journeys abroad, it didn't stretch very far. Not when sugaring the bait for people like Ingrid. We all had access to an expense account but it was subject to haphazard pruning and querulous complaints passed down to Charles. Nothing connected with central government is ever without its irrational and restrictive economies.

The few of us so employed possessed in common a tedium with contemporary society; rebelling against its inability, its disinclination, to prevent itself being used as a milch cow by supranational dishonesty. Charles had offered me Ingrid and her bed-fellow, Danger. I'd accepted her and it blind without demur. That I thought Ingrid the reincarnation of a Coptic high priestess was incidental to the job I had to do. Charles had me docketed as a linguistic ladies' man. It was an exaggeration, but one I could live with.

My real target, of course, was the syndicate behind Ingrid. She could be taken any time. The Syndicate possessed agents in every country in the world. Paymasters, they were called. They were the links between big business and crime. Every

15

town of size had its Paymaster. He presented to the world the image of a lawyer, a politician, a businessman; sometimes a judge or a high-ranking policeman. They controlled prostitution, narcotics and gambling for the Syndicate bosses. They controlled and paid the enforcers. They had deputies, associates and hirelings. Like the Mafia, they were everywhere.

Deborah was somebody else altogether. She would certainly disapprove of Ingrid. And Deborah's disapproval was always a potent factor in our relationship.

I looked into our office in Berners Street where she was, as usual, busily signing correspondence and wrinkling her pretty forehead over life's indiscipline. We discussed the business of Tallis Properties for an hour or so. It would be true to say she did the talking while I lounged in the visitor's chair agreeing amiably with most of what she said. When I didn't, I was careful to be polite about it.

Deborah had a wonderful head for this sort of thing. She was beautiful as well. She and I, co-beneficiaries of my brother's will, got along like two cats in a bag. Aware of the likelihood of his early death and fearing her inexperience of predatory males, poor Robert had made me her partner. Deborah had been his secretary before he married her and her expertise in the handling of property deals rendered me very much an unnecessary business appendage. My absence was probably more profitable than my presence. Still, I cheerfully tried.

I sometimes thought Robert may have wished his widow and me to be a little closer than joint signatories on a cheque. If he did, Deborah thought differently. I meant no more to her than the heavy mahogany desk to which she seemed wedded.

I, unfortunately, thought she was wonderful.

When she had finished filling me in on the current progress of the company, I asked her if she had arranged the more pressing matter of my departure for Arizona.

'All's well with our El Rancho Madrito Incorporated?' I asked diffidently. 'You've fixed me the papers I asked for?'

She reached within a drawer and took out a large envelope. It was stuffed with dollars and credit cards and faked papers about my supposed reasons for visiting Arizona. 'Newton Gribble is expecting you.' She looked down the bridge of her neat nose. 'You might do a little work for the company while

16

you are over there.'

'I'll remember what you say, poppet.'

'Please don't call me that, Roger,' she said crisply. 'I don't like it.' The spectacles I didn't think she really needed flashed light at me.

I smiled at her. 'I love you, Deborah.' When she didn't answer, I said, 'Is the helicopter tee'd up for me?'

'I have arranged its ferrying from Phoenix to Los Angeles airport. There will be a clearance chit and a flight plan permission ready by the time you want it. Refuelling will be laid on at Yuma. Newton has fixed you up with a gun and a Police Permit. They will be in the helicopter.' She paused, disapproval sharpening her face and tongue. 'You have to do this?'

I lit a cigarette, not offering her one for she did not smoke. Her question was the preface to an old, never-to-be-resolved argument.

'Not have to. I want to.'

'Won't you tell me who you work for? I might understand then.'

I kept silent, smiling away my inability to confide in her.

'It's a sickness in you, Roger. It should have drained out of your system long ago.'

I let my eyes scrutinize her body, knowing it would anger and discompose her. 'I'll marry and let you drain it out any time you'll have me.'

'Shut up! Why do you act as if you are the Flail of the Lord?'

'I have unexpended violence in me.'

'I've said it before; why not settle down to your side of the business. You are pleased enough to spend its money.'

'Bottoms to you, Debbie darling,' I said rudely. 'You don't want *me* here mucking things about so don't pretend you do.'

'You could take up something acceptable and decent, like . . . like shooting.'

I gave a snort of derision. 'An Establishment Englishman hooking tame fish and shooting feathers out of a flightless pheasant's backside. It makes me want to puke. At least *my* target can fight back.'

'Don't be disgusting,' she said coldly. 'Swearing denotes a

lack of intelligence and breeding.'

I couldn't argue with this and kept silent.

She said, 'You'll get hurt.'

I shrugged. 'It's what distinguishes it from slaughtering harmless bunnies and pigeons. Anyway, if I lose out you'll own the firm. That'll be fun for you.'

She regarded me closely for some seconds, ignoring my nasty remark. 'From the papers you've had me prepare, I assume it's a woman?'

'You make it sound effete. She's supposed to lead me into a tiger's cave.'

'You'll finish up going to bed with her.'

I wish I could say I saw jealousy in her but I didn't. 'You can hardly complain,' I countered. 'I've nobody to be faithful to but myself.'

Her mouth was small with her annoyance. 'Don't deprive your filthy appetites on my account,' she snapped, reaching into a tray and taking out some papers, dismissing me. 'I'm not asking you. Just warning you that promiscuity may be your undoing.'

Her irritation pleased me. I thought I might—fractionally—be getting somewhere.

After I left the office I was bored and time dragged. I visited the Museum of Natural History, leaving after a deflating eye-level view of the 75,000,000-year-old knee-cap of *Stegosaurus*. Waiting a few days for a woman with coffee-cream skin seemed not so tedious after all.

I drowned my impatience in an evening of Sibelius at the Albert Hall and, on another, sat through a watery performance of Rigoletto at the Coliseum.

I read the newspapers and studied the Personal Columns, deciding I wanted neither to be given colonic irrigation nor to share a Chelsea flat with a personable, broad-minded bachelor.

Always I returned to my rooms and the thoughtful waiting in a deep armchair; a tray of drinks at my elbow to provide solace and to anaesthetize my thalamus against the possibility of failure.

When the anxiously awaited call came it was morning and I was in the bathroom. I heard the subdued summons of the telephone bell faintly above the splashing of water on the shower screen.

'Roger?' The foreign intonation was immediately recognizable and the blood thumped in my veins. I smelt the resin of Corsican pines and saw the blue of the Mediterranean again as memory brought it back.

I was towel-less and stark naked, exposed to the view of most of Hyde Park through the undrawn curtains and dripping water on the management's Bokhara. With the courtesies out of the way and sitting damply in a leather chair, I asked her if she had just arrived.

She said, 'No, last night,' and told me the name of her hotel. It was a good one, needing a pretty fat wallet and a full suite of real hide luggage even to be allowed to talk to the receptionist.

'I'm glad you called me,' I said, pouring myself a drink with one hand and then manipulating a cigarette and my lighter.

'I said I would.'

'How is my singed friend Gost?'

She didn't answer for a second or two. 'I don't know. I hope I don't see him again.'

Gost didn't interest me enough to pursue the subject of his well-being with Ingrid and I asked, 'Are you going to share a sandwich with me? For lunch, I mean?'

'I'd love to, Roger,' she said with regret in her voice, 'but I have many things to do today. You will ask me to dinner?'

'All right. I'm asking you.'

'Thank you. What time shall I be ready?'

'At eight?'

'That will be nice.'

After I replaced the handset on its cradle I sat for a time nursing the glass of whisky and finishing my cigarette. I knew exactly the sequence of events which would follow the invitation and, predetermined though they were, the thought excited me. I returned whistling to the shower. Something I had not done since my return from Spain.

Perhaps I should not have been so confident: or it might have been that whistling in a shower is unlucky.

3

She was even more lovely than I had remembered, her coffee-brown skin smooth with a nacreous bloom to it; her eyes big and dark in the subdued glow shed from the inverted flower-pot shades of the table lighting.

Her short white dress was severely formal and showed her slender body and long legs to advantage. She wore a pale lipstick and black eyeliner emphasized her lustrous pupils. She still used the long cigarette holder.

I took her to the Brasserie Provençale in Greek Street where the pebbled squares of glass and the cigar-scented brown velvet hangings provided the atmosphere I sought. Although not a feasting with panthers, there existed a pervasive air of latent excitement; a proper contrast between the entrecote steaks and Chateau Lafite-Rothschild inside and the frank-furter sausage and onion taint outside; the hot fragrant food on silver platters and the squalid mess of cabbage leaves and discarded fruit wrappings in the street's gutters.

I kept the meal simple and light. I knew a surfeit of food to be the death of any aesthetic enjoyment of the wine. More to the point, I wanted no gorged crop between myself and the plans she had for me.

There was no dissimulation in her when I asked her to take our coffee and liqueurs in my flat. She saved me the mock modesties and hesitant pretensions of lesser women.

'That would be lovely, Roger,' she said gravely. 'I would very much like to see your apartment. Is it a long climb to the attic?'

I had taken the precaution of retaining my taxi and there was no off-putting delay between the ending of our meal and our arrival at the flat. I paid and dismissed the taxi-driver without any objection from Ingrid.

She carried a large handbag and I had no doubt that in among the hardware women carry around with them, she had found space for a nightdress of sorts and a toothbrush.

Hubbard, gorgeous as a bird-of-paradise in his porter's uniform of gold-frogging and cherry-red serge, checked us through the big revolving doors and into the lift. If he suspected Ingrid was not my mother, he forebore mentioning it. I paid enough rent to justify an automatic assumption of innocence. It is only the smaller hotels and cold-water flats which employ dirty minds.

In the flat she looked around her, a wisp of a smile on her lips. 'Yes,' she said with approval, 'this is a very nice attic.'

It was indeed. A decked stereo tape-recorder and its equipment took up most of the far wall, an expensively-stocked bar the wall near the door we had entered. The furniture was for sitting on and its sage velvet covered well-stuffed comfort.

All this left acres of convenient moving space on the mushroom carpeting. There were a few books around for the times I wasn't doing something else and, to stop me feeling lonely, lots of plaster and terra-cotta busts of Roman emperors.

I liked foliage to break up straight lines and angles and there were spinneys of swiss-cheese plants in the corners. Somebody from downstairs kept the bowls overflowing with white flowers.

Discreet behind a big leather screen, was the door to my bedroom. It seemed to be the sort of thing needing to be screened but that might have been just my peculiar mentality.

I took her coat from behind, smelling her Princess Nefertiti's bedroom fragrance again, savouring its strangeness. 'Would you care for a background of music to your coffee?'

She sat in one of the chairs in preference to the more companionable settee. A subtle touch, I thought. 'May I choose?' she asked. She was poised and queenly.

'Of course.' I held a silver box of cigarettes in front of her. 'I can offer almost anything unconnected with the Beatles and suchlike. Offenbach, Delibes, Ravel, Delius, Wagner. Or, perhaps, Gershwin, Rodgers, Berlin . . .?'

She laughed. 'I would like to stay with the French atmosphere for the rest of the evening. Delius, please.' Her eyes were reading mine as I held the spear of butane gas flame to her cigarette. I was glad to see there was no tremor transmitted to it.

When I had fed the wired-up monster stereo with tapes, I went to the bar. 'You'll have a cognac?' I said as 'Summer Night on the River' suffused its bitter nostalgia into the room.

She warmed the balloon glass between her palms like a

21

connoisseur, then swirling the liquor and inhaling the fumes. It was prettily done. Merely liking to drink brandy, I sat opposite and did so without ceremony.

'You left very abruptly, Roger,' she said out of the blue.

'Left . . .? Oh, yes. You mean from Malaga?'

'Yes.'

I shrugged. 'Gost had upset you. So much was obvious. You weren't with me: not on the same wave-length, that is.'

'Oh, Roger! Did it show? I am sorry . . .'

I laughed. 'You have the English habit of apologizing for nothing at all. It wasn't your fault he married your sister.'

She shivered and buried her nose in the balloon. 'He frightens me. He must terrify poor Karin.'

'He's dangerous all right. A man who smiles like he did under those particular circumstances has the soul of a hyena. He's an American?'

She wore a ring: a small, non-committal diamond ring on the second finger and she was twisting it around. 'Yes,' she said. It was obvious she was not going to talk herself into difficulties.

'What does he do to scratch himself a living?'

'I always thought he was in marine insurance. But,' she waved a hand vaguely, 'now I am not so sure. He deals in things.'

'His buttoned-down shirt collar suggests he's probably an ex-Ivy League College man.'

'He played football for . . . is it Alabama University?'

'It exists,' I guessed. 'Another cognac?'

I was dribbling it into the glasses when the outer door burst open with a shattering crack, sending splinters of wood and the remnants of the lock-casing flying into the room.

Ingrid screamed and I froze with the bottle in my hand.

Filling the empty door frame, Gost stood with his shoulders hunched like an angry gorilla, his face flushed red under his grey hair and the yellow eyes alight with purpose. He was a sobering sight on any reckoning and more so as his right hand was already darting sideways under his lapel towards the shoulder holster.

He had been facing Ingrid on his eruption through the door; not, in the first instance, seeing me at the bar. We formed the classical set-piece of *The Adulterer and his Mistress Surpriz'd.*

When his head did turn and fix my position, the cognac bottle was already on its way. Between the beginning and ending of Ingrid's scream it hit him soggily on his chest, knocking him off balance as he tried to dodge and get his gun out at the same time.

Then I leapt the bar counter and was on him, straight into the clutches of a grizzly bear with the stunning force of thunder in his fists.

Judo is, I know, a useful enough science if you can get the time to use it. Gost was scrambling over me, mauling and kicking; hitting hard with his heavy knuckles and grunting his pleasure at having me all to himself. Every time I got hold of a part of him to put on a lock or to throw him, he hit me. Had he not also been trying to get at his gun, he would have hit me a lot harder and a lot more often. He was beginning to smile with his thick lips.

We rolled and tumbled over the floor, banging into the furniture and bleeding on each other. He had fuelled himself up on whisky and stank of it. The brandy I had wasted on him added to the pervading reek of alcohol.

I hoped Ingrid would join in with a table lamp or a bottle (for I was weakening and bleeding from the nose) but she stood, apparently incapable of movement.

Then, with a thick arm around its throat, the grinning malevolent face was pulled away from me and I saw the cherry-red coat and fierce moustache of Hubbard. Gost twisted himself free and threw a blow at the porter who deftly blocked it.

Hubbard shook his head sadly. 'You shouldn't 'a done it, sir,' he said. 'You shouldn't 'a done it.'

Nor he shouldn't, for the porter hit him on his chin with a cracking right cross that could only have come from a professional. It was beautifully timed and Gost's eyes slid backwards into their sockets as he folded in the middle and fell on his face. He hadn't even time to look surprised. Delius was still providing what was now incongruous background music.

I got up from the floor and held a handkerchief over my nose. 'Good man, Hubbard,' I said. 'Watch him a moment.' I stepped over the unconscious Gost and slid my hand beneath his jacket, unsnapping the button of his shoulder holster and removing the short-nosed .38 revolver nestling under his armpit. While my hand was there, I also took his wallet. I put them both in my pocket. He was breathing stertorously and not far from coming round.

I straightened my tie and moved to Ingrid. She wrapped her arms around me and put a cheek against my dusty lapels. She was trembling.

'It's all right,' I soothed her. 'No bones broken.'

She stood away from me and took the handkerchief, wiping the blood with it. 'Oh, Roger,' she said. 'He's a beast of a man. You should have killed him.'

I laughed shakily from a sore jaw. 'With what. An Inter-Continental Ballistic Missile?' I indicated the bathroom. 'The medicine chest's in there. And a wet towel wouldn't do my face any harm.'

While she was doing this, I took the revolver from my pocket and hinged the cylinder sideways, ejecting the shells into the palm of my hand. I opened the wallet and glanced at its contents, seeing what I wanted to see.

'How did he get in?' I asked Hubbard, preparing to be annoyed.

'I'm sorry, sir. 'E said 'e was a friend of yours. While I was fiddlin' with the telephone 'e ran into the lift and took off.'

'You didn't give him my number?'

'No, sir. I didn't 'ave to. 'E saw it on the key board. Anyway, 'e left the bleedin' lift open and I 'ad to climb the stairs. When I caught up with 'im, you and 'im was mixing it on the floor. So,' he added portentously, 'I didn't think 'e really was any friend of yours.'

Gost stirred and his yellow eyes opened, taking us both in. He elbowed himself to a sitting position. 'You goddam limey bastard,' he said quietly to Hubbard.

I stood nearer to him and showed him the gun in my hand. 'I've emptied it,' I said, 'but don't feel too happy on that account. It won't stop my belting you with it if you start anything again.'

Ingrid had returned with some cotton wool and a towel but I waved her back with my free hand.

Gost stood slowly, shaking dizziness from his head and wobbling on rubber legs. Even in this extremity he was a tough-fibred, powerful man. His greying hair would never invite liberties or compassion from anyone not myopic. He bled, I was pleased to see, from a badly split lip and was, if anything, in worse shape than I. Nobody offered to mop him clean.

'Why?' I demanded. 'Because I used you as an ashtray?'

He wasn't looking at me but at Ingrid. An intense, steady and rather pathetic gaze. 'Vad gör du här? *Din ko*!' he said to her.

'Ingenting. Han bad mig stiga in,' she replied uneasily.

He said, 'Hör nu vad jag . . .'

I interrupted him. 'Speak your usual Bronx English,' I said. 'Your bad manners are showing again.'

One of my qualifications was a halting knowledge of basic Swedish. Enough to know that he had called her a cow.

He turned back to me and suddenly grinned. Not with his eyes, nor anything behind them. Just his mouth. 'This wasn't the time or the place, bud,' he said, almost fondly. 'But it'll come; it'll come.'

I said to Hubbard, 'Get the police.'

'*No!*' It was Ingrid behind me. '*Please*, Roger. Not the police.'

The smile was still on Gost's thick mouth and it irritated me. 'Why not?' I snapped, not taking my eyes from him.

'Go on, babe,' Gost said. 'Tell blondie why not.'

She faltered. '*Please*, Roger . . .'

It was very quiet in the room for long seconds. Then I pushed the gun roughly into Gost's breast pocket, tearing the lining of it. 'Throw him out, Hubbard,' I said. 'If he shows again, telephone the police and I'll make a charge.'

Gost checked the empty cylinders of the revolver and holstered it with menacing expertise. He rubbed the point of his chin with the back of his hand, making a small rasping sound. He looked again at Ingrid and then at me, swivelled on his heel and was gone with Hubbard close behind, shepherding him dourly.

I closed the shattered door and wedged a chairback under the remains of the lock. Then I sat on the settee and let Ingrid plaster the bridge of my nose and wash the worst of the blood from my bruised face. 'As I think I said before, you've some cuddly friends.'

She was intent on my nose. 'We do not choose our brothers-in-law.'

'Why didn't you want me to hand him over to the police?'

She hesitated. 'Because I thought tonight was important to us.' She stooped and touched my nose with her lips. 'Not something to spend making statements.'

I kissed her then, standing to do it with what I judged to be the right amount of fervour. A not very difficult exercise. 'Why are you frightened of him?' I asked, disengaging my mouth.

She stirred in my arms, making me feel the shape and softness of her body. 'Cannot we forget him? He is not important to us.'

'He's important to me if he shoots off that gun of his,' I said, releasing myself from her. 'How would he know you were here? Did he follow you from Malaga?'

She was perplexed. 'I don't know. If he knows I am here then he will know my hotel.' She bit her lip. 'It would not be difficult, would it? I mean, to follow me.'

'No,' I admitted. 'It's an easy talent to acquire. You flew back?'

'Yes. I did not begin to imagine he would . . .'

'He must think a hell of a lot of your sister.' I watched her closely. It was fascinating watching a Coptic priestess lie.

'I am worried, Roger. About Karin.'

'She's the other side of the Atlantic. Why should you be?' I went across to the bar and opened a fresh bottle of cognac. There was no point in mixing the drinks and brandy was as good an aphrodisiac—if she or I needed one—as anything else.

She took the glass from me and drank it, not worrying about any bouquet it might have had. 'His following me shows his determination. He will find ways of discovering Karin.'

'He was going to shoot one or both of us. Why me? Or why you, if it comes to that?'

She was watching my mouth and again I felt like a rhum baba. Her own mouth was moist and greedy. 'He might be jealous.'

'You mean, he wants you as well?' This was a contrary opinion to one she had expressed before.

'He would not be the first man to want to . . . to love his wife's sister.' She lowered her eyelids as if the thought of it shamed her.

'No, he certainly wouldn't. I know some dirty jokes on the

26

same subject.' I lit two cigarettes and gave her one. 'But he doesn't have to shoot me to make his point. I'm just as easily persuaded by threats.'

She patted my sore cheek and smiled. 'You are being very English and modest,' she said, 'and you are also very much covered in blood.'

'At the risk of being thought obvious,' I said, 'I *do* need a shower.'

I put some Cole Porter tapes on the stereo and poured us each another brandy before I went into the bathroom. She did nothing so obvious as to join me there and it made her a craftswoman.

When I came out, no doubt very pink and blond, she was sitting on the settee; very sure of herself and waiting with the right degree of confidence. It was clearly my move.

I grinned at her. 'What do we do now? Talk about smörgåsbord or Walpurgis Night?'

'You may,' she said coolly, 'but, for myself, I did not come just to listen to that or your music.'

I took her in my arms then and experienced that never-cloying pleasure of holding a strange and unfamiliar body pressed against my own, replying to the movements transmitted from the whole of the surfaces touching. I remembered the coffee-cream colour of her flesh and my legs weakened.

After I had taken her into the bedroom, she asked me to undress her. We acted just like ordinary married people except that she climbed all over me before I'd properly got into bed, biting and bruising me as if she were a hungry leopard.

Like me, she had a job to do and she did it superbly and with finesse, giggling as she did so and scratching weals in the flesh of my shoulders.

Had she been fifty-odd with scrofula, acne and a mouthful of plastic teeth, I would still have done what I had to do. As my good fortune had it, she was Ingrid and as lovely and talented as I believed her to be wicked.

*

When I had been thoroughly subjugated by her sex—Cole Porter had switched himself off unnoticed a long time ago— we lay with the curtains pulled aside and listened to the hissing

27

of the wheels of late-night traffic in the road below. The flat was too lofty for us to see anything but the winking lights of aircraft taking off from Heathrow and occasional stars blazing out there in the loneliness of the sky.

'Roger,' she said, her fingernail tracing arabesques on my chest. 'I am a good lover?'

'Of the utmost magnificence and panache. Did you take a correspondence course? Or are all Swedes like you?'

'You are teasing me.' She leaned forward, the globes of her breasts pale in the starlight. 'Kiss me, Roger.'

I kissed her. She was so predictable I could have written the script for her. It was difficult to believe she mightn't mean a word of it. 'I'd like a cigarette,' I said. 'Will you join me?'

I went into the other room and lit two cigarettes, returning to the bedroom with them. I stood for a moment at a window, looking down on to the wet shining street with its few parked cars and late-returning pedestrians. Beyond it was the darkness and quiet of the park. In a patch of shadow thrown by a bush I made out the figure of a man. A big lean man with tousled grey hair and, no doubt, could I have seen them, two fierce yellow eyes watching the windows of my flat.

If I shrugged, it wasn't with complete indifference. I felt I had treated him too casually. He was a tiger I shouldn't ever mistake for a domesticated cat.

When I rejoined Ingrid on the bed, I mentioned none of this. I guessed he would get bored with the waiting and watching long before daylight.

'What are you thinking about, Roger?'

I had lain for some time in silence, drawing on my cigarette. 'I'm leaving for Arizona on Wednesday,' I said with regret in my voice, 'and I'm not looking forward to it very much.'

She caught hold of my free hand and put it between her hot breasts. 'Are you saying you will miss me?'

'I don't meet a Coptic priestess those many times,' I said, 'that I want to lose her too quickly . . .' I stubbed my cigarette out. 'Still, *c'est la vie*.'

'You believe I am a Coptic priestess?' She wasn't quite sure how to take it.

'It's a compliment, Ingrid. You remind me of one. A beautiful, coffee-coloured, greedy one.'

'I am very flattered.' She inhaled at her cigarette and the glow gave her features a reddish cast, making her eyes large and shiny. 'You do not have to miss me.' She was smoothing a hand on my flanks.

'Oh? I don't?'

She discarded the cigarette and threw one of her legs over mine. 'I am worried about Karin and that terrible man, Roger. I would like to see her. To make sure.'

'America's a big place. Where is she?'

'New Mexico,' she said, sounding doubtful. 'Is it anywhere near—where did you say—Arizona?'

I put a shade of astonishment in my voice. 'It's the neighbouring State. Mind, that doesn't make it from here to Knightsbridge, but it's near enough in American terms.'

She hugged me in her excitement. 'Whoa, steady on, old gal,' I said in my best Marlburian accent. 'You'll be setting fire to the sheets. Whereabouts in New Mexico?'

'Albuquerque.' She was swarming over me now in her own aroused passion and we forgot New Mexico for a time. I thought Charles would be proud of me.

Later, I said, a little offhandedly, 'I suppose it could be arranged. I'm flying T.W.A. They'll no doubt have a seat for you. If they have, I'll be delighted to have you along.'

Kissing me, she said into my mouth, 'I insist, Roger, I shall pay the passage . . .'

'I'm a proud man, Ingrid. I *always* pay the fares of my . . . my friends.' I had been about to say mistresses. It would have been tactless.

'You will stop over in New York?'

'Not this time. Does it matter?'

She hesitated for some time. Then she said, 'No-o-o. I do not think so.'

'Reverting to an unpleasant subject, what about Gost? He could be a problem. It wouldn't need a very active brain to discover where we'd gone. And how we went.'

'I will change my hotel. You said Wednesday?'

'Yes.' I wanted to get some sleep.

She sighed contentedly and hooked the sheets up over her shoulders. 'That will be lovely, Roger. Please do not get tired of me.'

4

In the morning, Gost had gone. I could have convinced myself he had never stood in the blackness of the park but for the stub of a pale cigar discarded on a patch on trodden grass.

I put Ingrid into a taxi by way of a rear door debouching into Hogarth Mews. When we passed through the hall and under the scrutiny of Hubbard, he acknowledged only me. For him, Ingrid would not exist.

Back in my rooms I telephoned T.W.A. and confirmed the bookings. Then I checked the time. It was past nine and Charles would be in office. I called him on his ex-directory number.

He answered, 'Yes?', non-committally and anonymously. If you didn't know who was answering you weren't supposed to be dialling that number anyway.

'I can speak, Charles?' My voice was my introduction and he wouldn't want a name.

He said, 'Yes,' again.

'I've made contact with *Sphex*.' *Sphex* is a tiny sand wasp who lays her single egg on a caterpillar she first paralyses by stinging. The egg hatches out a murderous grub which eats pretty painfully into the tissues of the doomed caterpillar. It was not an inappropriate code word for Ingrid. Charles's humour was as black as his bowler hat; his imagination macabre.

'Aagh!' He sounded satisfied. 'Close enough?'

'I'm living in sin.'

'Lucky you. It won't hurt when the crunch comes?'

'It might bruise.' I kept my fingers crossed. 'There's a brother-in-law. He followed her over from Malaga and we had a bit of an Indian wrestle. The name's Paul Gost.' I gave him the facts and figures I had memorized, including the name of the hotel I had read from the papers in his wallet. 'Can you do a run-down on him with the F.B.I.? Perhaps Stockholm? And ring me back at the flat?'

'Will do,' he said. Charlie's Bar had a liaison with New Scotland Yard, the F.B.I., the Bundeskriminalamt, the Sûreté Nationale and the rest. It was a fact of life defying establishment procedures. 'When are you leaving?'

'On Wednesday. By T.W.A. to Los Angeles: the caterpillar being accompanied by *Sphex*.'

'You are sure you don't want help over there?'

'Quite sure, Charles. It might prove awkward. I'll play it by ear and scream if I have to.'

'Take our contact's details then,' he said. It was a matter of policy that we called on the established law-enforcement agencies only as a last resort. It represented an embarrassment if we did. Usually a ministerial one, if things went wrong.

I memorized the San Francisco telephone number he gave me, slotting it next to that of a flaxen Brünnhilde I knew from the New York Metropolitan Opera.

'I'll telephone you back, Roger,' he said, 'if I get anything on Gost. If you're out, I'll leave it on your tape.'

I had three days to kill and I continued to meet Ingrid. We went to the little places. Places where it was unlikely we would meet or be harried by Gost. We ate Italian in the Genazzini, Turkish at the Istanbul and saw some Cockney belly-dancing and stripping in a night club off Wyndham Street.

It wasn't terribly exciting but it gave us enough activity to avoid discussing anything serious about her background or mine. That part had served its purpose. I spent most of the time building myself up as a rather decent, slightly dim rugger type with an intellect not much heavier than an airmail letter. It seemed to accord with what she already thought of me.

I didn't take her for granted and didn't sleep with her again. It was there all right, waiting the right time and place. Which wasn't a wet, depressing London. There is no profit in acting the glutton for either food or sex and I preferred breathing space between the ingestion of either.

The shadow of Gost affected Ingrid although she was too much of a woman to let it show. I was conscious of it and reacted accordingly. I left my flat by the mews and met her in isolated places by circuitous ways, changing taxis and using the underground trains to confuse our trail.

While I wanted him to follow us to America—indeed, I'd done everything but send him a postcard to ensure he did—I didn't want him treading on my heels. He made me feel like a hunted rabbit, denting my *amour propre*.

It rained most of the time. When it did not, it was windy and gritty. I gave instructions to Hubbard that if Gost or anyone else asked where I was or was not, he had my full authority to blabber it out that I was flying by T.W.A. to Los Angeles and from there to Shiloh City.

I also left one of my spare cases in the hall. It was plastered informatively with hotel labels and air-line stickers.

There wasn't much else I could do to get Gost irretrievably involved. I needed him to stir things up and he couldn't do that sitting on his behind in England.

I found the recording of Charles's message on the second day. It told me that Paul Andrew Gost was forty-two years of age and a citizen of the State of Alabama. A graduate of Tuscaloosa University, he had majored in law although never bothering to hang his shingle on the front porch. That Tuscaloosa was also the headquarters of the Ku-Klux-Klan may have been a coincidence.

That there were no convictions recorded against him seemed just a matter of luck.

He had been a Captain in the 1st Cavalry Division (Airmobile), being given an honourable discharge some two years previously. While serving in Vietnam, his legs and buttocks had been mangled by seven bullets fired into the belly of his helicopter from a friendly but unselective automatic rifle. His stay in hospital was minimal, the effects of his wounds being shrugged off like so many bee stings.

The Army had been sorry to lose him. He had been impressively indoctrinated at Fort Benning, Georgia, with the need to kill and the expertise to do it with the minimum of soul-searching or emotional wear and tear. He was a cold killer-type character who would use a weapon by preference but his hands, feet and teeth if otherwise necessary.

It made me feel better about the outcome of our little fracas in the flat. It had its corollary that I wished I hadn't been quite so free with the indications of my departure and destination. I wouldn't always be able to count on Hubbard.

Gost had divorced his first wife. She had been messily raped by a then unknown negro and injudicious enough to allow it to be known. Gost came from the wrong stratum of Southern society to be able to tolerate this tainting of his well.

32

Two days after his honourable discharge he returned his Silver Star, Purple Heart and Sharpshooter medals by mail to the State Department and left in a hurry for Europe.

A week later, a negro was discovered crucified on a tree in a wood a few hundred yards from Gost's backyard and very dead indeed. His penis and scrotum had been savagely hacked away and his throat cut.

Suspicion is one thing and proof another. A face-saving warrant was applied for by the sheriff. Gost was then perfunctorily listed as sought for inter-state flight to avoid lawful arrest. Nobody appeared overly zealous about executing the warrant and it became elapsed.

The American Embassy later reported his arrival in Stockholm and his subsequent marriage to a Swedish national. To somebody called Ingrid Hansson.

Which made his nastiness to me that bit more understandable.

*

That last night I borrowed Hubbard's tiny mini and parked outside Ingrid's hotel for several hours, dismounting occasionally and prowling about in the rain looking for Gost.

Although I knew she would be taking a delivery at some time, I didn't spot her doing it. That part of the operation was done with a polished professionalism. On her part, at least.

It wasn't important I knew of it. I would know by tomorrow my role in the courier system. I was beginning to tingle with the anticipation of being at last in total involvement.

It was pinking to dawn when I returned the mini to its stall in the mews and let myself in by the back entrance.

As I entered the flat my mind was ahead of my body, already anticipating the ritual of a hot shower. I didn't immediately identify the stale bad-cabbage smell of smoked cigars signalled by my nose.

When I did I was in the room and flinging myself sideways, alarm bells jangling in my cortex, the hair on my neck bristling with anger and fright. I had the beginnings of a snarl on my lips. At that moment I wasn't so far removed from a savage brute animal that you would notice it.

I waited for a moment behind the safety of the bar but there was only that dead feeling that emanates from unbreathing empty space. When I searched the rooms, I found a bedroom window further open than I had left it. There were crumbs of earth on the sill and smears on the fall pipe outside. He wouldn't need to climb the full height of it. A ladder ceased only feet below my window. But it was an active enough malevolence to impress a braver man than I.

An unopened bottle of my whisky stood ready on the end of the bar nearest the door. I couldn't doubt its purpose had I blundered into the flat earlier. A disintegrating bottle full in the face can produce a fearful wound. The cold menace of the man chilled me. It had only been the coming of daylight that had driven him back down the fall pipe and saved my face from being pulped.

Two cigar stubs were ground heedlessly into the carpet and there were signs of an unhurried search of my belongings. I had left the paper wallet of our flight tickets on a table. He couldn't have missed seeing them and their message must have been plain. My previous efforts at leaking him my intentions were so much scratching at the wind. Now he *knew*.

I looked in the wardrobe and the cupboards and stripped the clothes from the bed. There was nothing obvious like a primed grenade in the toe of a shoe or a bad-tempered King Cobra coiled round the lavatory pedestal.

I undressed and went yawning into the bathroom for the shower I had been promising myself. I pushed through the rubber screens and reached up, grasping the sprinkler chain. I was hit by a stunning, paralyzing shock which contorted my body in a paroxysm of pain and tore a scream from me. It sent me writhing naked in darkness to fall through the rubber curtains and on to the carpet outside the cubicle. My hand pulled from the chain and broke the contact. Slowly the paralysis passed and I groaned back to consciousness with an aching numbness in my chest and right arm. Yellow light was creeping back between the slits of my eyelids. The nap of the carpet close to my eyes was a coarse jungle grass. Water still splashed in the shower. I shivered, salivating from the corner of my mouth. The soap I held in my hand was crushed and forced between my fingers like soft butter.

Early though it was, I poured and drank a large brandy.

Only my falling through the curtains allowed me to be able to enjoy it. Without that luck, I would have been dead in the shower with *rigor mortis* waiting to set in.

When I examined the booby trap, I saw that the rigging of the wiring from the ceiling light to the shower mechanism was crude. Gost had probably learned it from the Viet Cong. I disconnected it and finished my shower in a halo of brandy.

I was now prepared to believe he disliked me enough to kill me. A natural enough reaction, I admitted, considering I was enjoying his wife. At least, his intent allowed me no emotional compromise. If there had to be a choice between killing him or not, I knew I would. If I was able.

5

When I met her later that morning she was loaded down with a white leather cosmetic case, two pieces of hand luggage, a handbag and a battered Hasselblad camera; the latter's strap hung with a light meter and a spare lens. She also carried a wide-brimmed hat and a pair of sunglasses. A hotel porter stood by with two large travelling cases. There was no doubt I would be paying excess baggage fare.

She made a pretty show of confusion and total ineptitude as she struggled to climb into the taxi. I took the cosmetic case and hand luggage from her.

'I didn't know you were interested in photography,' I said helpfully.

She gave me a bright smile. 'I have a Swedish passion for recording my travels.' Unslinging the camera from her shoulder she handed it to me. 'Would you be a darling, Roger, and carry it for me? I seem to have overloaded myself.'

We were processed and rubber-stamped without difficulty through Passport Control and the T.W.A. check-point where I cheerfully paid the expected excess fare.

The jet engines clustered on the tail unit roared and lifted us irresistibly, unsticking the pounding wheels from the runway unreeling behind us. With the earth dropping away below and our safety belts unclipped, we lit cigarettes and adjusted the air jets from the bulkhead above.

Ingrid was as lighthearted as a butterfly and wriggled herself as close to me as the separate seats and propriety would allow. I ordered two brandies and settled back to pass the next twelve hours or so with the minimum of discomfort and boredom. I had stocked up with periodicals and a pack of cards while waiting at the terminal but they were an insurance against tedium I didn't believe I'd need.

We were now in the rarefied air above wispy cirrostratus and the grey Irish sea showed as dark patches between the gaps. I dismissed the thought of the empty miles between us and it and worried about them with only nine-tenths of my mind.

We drank the brandy and ate Russian salad and tongue from plastic trays with plastic cutlery. It was uncomfortably hot in the cabin and I removed my jacket. I twisted the cold air jet full on and it hit my face like an icy laser beam.

Ingrid wore a pale blue dress and looked cool as polar ice. Her eyes were protected by her dark glasses from the fierce sunlight flaring in through the portholes.

We talked without purpose of the people travelling with us and of the pattern of our journey from Los Angeles. Then she laid a hand on my thigh. 'I have a little confession to make,' she said.

'I'm going to be a father?' I asked lightheartedly.

'*Please*, Roger. Do not joke about such things. I would hate you. No,' she murmured, 'I was going to say . . . so that there is honesty between us . . . that I am a widow.'

I put my hand on hers and squeezed it. Then I considered her remark and looked gratified. 'My very good fortune if not your husband's,' I said. 'You thought I would object?'

'I wanted you to understand my position . . . why I am without ties. Able to travel, to meet people . . .'

'I'm sorry, naturally,' I hastened to amend. It was difficult to express sorrow for a widow whose allegedly dead husband had failed to electrocute me only by bad luck and a hairsbreadth. 'Was it recently?'

'About ten months. We had been married only three years.' She finished her brandy. As with love, she was an expert at it. 'He . . . he committed suicide.'

'It must have been a terrible ordeal for you.'

'He was older than I, Roger.' She bit her lower lip. It gleamed pink and moist and was surely never meant for mundane purposes. She really *was* a fascinating creature. So, I thought, must a Venus Flytrap appear to a hapless bluebottle.

'What did he do? For a living, I mean?'

'He owned a wood-pulping mill. Poor Henrik.' She said it lightly. I wasn't intended to think that widowhood made her less available.

'And poor Ingrid. In fact, poor Karin as well.'

She hesitated for a moment, baffled at what I meant. 'Of course,' she said, catching on. 'You mean, both of us unhappy in our marriages.'

'And you've been trying to forget?'

I received a white smile and dimples from her brown face for

37

my understanding. I ordered two more brandies. It is never too early or too late to be drinking duty-free alcohol with a beautiful widow.

'I sold the mill,' she said. 'It was a big one. So now, as you say, I am trying to forget.'

'Why suicide?' I smiled back at her. 'Or am I being rude?'

'It is the Swedish temperament. The winters are long and dark and very cold. There comes to some a blackness of the spirit and the pleasures of life are as nothing.'

We thought about this in silence as I lit fresh cigarettes. I had switched over to Lucky Strikes. There is no profit in being insular about the necessities of life.

I found it difficult to reconcile Ingrid and long winter nights with a blackness of the spirit. Even fictionally.

Cumulonimbus clouds were boiling up over Ireland and, although we flew well above the bad weather, up-currents of air jolted against the metal under our feet. Occasionally the enormous wings shuddered and their aluminium skins wrinkled.

'You had business in London?' I asked. It was open season for pointed questions.

'Don't you know, Roger?' she said, her eyes wide open and guileless. She put her mouth close to my ear and then nuzzled warm-breathed along the line of my jaw. 'Don't you *really* know why I came?' She pulled my hand against her breasts, ignoring what the other hundred or so passengers might think about it. I hoped we wouldn't be reported to the Captain for lewd and libidinous practices.

'And this flight?' I laughed disbelievingly. 'Surely not for the same reason?' Beneath my professional cynicism of human motivation, I wanted to believe it.

'Oh, yes. Very much yes.'

'And Karin?'

'As well. She comes into it, of course.'

'Of course. And what about the unspeakable Gost in hot pursuit?'

There was no need for her to feign fear. It lurked in her eyes, a small back spider's shadow. 'He cannot, Roger. He must not.'

'Perhaps I'm exaggerating his initiative.'

The expression on her face said I wasn't. She knew him so

much better than the mythical Henrik. If Gost didn't like me for sleeping with his wife, it was a fair bet he liked her even less for permitting the privilege. *I* was a matter of losing face. *She* was an emotional issue. In Gost's particular world, sudden death and amputation of the genitals seemed the salve for both.

She shook herself back to being a butterfly again. 'Tell me about Arizona,' she said. 'I am getting so excited.'

I told her of Newt Gribble and El Ranch Madrito. I even tried to sell her a plot of building land there. It was a tribute to the latent salesman in me that she was interested enough to ask to see the high-flown brochures and plans I carried with me.

'Where are we going?' she asked. 'What hotel? I must tell Karin.'

'The Thunderbird in Shiloh City. Shiloh,' I explained, 'is the nearest town to the development.'

I kept her mind occupied, away from chewing at the thought of the pursuing Gost and even to a point where I believe she was able to minimize his threat.

When she reached her optimum capacity for brandy, she picked up her handbag and headed for the tail of the aircraft. As the door closed behind her, I went to work.

I pulled the Hasselblad down from the rack and unflapped the front of the case, exposing the face of it. Unscrewing the lens turret, I hooked an impatient finger into the aperture and felt the smooth polythene packets taped inside. The cocking and triggering mechanism could be operated but it wouldn't take a picture.

With a newspaper held ready to conceal my activities from the wandering, attentive hostesses, I unstuck the packets. My fingers worked rapidly against Ingrid's return and I dropped one between my knees. I scrabbled frantically beneath the seat, cursing with one breath and praying with the next that she would dabble in there as long as most women do in similar circumstances of personal discomfort. I retrieved the packet, gulped my relief and screwed the lens back.

Then I opened the light meter and spare lens cases and took out the packets I found there, stuffing them into my pockets. I estimated they contained a total weight of eight ounces of white powder. If it was icing sugar, I was carrying about a shilling's worth. If, on the other hand, I chose to believe it was heroin, the eight ounces were the equivalent of 3,500 grains and many times more valuable than its weight in gold. I thought it might retail in the United States at up to twenty dollars a grain.

I blinked. Partly, I must admit, with a sudden unworthy greed for the more than £20,000 it represented.

Ingrid's courier fee from this could inspire an exuberance of physical passion for any man who might be found and persuaded to act as the innocent carrier. I needed no blueprint to show me the drill she was required to adopt were the Customs unfortunate enough to detect me bringing it in. She would regard me with unknowing, indifferent eyes and deny me like a bad smell.

As a container for the drug, the camera had been dangerous enough. Empty and back in her hands, it was nitro-glycerine and boiling lava. For her, not me. Nobody can lose £20,000 belonging to the merciless thugs of the Syndicate and not expect to suffer for it. This was something I had considered. The retribution that must follow was a thing that touched my compassion.

When she returned, smelling nicely of talcum powder and soap, the camera had been reassembled and was lying innocuously on the rack. I noticed her eyes checked its presence. As they had done throughout the journey. If fate decreed I was going to fall out of the aircraft, she was hoping to ensure I fell without the camera.

After a polite length of time, I slung my jacket over my shoulder and went to the toilet. There, I distributed the packets about my clothing. Stowed in odd pockets like custard samples, they were more likely to be found by a suspicious customs officer. But I had no choice. Luggage can be checked at the drop of a hat. A passenger's clothing is sacrosanct until he arouses suspicion. I had, too, a great faith in Charles's connections should I fail to survive the short walk between landing apron and passenger concourse. It was a faith like armour plating except I never knew when I was wearing it.

Alone and busy with the concealment of the drug, I allowed my face the luxury of expressing its loathing for the murder-making filth I was carrying: the seemingly innocent white powder whose miseries crawled under the skin like mad beetles. The stuff called 'horse' that turned young girls into uncaring prostitutes and young men into twitching, watery-eyed thieves and perverts. All for the money to buy more of it.

My attitude to Ingrid was ambivalent. On one level I was set irrevocably on a course that would end in her death or her destruction as a free human being. There seemed no alternative. For her part in this trafficking in degradation and squalor, there shouldn't be.

I could forgive her cold-blooded, cynical use of me to serve the ends of the Syndicate. I had no complaint of that. I was the bait offered and she took me. That I was, in my turn, using her to enable me to penetrate the Syndicate made it a *quid pro quo*.

The other side of the coin was my growing subjection to her sexuality and sheer physical attraction. I rationalized it by convincing myself there existed something nice beneath the hard rind of her greed and calculation. I feared as an end product I might be more than bruised. We do not choose with the mind those to whom nature ordains we shall be attracted. I was beginning to wish she *had* been fifty-odd with acne and plastic teeth.

Putting on my slightly dim, rugger-style affability, I let in the beginning of the small queue forming outside the door and rejoined Ingrid.

I caught my breath when I saw her. She had the camera in her hands and was pointing it to take a picture of the clouds outside. I heard the shutter click. A smooth, well-oiled click but not to my sensitive ears so expensive a click as hitherto. She looked back at me and smiled, obviously not aware of any difference. Then she returned it to the rack.

I sat and yawned. Watching her hotel for most of the past night was eating into my alertness. 'Do you mind?' I asked. 'Travel tires me and we've a long way to go.'

It didn't do me much good. I was hagridden by a horrifying nightmare lasting several life times. A gigantic pallid-fleshed wasp with Ingrid's face and breasts bit at me with porcelain cat's-teeth. Then it sprayed my body with a white powder from red-rimmed nostrils. The powder came alive, scurrying

41

over me and changing into knots of filthy black cockroaches burrowing beneath my skin.

I awoke with a heart-stopping start to find the aircraft tyres screeching and burning rubber on the O'Hare Airport runway. My seatbelt had been fastened over my thighs, the fresh air jet angled away from my face. I had slept deeper than I imagined. My watch said it was early evening in London. It was ten past three here in Chicago.

Ingrid smiled at me. She had prettied herself up. I felt tired and stale with a taste of zinc-plate in my mouth.

'You looked so beautiful, I let you sleep on,' she said.

Once trundling along the apron we were allowed to unbelt and I went to the toilet. I washed some of the tiredness away with cold water and an alcohol rub. My inside felt bile-green as if I'd been eating a salad of raw baby alligators. I needed something medicinal: alkaline, effervescent and preferably cathartic.

We stretched our legs outside and breathed some unpressurized city air while the aircraft took in more fuel. We were not clearing Customs or Immigration and she felt confident enough to carry the Hasselblad and take my picture against the impressive backdrop of office blocks.

A man would have noticed the difference in the weight of the camera. She knew no more about it than how to cock and trigger it off.

When the plane lifted off again with a full belly of fuel, I moved to the bar in the fore compartment. Ingrid pleaded tiredness but asked me to order her some coffee.

A man in a gunmetal-grey suit was holding himself upright by hitching his elbows on the bar counter. He called out to me, 'Hiya, mack! You ornery ol' buzzard!' He had had more than his fair share of wobble.

I looked round. There was nobody behind me. I showed my teeth as a token and said, 'Good afternoon.' It sounded stuffed-shirt as sobriety always does in the presence of drunken bonhomie.

He held out a hand and I shook it. He managed not to fall off the counter. He was drinking an American-style martini with a plum-sized green olive in it.

'You remember me?' he said. 'Good ol' Philip O'Brien from

Wickenburg?' He was a slim, hard-looking man with liver-coloured eyes and a neat Elizabethan beard on his chin. I had never seen him before in my life and he had obviously joined us at O'Hare.

'I'm sorry,' I said. 'There must be someone else who looks like me. My name's Roger Tallis.'

He goggled a little although his eyes were alert enough. 'Ol' Roger Tallis.' He hiccuped. Then he pointed a thumb at me and squinted his concentration. 'You ol' bassard. Shriners' Lodge in Phoenix,' he cried triumphantly.

'All right,' I lied. He wasn't going to be refused agreement anyway. 'You win. The Shriners' Lodge it was. How are you?'

'A drink,' he insisted, turning back to the bar. His elbows were taking a terrible beating. 'You gotta have a drink.'

Several of our neighbours were, understandably enough, edging away from us. I said, 'Can I start with an Alka Seltzer? I've had a rough trip.'

O'Brien waved an arm grandiloquently at the barman who was already dropping the chalky discs into a glass of water. 'Of course you may, my dear feller,' he said in a horrible parody of what he thought to be an English accent. Then he added, 'Begorrah, bedad and bejasus, I'm from the ould sod meself.'

Even the Alka Seltzer could do me no good after that. 'I don't know the place,' I said, drinking my medicine and turning to leave.

He lurched in front of me, cutting off my escape. 'You going to L.A.?' he asked amiably. He was demonstrably anxious for company.

'The plane is. *I* shall be going further.'

His face lit up. 'Not good ol' Arizona?'

'As a matter of fact, yes.' He was making me feel more stuffed–shirt than ever.

He pushed a cigar at me and I had a close-up whiff of martini fumes. 'Not good ol' Shiloh City?'

I refused the cigar but took some cashew nuts from a saucer on the bar, asking for an iced beer. It was warm in the bar and I wore my junk-stuffed jacket. 'Thereabouts,' I said guardedly.

'Guess what, Roger you ol' bassard. Me too.' He dragged a billfold from inside his vest and put a ten-dollar note on the counter. He lowered his voice. Probably the crew on the flight deck mightn't hear him but I guessed everybody else would. 'I'm a computer jockey at NORAD's I.C.B.M. site just outside good ol' Shiloh.' He winked confidentially at me and put a finger to his lips. 'So ssssshhh, Roger ol' buddy.' His acting wasn't up to the standard of his beard.

'Should you be telling me this,' I asked cautiously. I could feel the cold breath of the C.I.A. frosting the hair on the back of my neck. 'I might be Andrie Gromyko's uncle for all you know.'

He breathed martini over me again, his mouth a pink cavern of laughter. 'Ol' Roger a commie spy?' he guffawed. 'You wanna know what sort of propellant lifts good ol' Titan Two's ass off the ground? How many megatons of biff-bang she sets off?'

'No,' I said shortly. 'And you're talking a lot of tit.' I wanted to hit his stupid, drunken face. 'Excuse me, will you? I've someone waiting for me.' I had him tagged as a hostile.

He slapped my back and leered at me. 'You married? Good ol' Roger! Eh?' His eyes, I noticed, were calculating and not very friendly.

'My fifth,' I said curtly. I added, inconsequentially, 'Did you start your boozing in Chicago?'

'I sure did,' he beamed. 'A good ol' tankful to last me out the week. I also collected myself some high-grade pussy while I was there.'

'It's a long way to go. Even for high-grade pussy.'

A girl in a tight-stretched orange skirt and frilly blouse stopped at the bar and O'Brien fell upon her with good will. 'Katey!' he cried. 'Good ol' Katey. Come'n meet good ol' Roger. We've done some good ol' orbiting together.'

Katey and I shook hands solemnly. She wore a dollar or two's worth of lipstick and eyeshadow but it suited her young face. Rimless spectacles were crooked on her small nose. She was the organizational type. She looked quizzically at me. 'Glad to meet you, Roger. The name's Janet, by the way.'

O'Brien was weaving on boneless legs towards the main cabin. 'Your friend's a hell of a lush, isn't he?' she said to his departing back.

'Have a drink,' I offered, thinking O'Brien had played his hand very deftly indeed. 'He's no friend of mine. I take it not of yours either?'

'A bourbon,' she replied, 'on the rocks.' Then she laughed. 'I don't know the guy from the Empire State Building.' She regarded me closely. 'You belong to somebody, Roger?' she asked crisply, as if about to exercise an option on me.

I nodded. She was probably myopic anyway. 'Regrettably. Lock, stock and both barrels. Perhaps you'd wait for me to come back into the market?'

'No,' she said. 'It was a passing thought. You've got nice teeth but I've got things to do.'

I was glad of that. We laughed together because we both felt we'd escaped from something and because the sun went on shining happily through the portholes. Sexual need is a terrible tyrant.

I was still laughing when I went to rejoin Ingrid. O'Brien was asleep in his seat, croaking disgustingly like a bearded toad. Two things I knew about him. He wasn't as drunk as he would have me believe and, like Gost, he sported a gun in a shoulder holster.

They seemed to be part of the national psyche. Like bossy women.

6

Walking down the gangway, the heat hit us like a slammed door, bouncing up from the baked sandy earth of the airfield. The sky was a bubble of thin blue circled by droning metallic insects intent on entering the traffic pattern.

My watch and my metabolism assured me it was the middle of the night, although the clock on the control tower showed the time to be only seven-fifteen.

Los Angeles International Airport was a sudden impact of flat American accents and a shock-wave of new smells. The Customs and Immigration people looked at us morosely and without interest; their examination of our papers perfunctory. Had I not been bulging with heroin I could have felt slighted.

While within their orbit, Ingrid made it seem as if we were chance-met strangers. She was prepared to disown me at the blink of a suspicious eyelid. Once out into the concourse, I was back into the fold and she relieved me of the Hasselblad as deftly as I had been saddled with it.

It was as we were sorting the hand luggage that I saw the man. As casual as a pair of old flannel trousers, he leaned against a pillar, his identity concealed behind a copy of the *Los Angeles Times*. Focusing my eyes to the distance, I could make out the small hole he had torn in the sheets of paper. It was the oldest, most-worn dodge in the field of surveillance. I'd used it myself in my detective days. Years ago when one's status lay in the choice of newspaper used. I'd been a *Daily Telegraph* man myself.

I noticed the man because he was wearing Gost's black-faced, diver's watch. Or the twin of it. And on much the same thick and hairy wrist. I didn't need any further convincing. My cortex was thumbing alarm bells again.

Knowing our destination, it would be a sound military tactic for him to get there first. To follow from the front and not to trail along behind. My respect for his ruthless tenacity deepened. And, with it, came tension.

I wasn't remotely as unconcerned as I hoped I appeared. I was praying, '*Oh, Christ, don't let the mad bastard shoot me here. Not to bleed like a stuck pig all over the terrazzo. Not to have to explain—were I able—about the fortune in junk I was carrying.'* I knew that outraged husbands are as dangerous and unreasonable as trodden-on snakes and rarely deterred by any thoughts of punishment. I knew also that in Texas a cuckolded husband may, by law, shoot out of hand his wife bedding it down with another man. I knew we weren't in Texas and that I wasn't bedded down with Ingrid. I wasn't so sure Gost would care about a technicality or two. His fists had that look about them.

I sucked the devitalized air of the great hall into my lungs and steered Ingrid away. But Gost wasn't in a shooting mood today, remaining smouldering behind his newspaper.

When she saw the block of telephone booths, she said, 'Please, Roger. I must telephone Karin.'

I pulled open the door of one of them for her, preventing its closing completely by jamming it with the handle of the bag I placed near by. I walked away but circled and came back on her blind side. It was difficult to distinguish her voice above the noise in the hall but I heard her making an inter-state call to New York. While she waited for the connection, I showed myself in front. I was smoking and interesting myself in passing female traffic: a typical male waiting with resignation for a woman to finish a telephone conversation.

Gost had moved and was nowhere in sight. I didn't feel reassured on this account. He still had me in his sights. I could almost feel his yellow lion's eyes on me.

I observed through the glass door that when she spoke, her lips moved in an unsmiling face. Once she frowned and pushed the bag handle away with her toe. I couldn't hear what she was saying other than the words were English, not Swedish. Not hearing didn't matter. Not when I could see her mouth. I read, 'delivery . . . Thunderbird Hotel at Shiloh City . . . tomorrow . . . Englishman, Roger Tallis . . . Phoenix no . . . I understand . . .' She then whispered to herself with a look of intense concentration. She was memorizing instructions or a name and address. I couldn't read it and it didn't matter. All this confirmed for me she was arranging for the handing over of the camera. That she could have been gossiping with her sister—if, indeed, she had one—was extremely unlikely.

When she came out, she was gay. 'I could not get her,' she

smiled. 'Her landlady said she was working.'

'Try later from our hotel,' I suggested. 'I think they have a telephone or two there.'

Out through the big plate-glass doors and on the sidewalk, we took a yellow cab to The Biltmore. I had no illusions that I'd lost Gost. Following a cab in an urban go-slow is child's play. At no time did we go faster than a road-roller or get out of the close-packed ruck of elbowing vehicles.

Ingrid was now in firm possession of the Hasselblad and set up for the *chagrin de vie* that was her due.

With a delicacy unusual for me, I had booked separate rooms although taking the precaution of ensuring they were adjacent. At the door to her room she paused, waiting for the departure of the porter and said, 'Darling, do you mind? I am exhausted. I *must* have a bath and bed.' She looked pale and fatigued. Even the wide-brimmed hat she still carried was wilted.

'No dinner?' In truth, I wasn't in much better shape myself but I knew I couldn't sleep yet.

'No.' She transferred a kiss to the tip of my nose with her forefinger and smiled, leaving me in the corridor.

I wasn't too worried about what she might do. It was doubtful if she would go out, knowing I was still up and wandering.

Outside in the street there were neon lights and the red tail lamps of passing vehicles. The muted growling of crawling machinery added a background to the blaring of car horns and the music seeping out from the bars and restaurants. There was a stink of exhaust gases in the warm air that rasped the back of my throat.

I found a saloon immediately opposite the hotel entrance. It provided a convenient place from which to watch for Gost. I sat on a stool at the window end of the counter and the bartender and I stared at one another. He looked an ex-pug in the middle-weight division and as if he didn't care whether I had a drink or not.

I ordered a beer and got one half liquid, half froth. He never offered change from the dollar I gave him. I was glad I didn't live with him. We would not have got on together.

I felt unusually morose. At that moment, even the company of Gost might have had its points.

Across the room a woman sat alone at a small table. She was thirty-ish, bleached and a potential, if not actual, divorcee. She was slightly over-ripe and over-bosomed. Very, very edible, I thought to myself. It probably showed on my face. In front of her was a tall glass filled with crushed ice and what looked like raspberry syrup and clotted blood. A shrubbery of mint sprouted from it.

We exchanged what could be called calculating stares, each weighing the other's intentions. I knew that if she could assess me as a well-nourished Caucasian with a clean bill of health and silk underwear, I was on the short list.

When she eventually smiled at me, I lifted my glass. I saw her teeth were her own and very white. She was as wholesome as yoghurt and I wanted her as an antidote to what Ingrid was doing to me. Carrying my beer, I walked over to her. At close quarters she smelt as discreetly and expensively as I had hoped. The whites of her eyes were beautifully clear. The men in her life hadn't worn her too ragged.

'You are waiting for someone?' I asked politely.

She shook her head. 'Avoiding my husband.'

'I'm sorry, I'm intruding.' I started to return to the bar.

'Wait,' she commanded. 'Unless you're scared of a guy of sixty-five, a hundred-ten pounds in his long-johns and sixty-two inches standing on a stool.'

It didn't fool me for a minute. She was more than likely married to an All-American football player with a nasty temper.

'Please sit down,' she said when I hesitated.

I sat. 'I wouldn't like to hurt his feelings,' I said.

She laughed, showing a curling pink tongue. She had a small fortune in gold cappings on her back teeth. I liked her. 'Would you let me worry about that,' she scolded me, her eyes creasing with good humour.

I bought her another of the blood-coloured confections and myself a whisky. The bartender's face was expressionless. I suppose he had seen it all before. No doubt it irked him to be a permanent bridesmaid.

We sat face to face over the tiny table with its bottle-supported lamp, our knees touching companionably. I was clearly making the grade.

'Poke your fingers out,' she ordered, extending her own like two pink starfish with scarlet-tipped pseudopods.

We touched finger-ends for a few seconds while she closed her eyes. Then she nodded her head approvingly.

'What was that for?' I asked, returning my fingers to coil around the whisky glass.

'It's Contact Empathy,' she explained. 'It tells me whether we are in harmony with each other.'

'And we are?'

'Yes-s-s.' She made inroads into her raspberry syrup. It smelt as I imagined rocket fuel to smell, well laced with Eau-de-Cologne. 'It also measures a man's potentialities.'

'And mine?'

'It has a deep humming noise like an automobile engine.'

I looked pleased. It was obviously meant as a compliment. 'And that's good?'

She nodded her blonde head, her diamond earrings glinting. 'My husband's has a dry crackling sound.'

The conversation was trivial, a disguised sounding-out of our intentions and backgrounds. It was a little more polite than exchanging the contents of wallet and handbag but it took longer.

After a while, she said, 'When are you going to stop being so goddam polite to me? It's not natural.'

'There's an old Chinese proverb about, "Softly, softly, catchee monkee," ' I said, 'if you'll excuse the analogy. It isn't original either but it still works.'

She regarded me with the how-much-does-the-bastard-weigh stare of a slave-trader. I felt naked on an auction block. 'Men want so much,' she complained.

I looked astonished. 'We do?'

'No,' she said, 'not *that*. I mean, it doesn't stop there.'

'There's something else?'

'They get too involved.' She was impatient with her memories of past, involved men. 'They fall in love, want to get divorces and such-like. I won't do that. I don't mind being borrowed . . .'

'I'm a great library-book borrower,' I murmured. 'I never forget to put a book back on the shelf where it belongs.'

We were pursuing the subject of her town apartment and its

degree of accessibility to a suspicious husband, when I looked up and into the bearded face of O'Brien.

He was outside in the street, watching me intently through the glass front of the saloon. Obviously as startled as I, he dodged back out of view.

'I'm sorry,' I said, rising quickly from my chair and knocking it backwards. 'Somebody I know . . .'

By the time I fell out onto the sidewalk, he was disappearing round the corner of the block. I flung my legs in a fast burst and caught up with him as he was handling open the passenger door of a big car. Another man was in the driving seat. A square-jawed tough with a bent nose and a stubby pipe clamped between his teeth.

I was panting. 'Just a minute, my friend,' I said to O'Brien. 'Why the disappearing act? You were following me.' I watched his hands, remembering the shoulder gun.

O'Brien glanced at his companion and then back to me. He smiled but it was congealed. 'You're drunk, mack.'

Although it was dark where we stood, I couldn't be mistaken about the small beard and the liver-coloured eyes. He put his hand back on to the door of the car. I should have watched it more closely. He suddenly twisted, dropping his shoulder and swinging the hard edge of his hand like a lightning stroke solidly against the side of my neck.

All support went from my leg bones and I started to fold. My mind remained clear until the back of my head hit the concrete ground with a dazzling, blinding light that suddenly changed to a black nothingness.

The patrolman's gilt cap badge glittered in my opening eyes. His face looked grim under the shiny peak as I goggled at him, swimming up from the depths of my unconsciousness. He had the expression of a man classifying something as municipal garbage.

This couldn't go on, was my first thought. I had to win sometimes, if only on the law of averages.

'You've been drinking, friend?' the patrolman asked me.

I propped myself up on my elbows and explored the mole-hill on the crown of my head. There was blood on my fingers and I showed it to him. The small crowd that had gathered peered eagerly at me over his shoulders. 'Yes,' I answered him. 'But not enough to give me concussion.'

He had a large nose and the nostrils flared as he sniffed hard at my face, disappointed I didn't smell like a brewery. 'Somebody mugged you? You lost your billfold?'

I patted the wallet still in my hip pocket and shook my head. It felt as if it was going to drop off. 'I fell over.' Neither O'Brien nor his car and driver were in sight.

The patrolman heaved me to my feet with one hand. His other was holding a long wooden club. I swayed, locked my knees and managed to look as if I was here to stay.

He grunted deep in his brass-buttoned tunic and rubbed thumb and finger at me. 'You got papers, bud?' He was a man given to taciturnity.

The papers I produced irritated him by being acceptable. Something about my being unconscious on the sidewalk excited his deepest forebodings. 'You making a complaint against anybody?' he finally asked.

'I'm sorry,' I said. 'A complaint?'

'Any complaint of a felonious assault.' He didn't believe my story any more than I would were I in his shoes.

'No,' I said. 'It was an accident. Thank you for your help but can I go now?'

'To where?'

'Back to my hotel. The Biltmore.' If I thought that would impress him, I was mistaken.

'You're British, ain't you?'

'It was on the passport you looked at.'

'Yeah, it was. You staying in L.A.?'

'No. I'm on the way through.'

'All right, bud,' he said impatiently. 'So where?'

'Shiloh City.' My audience had vanished now it was evident I wasn't either going to bleed to death or be arrested. 'It's in Arizona. Population 150,000, seventeen drugstores . . .'

He scowled at my ill-timed sarcasm. 'I know where it is,' he interrupted, not liking me at all; obviously suspecting I was one of the F.B.I.'s Ten Most Wanted Criminals.'

I said again, 'Can I go now?'

He shifted the gum from his left cheek to his right and twisted the strap of his club further up his wrist. 'I shall be watching out for you, bud,' he said in parting.

My lonely, over-endowed, tee'd-up-for-the-kill pigeon had flown the loft. The P.V.C. of her chair was still indented with the impression of her bottom and a tall glass stood empty on the table.

If I felt deprived, I consoled myself with the knowledge that I would meet her in New York, London, Tokyo, Berlin, Mexico. In fact, any place where tall, handsome women find themselves married to little old men no higher than five feet two inches standing on bar stools.

I stopped outside Ingrid's door on the way to bed. The matchstick I had pushed into the hinge was still there. She had not gone out; nobody had gone in.

Inside my own room, I thought deeply of O'Brien. The bearded clown was causing me some concern. That he was the link, the pick-up ordered to contact Ingrid seemed only too probable. Why he chose to hit me so unexpectedly was another thing altogether.

With an aching skull, a bruised sterno-mastoid and a wilting ego, I was in no mood to think too long. I took three aspirins, flooding them down with water. They would almost certainly eat holes in the lining of my stomach but, psychologically, calm me down enough for sleep.

Before I slept, I took a cautious shower. I was getting quite a complex about showers and the enterprising Gost.

7

The morning was clear and sunny with only the normal amount of Los Angeles sulphur dioxide in the air.

I said nothing to Ingrid about the previous night's débâcle and nursed my wounds privily. Once in the cab and away from the hotel, she was butterfly gay again.

The blue-and-white helicopter stood ready on its tricycle undercarriage straddling the take-off pad, the blades of its rotor swishing through the warm air in flight idle. A mechanic was inside the cabin, awaiting my arrival.

He packed our cases into the baggage compartment, obtained my signature on the clearance chit and left. In one of the cases, I had concealed the heroin.

The sponge-soft upholstery was hot where the sun was striking through the fish-bowl canopy. While Ingrid was interesting herself in the fittings of the cabin, I checked the First Aid Box. Inside, nestling among the bandages and Sal Volatile, was an automatic pistol with a full clip and a spare box of shells and two pen projectors of Mace tear gas. Suddenly, Gost didn't seem so irresistibly formidable. And what Charles didn't know, he couldn't get steamed up about. I wasn't prepared to fight Gost with an Old Marlburian tie and a walletful of credit cards.

I pulled the nylon safety strap over Ingrid's thighs and buckled her down. Then I clipped a throat microphone round her slender neck and adjusted her earphones. I admired her *sang-froid*. For all she knew of my capabilities, we might be within minutes of zooming straight up into lunar orbit or hurtling headlong for one of the unmissable hangars around us.

I, myself, wouldn't fly three feet above the ground with a pilot I hadn't personally known to be checked out. Too many things can go dreadfully wrong with such an unstable flying platform.

When I touched her thighs, she shivered. She wore a thin oatmeal-coloured dress with shiny gold buttons down the front. I touched her cheek with my mouth. 'If you threw a bucket of water over me now,' I whispered, 'I'd sizzle.' It wasn't Shakespeare or Gabriel Rossetti but she knew what I meant and was pleased.

She was beginning to trust me. And that hurt.

I removed my jacket and tie and settled in my bucket seat, my feet on the tail rotor pedals. Obtaining wind direction and speed from Air Control, I busied myself with a map, a straight-edge and a navigational protractor. Then I set a compass bearing of 146° for Yuma, although I knew I would rely mainly on visual navigation. It is difficult to get lost in a helicopter. If I managed to, I could always go down and ask. Or read a town's name on a water tower.

Having done a rapid instrument check and received per-mission to lift, I taxied her out for a running take-off. There were some flies inside trying to hitch a free ride. I chased them back out through the open windows with the folded map I kept on my lap.

Ingrid lit two cigarettes and put one between my lips. I started to object to it as a fire hazard but didn't. The French do it all the time.

I opened the throttle until the engine and rotor blade noises married into one another and eased the stick forward. I pulled the collective-pitch lever up a couple of inches and then higher as the blades thrashed with increased lift, vibrating the metal fuselage. She took to the air like a glass-stomached tadpole, the yellow earth dropping away as we crossed over the airport buildings.

In the shadow of the administrative block, I saw a man. He was talking intently to another, his grey hair and lean foot-baller's build, foreshortened though it was, unmistakably identifying him as Gost. It wouldn't be long before he dis-covered I had filed a flight plan to Shiloh City.

I smiled around my cigarette at Ingrid, engaging her attention, ensuring she did not look down and see her husband.

Lifting the helicopter in a steady slanting climb, we left the ordered rectangles of masonry and patterns of freeways and flyovers behind us. To our left, in the middle distance, were the brown and mauve upthrustings of the San Bernadino Mountains.

With the sun striking more fiercely into the perspex bowl of the cockpit, I pulled across the green-tinted glare shield. Even with her smooth flesh bathed in this sickly luminescence, Ingrid's loveliness was heart-stopping. She remained a cool crème de menthe while I sweated like an Egyptian field-hand. I had closed the windows against the noisy whacking of the rotor blades and I now partially opened them to the cooling air of the higher altitude.

I levelled out at 6,000 feet and reduced rotor speed to maintain my optimum cruising. Yuma was 240 miles southeast as the buzzards flew, nearly two hours' flying time for a helicopter.

Crossing the Santa Rosa Mountains and checking my position by locating Palm Springs, we peered down into massive canyons gouged from the rock and saw in their bottoms the silver ribbons of fast-running streams.

Soon the eroded mountains receded to give way to desert flats, the parched arid landscape reaching to the lower shore of the inland Salton Sea. South of El Centro, I fixed my nose-wheel on an irrigation canal and followed it to Yuma.

We had passed over a prehistoric world of sand dunes and gaunt stone outcrops scoured by abrasive desert winds. Now thunderheads built themselves up across our path and I reduced altitude to ride beneath where the clouds were dragging wet skirts over the dusty ground. Soon large fat blobs of water splashed on the curved perspex and flowed backwards. I dropped the helicopter on to the pad in a hurricane of driving rain and we ran for it laughing, our hair wet and plastered to our faces.

While we ate sandwiches and drank coffee in the airport restaurant the storm passed over, leaving a dripping landscape which steamed under the newly-emerged sun.

I didn't bother with the flight plan. From Yuma, the broad Gila River runs without break or curve to Shiloh City, a distance of ninety miles. Parallel with it, stretches Route 80; on its other side, the Southern Pacific Railroad runs ruler-straight for the Mogollan Rim.

Shiloh City lies on Palamos Plain in a notch of encircling mountains. The plain itself is part of the Great Sonoran Desert. It is a stony wilderness of green telegraph poles called saguaro cactus. It is a savage waste of cholla and yucca; their foliage a bristle of spikes and thorns, burrs and ugly spines.

The land is as harsh as pumice stone; as are the animals and insects living on it. Rattlesnakes, black widow spiders, poisonous centipedes and scorpions are indigenous. Bear and cougar are found in the mountains while lynx, coyotes and peccaries hunt or graze beneath the unrelenting sun.

The periphery of the city has been tamed by irrigation. Melons, citrus fruits and lettuce grow large and tasteless in the flat fields surrounding the modern blocks of the business section and the Spanish-style villas of those who work in them.

When it rains in the Sonoran Desert, the solid water knocks unsheltered men to the ground and dangerous flash floods storm along the dried-up watercourses.

The city supports a mayor to manage it and a chief of police to keep out troublesome strangers. A sheriff pokes his nose into affairs outside the city limits. Occasionally a maverick prospector goes bush and gets a Navajo Indian woman with child. Or a friend of the sheriff's has a horse stolen. It keeps him occupied between shooting coyotes and looking after his voters.

All these officials have big offices and large shiny cars with rifle racks, flashing red lights and sirens.

As I understood it from Gribble, the Mayor is able to make the Chief of Police say 'please' and open doors for him. The Sheriff is known as an untamable and snarling dogsbody, getting along with nobody but the Indians.

Shiloh City isn't a place in which to get into a fight or lose your wallet unless you have political connections. It seemed always a far cry from Chorlton-cum-Hardy, the Women's Institute and the Bay Tree Tea Rooms in the High Street.

Making altitude and keeping the nose of the helicopter dead on the lines of gleaming iron, I asked Ingrid to light up again. She put the cigarette in my mouth and unbuckled her belt. Then she smoothed the palm of her hand over my hair and neck and down my back inside the shirt. 'Do not let us wait too long, my darling Roger,' she said.

'As soon as I'm able,' I replied. She was getting me into a lather with her hand-smoothing technique.

Changing course to starboard and crossing the Gila River and Route 80, I said, 'I want to show you El Rancho Madrito. If you ever get a Swedish blackness of the spirit, it's just the place. Six miles from the nearest flush toilets and only the coyotes for company.' This was an exaggeration.

'I'd like that,' she said, laying a hand on my knee. 'We could have lots of interesting talks.'

El Rancho Madrito was a red-tiled cabaña with outbuildings flanking it. White-painted rail fencing separated it from the building lots Deborah hoped to sell to homesteading Americans.

The ranch was set in almost the only natural oasis of green in the plain. It was overshadowed by the stark heights of Painted Rock Mountain. Streams shedding from the gullies fed a luxuriant growth of fan palms, desert willows and cottonwoods.

I banked the helicopter, putting on hard rudder to keep her in the turn and circled the buildings, reducing altitude to a thousand feet by gradually releasing the pressure of my foot. A knot of chestnut horses feeding in the corral separated and cantered away frightened at the sound of our approach.

Reaching the mountain side of the ranch, I put the machine into hover, unbuckled myself and opened the window fully on my side of the cabin. Immediately below us was a scree of tumbled rocks and stunted pines.

I reached an arm behind Ingrid and took the Hasselblad from where it rested on a rear seat. Before she could protest— and I saw the beginning of it on her mouth—I said, 'I'll take a picture of the ranch for your records.' I made it sound a wonderful idea.

Tightening the friction clamp on the collective-pitch lever and holding the stick steady between my knees, I unflapped the case, cocked the shutter and pointed the lens through the window. Then I followed with my head and shoulders, aiming at the view below. Abruptly, the helicopter lurched and I exclaimed in alarm, dropping the Hasselblad as I snatched at the stick. The aircraft staggered sideways and the landscape wheeled around us. We were thrown together in a tangled, helpless bundle and Ingrid screamed piercingly as she lay on the curved perspex with a thousand feet of air between her and the ground.

I felt the rotor blades shuddering in a stall as I clawed my way back to the seat. The helicopter was bitching it up more than I had anticipated and I prayed fervently I could bring her under control before she plummeted on me. We were falling fast and twisting sideways like a wounded duck. Being unbelted didn't help. It was, by ordinary air safety standards, a hare-brained action just to lose a camera but I had to make it convincing.

Jamming myself in the seat, I edged the stick forward gingerly, pushing hard on the rudder bar. As the aircraft stopped spinning I banged the collective-pitch lever down and she dived out. When stability had returned I lifted her back to a safe height and went into hover.

What I had meant to be a simple stall and recovery had nearly put us into the cactus. We had been near enough to the ground for the roof tiles of the cabaña to be sharply defined.

Ingrid, white-faced, pulled herself back into the seat. She wasn't the only one shaking but hers showed. She put a hand over her mouth, her eyes dark with utter fear. 'Oh my God, Roger. What have you done to me? Whatever can I do?'

Her distress pierced me but, so far as I was supposed to know, she had lost only a camera. I looked contrite. 'I'm sorry, Ingrid,' I said. 'I'll replace it, naturally. It was clumsy of me.'

She was miserable in her fear. 'It belonged to my father. *Please,* Roger. *Please!* Can we go down and look for it?'

I smiled reassuringly and put the helicopter in a steep angle back to the scree, a good five hundred yards from where I had dropped daddy's camera. I chose a level clearing on the boulder-strewn slope and landed, the lashing blades flattening the small bushes and tossing the pine branches as I reduced power to counteract the sudden ballooning effect of the ground air cushion.

The rocks were baking in the morning's heat and we were soon flushed and dishevelled from the pointless search. Fearsome mosquitoes were active and attacked our sweating faces as we slipped and scraped in our town shoes among the loose stones.

We both collected painful spines in the flesh from cholla cactus. I had no water in the helicopter and the dryness of our throats inhibited smoking. I wondered why nobody from the ranch had investigated our landing. I said to Ingrid, 'They possibly thought we were a flying saucer.' It fell exceedingly flat.

After that we spoke little. Her expression was one of a woman sentenced to death. I had to ignore it but her unhappiness burrowed beneath the crust of my deception and it hurt.

The shadows of the pines had shortened to indigo discs when she finally gave up the exhausting search and conceded defeat. I held her hot damp hand and helped her back into the cabin. I didn't know what to say and said nothing.

We were both glum and miserable and as I started my drill for take-off, she said, 'Roger! I am frightened.'

'Oh?' I was surprised. 'Of what?'

'Please do not think me silly . . . feminine,' she faltered, 'but I am sure Paul is following us.'

'Nonsense,' I said heartily. 'How could he?' I looked through the perspex at the empty desert and forbidding mountains. They were shimmering with the reflected heat. 'He isn't likely to be out there, is he?'

'He would find out. He is clever like that.'

'No,' I said briskly. 'Don't give it another thought.' The cabin was becoming a tropical hothouse and I trickled irritating sweat.

Her bottom lip trembled. 'Could we go somewhere else for tonight?' She put her hand on my thigh and smoothed it. 'Where we would not be distracted by worrying about him.'

I had a vividly coloured mini-picture of our undistracted night somewhere else. It was tempting. 'I'm sorry, Ingrid . . .'

'*Please*, Roger.' She pushed her black hair away from her forehead.

'No!' For the first time I spoke sharply to her and she was startled. 'Why should we skulk around in the cactus for a bush pig like your brother-in-law? He doesn't concern me that much.'

She opened her mouth to speak but I overrode her, giving no opportunity for further argument. 'I've booked in at the Thunderbird Hotel and that's where we're going. If I get any more interference from Gost I'll . . . I'll disembowel him.'

I put my thumb on the starter button and held it there until the engine fired. The rotor blades started to turn and I occupied myself with the mechanics of lift-off.

I gave her a metaphorical blue rosette for stomaching my male arrogance so gracefully. 'All right, Roger,' she said. 'But please look after me. I feel so terribly vulnerable.'

That was the worst thing she could have said. I wanted to dislike her and she was making it hard for me to do it.

*

I lowered the helicopter precisely and prettily on to the baked earth auxiliary strip off Shiloh City's pin-bright Montezuma Field. I gave instructions to a Mexican line boy to tether her against the dusty desert winds and to have the bowser visit her for refuelling.

A rented blue Chevrolet—as low and wide as a double bed and encrusted with multiple lights—waited for me beneath the canopy of the control tower. The sun was hanging overhead, searing the exposed metal of the car. When I opened the door the inside was a hot, leather-smelling oven. I stacked our luggage into the cavernous boot and helped Ingrid into her seat.

She was now under control, the nasty frightening thoughts pushed firmly into the cellar of her mind.

As I steered the great glittering monster out through the gate and on to the concrete slip-road leading to the city centre, I was conscious of a metallic brown car dogging our licence plates. I played stop and start on different pretexts for a time. Although there were intervening vehicles on the road, our brown shadow kept station some 250 yards behind us. The very obviousness had a kind of arrogance to it.

I kept the big flat shape with its distinguishing four head-lamps in my driving mirror. It was too far away for me to see anything other than the silhouettes of two men against its rear window.

When I reached the palm-tree lined freeway, I trod hard on the accelerator pedal and drew away. Using the additional yardage gained I turned suddenly with tyres squealing into a secondary road, pulling up on the forecourt of a filling-station.

Ingrid was startled. 'What is the matter?' she asked. 'What is wrong?' She had put a white silk scarf over her black hair to contain it in the turbulence beating in through the open windows. She looked very point-to-point English.

I frowned in irritation. 'The nearside front tyre feels sloppy. It's affecting the steering.'

The brown car slithered broadside round the corner in a wide sweep, straightened with rubber burning from the maltreated tyres and thrashed past us. But not so fast that I didn't photograph with my mind's eye the two men in it. I would know them again. The driver would also know me, for our eyes locked as he twisted at the wheel and I saw recognition in them.

He was Latin-swarthy with an eagle's beak of a nose inherited from an Apache Indian. His hair was black and oily and reached down his angular cheeks in sideburns. His mouth was nihilistic, a lipless crease over the strong chin. The eyes were black obsidian and glittered with burning arrogance. I read him as a man who would pull out fingernails for a laugh.

His companion was short, fat and greasy with sweat. His hair was a ridging of tight curls and he wore a pencil-line moustache. He looked a right man for the girls. Little innocent girls still carrying books to High School.

When they had passed, I gave the attendant a dollar for telling me I had imagined the soft tyre and drove off thoughtfully. Ingrid was attracting the attention of aggressive males in droves. There was no arguing she had every reason for nervousness although, so far, I didn't believe she had anything stronger than a foreboding of the Syndicate's ruthlessness with failures.

I reached the Thunderbird by threading circuitously through the back streets, not seeing the brown car again. I drove the Chevrolet straight down the steep ramp into the garage beneath the hotel, taking the lift to the Desk Clerk's office.

The rooms reserved for us were connected by a door. There was no key in the lock but I knew I could make short work of it with a straightened paper-clip. Given sufficient encouragement from the other side, that is.

The air-conditioning of the hotel restaurant and its newspaper-sized menu tempted us to fill up on top of the sandwiches and coffee we had taken at Yuma. The meal was, predictably, enormous steaks and french fries with side plates of crisp salad.

Ingrid had changed into a smooth sage-green linen dress with gilt buttons. I wore white cotton trousers, a bronze light-weight jacket and the automatic pistol. Its ugly snout was stuck down behind the elasticated waistband of my trousers, secure in a pocket specially fitted for such bric-a-brac. The thought of its discharging itself accidentally was a horrifying one but I could not stand the discomfort of a shoulder holster.

Through the meal she worried at me about the camera. With a ball-point pen I drew detailed plans of the supposed location of it on a linen napkin. This she put into her bag. Then she asked me if we could go back and search again. Properly, this time.

I allowed myself to show a little exasperation. 'Damn it, Ingrid,' I grunted. 'It's lost. I'm sorry it has a sentimental value but there's absolutely no chance of finding it.'

'Could I hire a car,' she insisted, 'and look for it myself?'

'You could. But even if you found it,' I added brutally, 'it'd be smashed to useless fragments.' *That* should make her think. She wouldn't want anybody else—particularly not me —to see its supposedly scattered contents.

She was looking about her, her eyes never still. It would be an obtuse man not to see she was worried sick again. I gave her a cigarette to canalize her attention. She fitted it to her long holder and smoked with the cool elegance I had so much admired in Malaga. The savour was fast going from my so-idealistic crusade. As it so often does when ideals stumble over warm humanity.

I squeezed her forearm. 'I'll see what I can do,' I said, 'but in the meantime I have business in Phoenix. Would you care to come?'

'I'd love to. Is it far?' That she was determined not to be left alone in Shiloh City was obvious.

'An hour's drive if I forget all about speed limits.'

'Not in the helicopter?' she said with disappointment.

'I don't think so. I want some fresh air. And I'd like you to see the desert from ground level.' I coughed over my cigarette. I was now on king-size and twenty a day weren't doing my taste buds any good.

We took the cut-out road through the Gila Bend Mountains

and joined Route 80 at Hassayampa, reaching Phoenix in mid-afternoon. I saw no brown car, no Gost and no O'Brien. It left me feeling a little neglected.

I dropped her in the shopping centre. 'You might find time to telephone Karin,' I said helpfully. The fiction was wearing thin. Until now we seemed to have agreed we could take Karin for granted.

She smiled. 'I shan't forget.'

'Give her my love.' I sat in the car for a minute or two, watching her walk away with her graceful cat-stride. Her fear was tearing my stomach to shoe-laces. I was becoming sickened with the calculated blue-print for the destruction of this beautiful woman. To hell with Charles! To hell with the Directorate of Special Services! I couldn't live with the thought of bacilli getting to work on her dead body. The hotel was a death-trap for her. I was like the man on the Clapham bus given the choice of saving his mother-in-law's life by pressing a tit that would destroy 5,000,000 Chinese peasants in their anonymity. The drug addicts were like the Chinese peasants. Unknown, remote and impersonal. Even, so far as I knew, personally obnoxious. They were certainly self-destructive and serve the silly bastards right. Who was I to stand between them and their chosen poison? I made the decision right then. Sitting in the big blue Chevrolet in a hot street in Phoenix, watching the sinuosity of a woman's walk with the basement of my mind.

The blonde with the bosoms and the dry crackly husband might have saved me from a divided purpose had she only waited a few minutes longer. So much of my thinking was being done with my genitals.

Gribble had his office on Van Buren. That in itself was an achievement. It showed all the liveliness and bustle of an old-fashioned mortician's parlour but looked as if it made money in discreet quantities on the side.

His inner sanctum was guarded by a new secretary; a gorgon dressed to look like a woman. She had chalky dentures, aluminium-coloured hair and chunky mottled legs. In between these tempting sex symbols she wore a purple woolly suit and pearls. Obviously, I thought, chosen by his wife. I had met his previous secretary. Brunette, nubile and complainingly pregnant.

Gribble himself was cadaverously gaunt and in a permanent fret about people not buying our little parcels of developed desert quickly enough. He owned a well-established ulcer which he regarded as an evil familiar, cursing it as he would a sentient being. He punished it with homogenized milk and filtered cabbage-water, drinking this medicine in equal nauseating quantities.

Nevertheless, I didn't think he was a man to begrudge me my health. He shook hands and asked after it. Then he poured me a whisky and we talked at length about his ulcer's malevolence. He drank milk himself, puckering his mouth at it as if tasting raw lemon juice.

We disposed of the small talk and minor business matters Deborah had trusted me to negotiate. They weren't much and could have been done as easily by mail. To Gribble, however, I was just a business associate who concerned himself with the minutiae of selling real estate. A play-boy type who ran about on not-very-important errands. A biggish wheel in Tallis Properties but not one allowed to trundle too far on its own. He knew nothing of Charlie's Bar.

I lit a cigarette. Gribble's ulcer wouldn't let him smoke. It wouldn't let him do a lot of the more interesting things in life. 'Thanks for the reservations at the hotel,' I said, 'but the steaks are a bit on the small side. Mine wasn't any bigger than a riding saddle.' We both laughed. 'I'd like to keep the reservations but spend a couple of nights at the ranch.'

He made a steeple of his fingers and leaned back in his executive-type swivel chair. His eyes were inquisitive. 'The other room? It was for a friend? The company auditor, perhaps?' He was being ponderously sarcastic. 'Tell me to mind my own goddam business, if you want to.'

'All right. Mind your own goddam business, Newt.' I laughed. 'Although I can't imagine you ever would. It's just I'd appreciate some isolation.'

'Of course Rog,' he said. 'There's only the caretaker in the bunkhouse. I'll give him two days' vacation in Phoenix. He can weed my yard at home.' He lifted the telephone handset from its cradle and dialled a number.

While we waited for the connection, I said, 'He's no

caretaker. I nearly pancaked the helicopter on the ranchhouse roof this morning without waking him up.'

'I'll skin the bastard,' Gribble muttered. 'He's one of my wife's eighty-three cousins. A useless, no-good bum with callouses on his ass.'

The caretaker was called Chuck and his tinny response sounded unco-operative and aggrieved. Gribble's voice hardened as he cracked the capitalistic whip and Chuck surrendered quickly.

'It's O.K.' he said, replacing the handset. 'What about a cook?'

I shook my head. 'It's only for a couple of days. I'll collect some food and drink in town.'

'No,' he said '*I'll* get it delivered. It'll be my pleasure.' He looked broodingly at the framed picture of his square-built wife on the desk. 'One day I might be able to have a dame there myself.' He had all the misplaced optimism of a long-term married man.

'You randy old goat,' I scoffed. 'I'll probably find the cellar littered with old cabbage stalks and empty milk bottles.'

When I rejoined Ingrid, I told her nothing of my arrangements but she surprised me by saying, 'Might I drive, Roger? I do not want you to feel you are a tame chauffeur.'

I opened the door for her. 'Pay your own speeding tickets.'

She proved to be a deft, competent driver and I relaxed beside her, narrowing my eyes against the glare that made nonsense of our sunglasses. She was very good at avoiding the big grey lizards that courted death by running across the road beneath the wheels of approaching cars.

I navigated for her. Crossing the Gila River by the turnpike bridge, I told her to take the left fork. 'I want to show you something wonderful,' I said.

Soon we could see the glint of brilliant kingfisher-blue water, a small disc of reflected sky wedged in by yellow rocks and shrub-covered canyon slopes. Its deserted, stark beauty took the breath away. Here was the peace of undisturbed nature.

When we reached it by the dusty dirt road leading from the highway, it opened out to a placid pool rimmed by a narrow strip of level sand. We sat in the car and looked at it, smoking peacefully in the cool shade thrown on us by the sandstone cliff that towered above. Except for the sounds of foraging bees and the gentle bubbling of water in the radiator, there was a vast quiet.

When she had finished her cigarette and flicked it through the open window, she turned to me and burrowed her arms beneath my jacket and around my waist. She kissed me with happy affection and rubbed her hair against my cheek. Then she stiffened as I felt her hand touching the pistol at my hip.

'Why have you a gun, Roger?' she asked. 'This is not like you.'

'Oh, but it is,' I said lightly. 'It seems to be a compulsory item of men's wear round here. Signifying nothing more serious than a wish to conform.'

'No. I do not believe that. You fear there will be trouble.'

'All right. The thought had occurred to me,' I admitted. 'If he does catch up with us, Gost might have another go.'

'And you will shoot him?' She didn't look particularly alarmed at the prospect.

I hardened my voice and meant it. 'Right in his navel. I said I would sort him out if he interfered with me again.' It probably sounded drastic to her, but then she knew nothing of his attempt to electrocute me. And the thought of the bottle placed ready to macerate the skin of my face furthered my resolve.

Surprisingly, she kissed me on the mouth. 'I feel safe with you, Roger. You give me a warm feeling.'

'Talking of warm feelings,' I said, skipping away from the subject of Gost and guns. 'I'm going for a swim.'

She unwound herself from me and pushed her door open. 'I will come with you.'

I licked my lips. 'We'll have to do it raw. As naked as two peeled bananas.'

She peered at me slyly and then laughed, kicking her shoes off. They flew yards away from the car. 'Would it embarrass you, Roger?'

Out of the car, we faced each other and undressed. As she slid out of her underclothing, her eyes never left mine. There was no pretentious modesty about her.

When we were both naked with our clothing dropped

67

heedlessly on to the sand, I said through the balloon of excitement lodged in my throat, 'To hell with the swim!'

We came together under the hot sun like two enemies fighting to eat the other alive. It wasn't the sophisticated, formalized twentieth-century coupling we had enjoyed with the cognac in my rooms. It was a primitive emotion satisfied brutally on both sides. A thrashing of sand and slippery sweat and destructive tensions unwinding as we panted to a climax.

I thought it more effective than consulting a psychiatrist; more therapeutic than a sauna bath.

There was a second, more restrained Roger Tallis observing the antics of his atavistic *alter ego* with a cool detachment. *He* saw clearly enough that I was sub-consciously punishing Ingrid for her criminality. I laughed at this. As Lord High Executioner I certainly had an enviable job if punishment took this form. Yet, beneath the self-mockery, I knew there to be a grain of truth in the analogy.

I lay spent on my back at her side and laughed shakily. I hadn't really known her before. Her face was flushed and it mirrored the violence of the past few minutes. She panted and her teeth showed between her parted lips. There was something elemental, almost self-destructive, about her expression. I hoped no other man would catch her alone in the same mood.

After a rest, baking under the reddening sun, she pulled me over and down on to her.

When we had time to talk, I said, 'I'm going to take you to the ranch. To stay there.'

Her arms tightened convulsively across my shoulderblades. 'Not back to the hotel?'

'No. You could be right about Gost. He might even be sitting on our tails now.'

She pulled herself up startled, her hands covering her breasts. 'Oh, Roger! You really think so?'

I pressed her back down again and laughed. 'Don't panic,' I said. 'There's nobody here but you and me and all this cactus.'

Nonetheless, I promised myself, I would on other occasions keep the pistol a little nearer to me than the six feet away I had left it. Gost was a man of most infinite resource and initiative.

8

El Rancho Madrito was more attractive, more spacious, viewed on our feet than from the air. Built in Mexican–Spanish style, the main living quarters surrounded an interior flag-stoned courtyard. Here there were palms and overhead vines to soften the impact of piercing sunlight. A bronze fountain sprinkled water on to cruising goldfish and broad lily pads.

The windows were green-shuttered in white walls, the roofs tiled in bleached terra cotta. A coarse-leaved crab grass lawn flourished against all the odds.

I was unlocking the door when I heard the drone of an approaching vehicle and saw the plume of dust stirred up behind it. It was a black and white car and it bounced on the pot-holed drive as it turned off the road. I saw the red light on its roof and, on the door, a badge. It was a seven-pointed star with the words *Semper Vigilans* beneath. In case anyone didn't get the message, SHERIFF was painted along the side in foot-high letters.

The driver put his brakes on hard and scored furrows in the chippings of the drive. He got out of the car as slow as a western drawl.

A bony, knobbly, late-middle-aged man, he looked as abrasive as the desert he claimed as his bailiwick. He wore a khaki shirt and trousers and a Texas-style hat with a band of plaited rawhide laces. Buckled round his hips was a stitched cowhide gunbelt. The bullets in the loops appeared to have been burnished with metal polish. The single holster carried a telescopic-sighted revolver.

He had a silver star pinned over his left shirt pocket and a pea whistle dangled from a button. Big ornate cloth badges covered his upper arms.

His skin was brick-red as if sand-blasted by desert winds. Much of it was covered by the hairy fringe of a large moustache. He creaked with homespun honesty.

He should have galloped up on a horse. The big, glittering, rifle-racked car was an anachronism. So was the purpose of his visit. 'Seamark's the name,' he said. He narrowed his pale grey eyes and nodded briefly at Ingrid. She was standing in the shade of a date palm near the door.

He looked about him. 'Where's the chopper,' he asked without preliminaries.

'At Montezuma. You want to see its papers?'

'Yeah. I want to know why you made an unauthorized landing at Painted Rock this morning.' He was unsmiling, making it a serious violation. His accent was clipped and trimmed by official rectitude. With a glass of beer in his hand, I thought it might be more drawled.

'I landed it in an emergency,' I said mildly. 'And I filed a proper flight plan with C.A.B. at Los Angeles.'

He took a small pad from one of his shirt pockets and a pencil from the other. He flipped a page and I saw he already had the helicopter's registration number written down. It was interesting because I was sure we had not been observed. Certainly not near enough for anyone to read the figures stencilled on the fuselage.

'What was the emergency?' he asked.

I looked at Ingrid and she made a small moue with her mouth. 'I dropped Mrs Hansson's camera. From a thousand feet.'

He regarded me unblinkingly for a long time. 'And what makes that an emergency?'

'It was a valuable camera.'

'Let me see it.'

'We didn't find it. I couldn't peg the exact spot it landed.'

He wrote words on his pad and put a thumb over them when he saw me looking. To Ingrid, he said, 'Is that so, ma'am?'

I hardened my voice. 'Suppose you go and chase a coyote, Sheriff. I don't expect to have you confirm my statements right under my nose.'

He ignored me, brushing my rudeness to one side like a cobweb. 'Is that so, ma'am?'

'Yes,' she replied. 'It is so.'

'Now, Mr Tallis,' he said with more geniality, 'tell me where you dropped this camera.' He had his eyes fixed on me. They were the grey of gun-metal and obviously good enough to read my fingerprints at fifty yards.

'You won't want Mrs Hansson to confirm it?' I said sourly.

He grinned behind his moustache, showing stained un-American teeth. 'No offence meant, son. Us law officers are an unbelieving lot. I'll make up for it by having a search made.'

He put his pad away and took a shagreen-covered gold case from his hip pocket, offering us cigarettes. It was a nice, civilized touch. But I was disappointed, thinking he'd roll his own smokes with Bull Durham tobacco and toilet paper.

'I landed the helicopter as near to the spot as I could remember it,' I said. 'There was a dry wash with a clump of cottonwoods near by. The camera landed in a pile of rocks.'

'How come you dropped it anyway?'

'I was taking a photograph of the ranch.'

'Mrs Hansson was with you?'

'Yes. We were en route from L.A. to Shiloh.'

'You were the pilot?'

I smiled disarmingly. 'One-handed. It *can* be done.'

'So how did you drop it?' Suspicion wasn't far below the weatherbeaten skin.

'I accidentally knocked against the stick. The helicopter fell sideways and I dropped the camera straightening her out.'

He nodded solemnly, seeing it happen as I was describing it. 'You saw it land?'

'No,' I said sorrowfully. 'I was too damn panic-stricken. You know how it is.'

'Yeah,' he agreed. 'Like riding a crawfishin' horse.'

He flipped his gun from its holster with a smooth dexterity. Checking the safety catch, he handed it to me. He was noting the clumsiness with which I handled it. It made me a lesser man in his eyes. 'Use the scope, son,' he said, 'and give me a fix on where you think it might be.'

'It's a lot of fuss for just a camera, Sheriff,' I protested.

Ingrid had realized the implications of its possible finding and she interposed anxiously. 'Yes,' she said. 'Please do not bother. Mr Tallis is getting me another.'

'Nonsense, ma'am,' he overrode her objections. 'It'll be a pleasure.' He was staring at her hard; wondering, I supposed.

She almost wrung her hands. 'It won't be any good, Sheriff,' she wailed. 'It will be broken . . . not any use . . .'

He thought about this, his chin sunk in his cloth tie. 'Perhaps not, then,' he conceded, 'but I'm sure surprised you don't want me to look.' To me, he said, 'Just for the record, son, take a fix.'

I pointed the revolver at Painted Rock Mountain and squinted through the telescopic sight, adjusting the cross-wires on the scree at the foot of the slope. It was over half a mile away. 'There's a sandy wash beneath the two sharp pinnacles on the east ridge,' I said. 'The camera fell in the area south-east of the cottonwoods.'

I returned the revolver to him and he checked the fix himself. He appeared satisfied and reholstered the weapon without further comment. He took his pad out again and wrote in it the description of the Hasselblad as I gave it to him. He said no more about my landing of the helicopter and I took it we'd kissed and made up.

He seemed an efficient and conscientious public servant. Certainly not the snarling dogsbody I had been led to believe he was. Perhaps not too high in his I.Q., but his equipment suggested he could shoot straight. Which probably mattered in these parts.

I noticed he had known my name without being told. It made him a that much more efficient policeman.

He snapped a fingernail on the wide brim of his hat and said, 'So-long, ma'am,' to Ingrid. He managed a nod for me.

The car jolted from a standing start to a roaring acceleration as he gave it the equivalent of spurs, scattering chippings against the wooden planks of the fencing. Then he was gone in his attendant plume of rolling dust.

I ignored the effect he had had on Ingrid. She was chewing away at her bottom lip and clearly worried. She followed me into the house docilely enough, keeping her worries to herself.

There was a shadowed coolness in the spacious rooms and the floors gleamed with hard polishing. It looked a place to be relaxed in. It needed only a wall of books and a grey-haired butler to bring in the occasional glass of iced beer.

I introduced Ingrid to one of the bedrooms. It had, incongruously, a tester bed hung with gold-coloured drapes. It was big enough for a couple of active bigamists. The walls of the room glittered with inlaid pyrites and polished porphyry. The furniture was white leather-covered and twice as bulky as it needed to be. If there was no company to be had, the occupier had a coloured picture television set to look at and a gold-plated telephone in which to talk.

Gribble had organized the delivery of the provisions before we arrived. He had exercised an epicure's taste in his choice of food. There were tins of boned Californian quail, roast pheasant in Burgundy, smoked sliced salmon, defatted Kentucky ham and, anticlimactically, half-a-dozen tins of lima beans. There were also some interestingly shaped bottles that could only contain wine.

I hoped Ingrid had done the Swedish equivalent of Domestic Science during her schooling and was willing to put it to good effect while I collected the luggage.

Before leaving, I kissed her nose and said, 'You'll be all right for an hour? You're not frightened? Not of Gost?'

'No,' she lied bravely. 'I just want you back again.' She pushed her body against mine and closed her eyes. 'The night cannot be too long, Roger . . .'

'I know you wouldn't be so mad as to answer the door to Gost,' I said, 'but it's safer not to open it to anyone. Not if you don't know them. Hide if you have to.'

She nodded. 'I shall not be foolish.' She squeezed me. 'Please hurry back.'

*

It was dark when I reached Shiloh City and a big buttery moon was rising from behind the mountains. The Chevrolet dipped its bonnet soggily as I braked to a halt outside the hotel. I had stopped it in a prohibited zone, relying on my status as an ignorant foreigner to excuse my social perverseness. It worked most of the time. When it didn't, I sent the ticket to Gribble. It was accounted, I assumed, a tax-deductible expense.

The man who climbed out of the black car sprouting radio antennae and displaying a badge on its door panel wasn't interested in parking offences. He produced a leather folder and opened it in front of me, showing me the silver shield it contained. It said he was a Detective Lieutenant in the Shiloh City Police Department. I was fast becoming popular as an object of official suspicion.

A sandy ferret of a man with pale eyelashes, he had pointed

—almost womanish—features. His left cheek was dreadfully disfigured by a hand-sized port-wine mark. He would never pass unidentified, unnoticed, in a crowd.

He wore a narrow-brimmed hat and a dark chocolate suit. I couldn't see the bulge of his gun but he looked the sort of man to carry one in every pocket.

He was very precise in his speech. 'Pardon me. You are Roger Tallis, sir?'

I said I was.

'My name is Sowerby,' he said. 'The Chief would like to see you.'

'Did he happen to say why?' Out of my car and standing beside him, I was the bigger man. I didn't consider him less dangerous on that account.

'No, he didn't.'

'Is he a friend of the Sheriff's?'

He lowered the sandy eyebrows. 'Huh?'

'Seamark. Sheriff Seamark of Caliente County,' I said patiently. 'The man with the Wyatt Earp moustache.'

'You being funny?' He really meant it.

'Not exactly.'

He struggled with his politeness and it bobbed to the surface again. 'Are you coming, Mr Tallis?'

'Now?'

'Yes.'

'Do I have a choice?'

He shrugged. The cancerous blotch on his face was like bubbling strawberry jam. It mesmerized me and the fact that it did irritated him.

I moved to get back into my car and he put a cautionary hand on my sleeve. 'Don't bother, sir,' he said, politely insistent. 'It will be O.K. where it is. The ride's on the Department.'

I could have stood on my dignity, quoted Magna Carta and the Bill of Human Rights and refused to go. It wouldn't have done any good. He was doing his job and there was no argument other than violence that would deflect him.

He opened the door of the patrol car for me and, not speaking any more, concentrated on navigating through the busy streets to City Hall. The blotch was away from me, which was something.

I was ushered into the office of the Chief of Police like a deserter produced before a court martial. I wasn't asked to sit and this tightened the flesh over my jawbones.

The room was coldly clinical with unshaded strip lighting and birch-grey emulsioned walls. The windows were shuttered against the outer darkness by venetian blinds. The upper third of the enclosed air was a hazy fog of cigar smoke. The lieutenant stood behind me and I could feel his eyes on the back of my head.

His Chief was squatting behind a big leather-topped desk, rotating a thick cigar between rubbery lips. In case there was any doubt of his identity, a gold-leaf sign on the desk said *CHIEF THOMAS B. GEBHARDT*. A heavy smell of sweat came from his gross body and there were damp patches of it under the armpits of his freshly-pressed shirt. On his chest he wore a line of medal ribbons and an enamelled shield repeating the admonitory motif, SHILOH CITY POLICE CHIEF.

Crossed flags decorated the wall behind him. There was also a framed photograph of himself having his hand shaken by J. Edgar Hoover back when Al Capone was alive and a power in the land.

A huge black Dobermann Pinscher bitch lay at the side of his desk, rumbling gently in her chest.

Gebhardt's eyes, watching me, were wet snail-shells. He snapped pudgy finger and thumb at me without speaking and I bristled.

'Don't flick your fingers at me,' I said coldly, not caring what he thought or said. There was certainly nothing he could do.

He looked at Sowerby behind me as if seeking to call him to account for my outrageous behaviour. Then, convinced he had heard right, his face became swollen and a dull red. He did a poor job of controlling himself in front of his subordinate.

'Gimme your papers, buster,' he finally rasped around the thickness of the cigar, 'and shut your mouth before I shut it for you.' He held out his hand. I noticed he didn't snap his fingers at me again.

I withdrew my wallet, selected my passport and gave it to him. 'If your chap behind tied me down, I might consider it a serious threat,' I said politely. 'As it is you look as if you'd have a coronary trying it.' Then I sat on the edge of a table near his desk. Nobody told me not to and I made myself comfortable.

There was a long silence and heavy breathing from my rear. Failing to outstare me, Gebhardt licked his index finger and turned the pages of the passport. 'You're British,' he said at last as if this explained everything.

'Yes.' I didn't care to elaborate on this. I could feel the sandy lieutenant's eyes boring into me; wanting, I thought, to shoot me in the neck. No doubt I was unfair. He probably owned to a grey-haired mother and a dog that loved him. It was just I didn't like him behind me.

Gebhardt did a little more reading about my travels, occasionally eyeing me morosely.

'You wanted to see me?' I said.

He took the cigar from his mouth and regarded the wet end with distaste, blaming me for it. 'You here for long?' he growled.

'It depends,' I replied. 'But certainly for as long as I think fit.'

'What's your business?'

'I'm an associate of Mr Newton Gribble of 1603 Van Buren, Phoenix. We deal in real estate.'

'Why come to Shiloh? Why not Phoenix?'

'Because it's nearer our development, El Rancho Madrito. Also because there's a sign outside the city limits that says, "Welcome to Shiloh".'

'So now tell me you've got political connections.'

'No, I haven't,' I said showing my teeth. 'But if that's what it takes to stop people leaning on me, I can get them.' If his scowl meant anything, I wasn't doing much to win friends or to influence people.

He took me through the details of my journey right up to the licence number of my car. When he had written the worthless rigmarole down, he yawned and I came in with a remark of my own.

'I saw your friend Seamark this evening,' I prodded him.

His mouth remained open in the wide yawn, his cigar held poised in front of it. Then he snapped his teeth shut, his eyes calculating. 'Sheriff Seamark?'

'Yes.'

It was bothering him. 'So?'

'He was worried about my losing a camera. A valuable one.' Total involvement, Charles had said and I practised it. 'He told you?'

'Told me? You're kidding,' he rasped. 'Sheriff Seamark's got his problems, I got mine. Suppose you pay attention to mine.' He shuffled some papers and selected one. It was a teletype flimsy. He said, 'There's an information from the L.A. Police Department about your being found unconscious on a sidewalk last night. That you weren't very co-operative. Did you see who slugged you?'

I was surprised. 'They thought that worth the sending of a teletype message?'

'It's the system, friend,' he said.

'Well, the system had better get it straight that I wasn't slugged. The Los Angeles Police are leaping to some totally unwarranted conclusions.'

Gebhardt stabbed at me with his cigar. 'If they say you were slugged, buster, you were slugged. Saying you fell over is a load of limey chicken-shit. You,' he said slowly, 'are an alien.'

'Not when I'm home I'm not . . .'

'Don't interrupt me,' he rasped, doing so to me. 'You look the sort of guy liable to attract plenty of trouble. Like buzzard meat. Some of it,' he added, 'from me.' The smell of sweat was stronger. 'I ain't so sure I won't get your permit revoked anyway.'

'It'll need the Secretary of State's signature to do it,' I answered, not really knowing, 'and a bit more than bloody-mindedness on your part to convince him of its necessity. Are you making it a crime to bleed on a Los Angeles sidewalk?' I lit a cigarette. Waiting to be offered one or directed to sit in a chair seemed a waste of time.

Without replying, he held out the passport to Sowerby. 'Process it,' he ordered.

I knew what that meant. A Xerox copy of the pages containing identifying data and a reproduction of my photograph and signature. Later, a cable to Interpol Office at New Scotland

Yard with a request to check me out at C.3. The answer would be, 'nothing known: no record.' Charles had already catered for such simple contingencies.

Returning his attention to me, he wheezed, 'This is a tight, friendly little town, mister. We got enough of our own hoodlums without importing any from Europe.'

'I'm one?' I couldn't honestly quarrel with his assessment of me on the facts he might have. And he wasn't someone I could whisper 'Charlie's Bar' to. There was no doubt I was already categorized as a villain. Someone—probably Gost—had stirred things up for me. An anonymous telephone call would be as good as anything. It made Gebhardt's surliness that much more understandable.

He said, 'That gun in your pants belt. You've got a Police Permit?'

I pulled out my wallet once more and gave him the right piece of paper. It had been issued by the Phoenix Police Department on the application of Gribble and was valid anywhere in the State. Reading it, he chewed balefully at his frayed cigar and then handed the permit back.

'It don't give you the right to wave guns about under people's noses,' he finally said.

'No, it doesn't. I've got it to shoot people with. When I'm entitled to do so to protect my own life. You want me to quote the statute?' I asked.

'I already know it,' he assured me. Then he bared his teeth. 'I know enough about it for you to have to be goddam careful in Shiloh City.' He scrubbed the cigar butt to extinction in a glass tray. There were four cigars like chocolate eclairs in a leather case protruding from his shirt pocket. He took one of them and crackled it lovingly between his fingers. 'Who did you come here with?' He was a great man for ignoring the courtesies.

There was no point in evasion. His eyes told me he already knew it was with a woman. A little elementary spadework at the airport, a talk with the hotel desk clerk and he would know as much about Ingrid as I did myself.

'A friend.' I wasn't going to make it easy for him.

'A woman?'

'Yes.'

'Her name?'

'Mrs Ingrid Hansson, a Swedish national.'

'Not your wife then?' He made it sound dirty.

'Does she have to be? Is there a law prohibiting it?' My jaws were beginning to tighten again. 'Do I have to produce a marriage certificate before I can book in at the same hotel as a friend?'

He became furious. For a policeman, his toleration folded up at a depressingly low level. 'That ain't the point,' he gobbled. 'It's an outrage against public decency.'

'Is it against the law?' I persisted. As if it ever could be and civilization still persist.

'You know damn well it ain't.'

'Then mind your own bloody business,' I snapped at him. 'I don't want any thickheaded blue-nose policeman interfering with my private life.'

He was on his feet, his palms flat on the desk, his red face yelling at me for a goddam smooth-talking son-of-a-bitch with no respect for the law or anything else.

The Dobermann Pinscher was barking at me as well.

The door opened and a tall slim man stood in the frame. He was smiling genially at the apoplectic Gebhardt who had halted in mid-torrent. 'Good evening, Chief,' he said pleasantly. 'I was passing by and heard you talking.'

Gebhardt swallowed his spit like a dry bread crust and screwed out a smile. 'Hi, Mayor,' he said. '*Siddown!*' he snarled at the over-excited bitch.

The newcomer held his fist out to me and I shook it. His fingertips were pressing in sequence as he held my hand but whatever it meant I didn't belong. 'Kezler,' he said. 'Donald Kezler and proud to be mayor of this beautiful city.'

'Roger Tallis,' I answered, 'and very pleased indeed to see you.'

He exuded personal wealth and possessed the sun-lamp tanned good looks of the successful politician. I imagined, and could have been wrong, that he had all the sincere *bonhomie* of a man who would kiss a citizen's buttocks for the promise of his vote. His teeth never stopped shining nor his eyes trying to peel the layers from my exterior image.

'I know your name, Mr Tallis,' he said heartily. 'I took the liberty of looking at your passport. Lieutenant Sowerby was stepping out of line but,'—his eyes crinkled—'he didn't like to refuse the mayor. You don't mind?'

'No,' I said, releasing my hand. 'Not so that I'd like to quarrel about it.'

He slapped me on the back and spoke to Gebhardt. 'I'm sure Mr Tallis is a right guy, Chief. Being a Britisher and all that.' He said it meaningly, conveying a message. 'He's not in trouble?'

Gebhardt looked uncomfortable and sat down. 'Not yet he ain't,' he answered, his face surly. 'But he's got plenty of time.' He picked up the teletype flimsy and handed it to Kezler.

The mayor read it and, as he did so, pinched his lower lip into a fold. He regarded me with a cocked eyebrow. 'Somebody doesn't like you very much.'

'I'm surprised,' I said. 'I'm usually so lovable. Who?'

He shook his head. 'You should know. If somebody slugged you, you should.'

'Look,' I said irritably. 'I'm not so stupid as to believe the Los Angeles Police took the trouble to send that message just because they thought I'd been slugged. There's something more.'

Kezler spoke to Gebhardt. 'What about it, Chief? He's entitled to know.'

From his expression, Gebhardt didn't think so but he took back the flimsy and read it again. 'After you left L.A.,' he said, choosing his words carefully, 'a tip-off was received you were engaged in the smuggling of valuable merchandise.'

I went cold. 'What do you mean? Valuable merchandise.'

Gebhardt looked at Kezler and the latter nodded. 'Narcotics,' the lumpy man said. He wasn't half so indignant over this as he had been over my presumed sexual liaison with Ingrid. He possessed a curious set of values.

But I felt the floor lurching sideways beneath my feet like a treacherous bog. 'Narcotics?' I said. 'You must be mad.'

Gebhardt shrugged his meaty shoulders. 'It's what we aim to find out, mister.'

'An anonymous telephone call,' I said derisively. 'Is *that* your tip-off? Because if it is, I know who made it. And why.'

Their faces were wooden, telling me I was right.

'You came with Mrs Hansson,' Kezler stated.

'That's right.'

'She would be subject to the same suspicion. You don't want to drag her into it too?'

'No, I don't. Nor myself.'

'Where is she?' he asked.

'Suppose we deal with me first,' I said to Gebhardt. 'Am I being accused? Or asked?'

'We can clear you,' he said, 'if you play ball.'

'Yes? How?'

He eyed me carefully. 'We could search your hotel rooms. Then your chopper at the airfield.'

'You've a warrant?'

'I could get one.'

'I doubt it. Not on an anonymous telephone call, you couldn't.' This was something I knew about.

Gebhardt's cigar had gone out but it stayed between his blubber lips. 'We don't have to put it to the test, mister,' he rumbled. He pulled open a drawer and took out a slip of paper. 'This,' he said, 'is a form of authorization for us to search. Are you willing to sign it?'

I took the paper from him. It read, '*I—————— authorize the Shiloh City Police Department (Detective Division) to search the premises in my occupation at—————— ——————. Signed——————Date——————*'

'I've no objection,' I said, 'if you promise you won't drop cigar-ash on my sheets. What about the helicopter?'

'I'll add it in,' he replied, 'but it ain't strictly necessary. Not being premises.'

'I could find a dozen lawyers who would say you were wrong. But I won't bother.'

When he had filled in the form, I signed it. He said, 'Thanks,' and put it back in the drawer.

There was a silence for a few moments. A beetle was banging its head against the strip-lighting tube and fell upside-down on to Gebhardt's blotter. He frowned at it waving its legs in the air but did nothing.

'All right,' I said impatiently. 'Let's get on and do it. I want to get to bed.'

'No hurry, fella,' he replied. 'We'll let you know.'

That meant they'd already done it and were busy papering over the cracks of non-success.

'As you aren't bothering,' I said, 'there's no reason to keep me here.'

Gebhardt looked at Kezler who was inspecting his nails. 'No,' he growled. 'But don't leave town.'

I had turned around to leave but this stopped me. 'I'm collecting my luggage and going out to the ranch,' I said, 'and that's leaving town.'

Gebhardt swore. 'You're not sleeping at the hotel?'

'No.'

He opened the drawer again and took out the authorization to search. 'We should have the ranch on this,' he said, reaching for his pen. He had obviously not known of my connection with the ranch before I had earlier told him.

'Not bl ——'

Kezler intervened. 'Leave it, Chief,' he ordered. 'There's no need for that. I know an honest man when I see one.' He was definitely on my side. Despite his politician's grin, I was warming to him.

'But *goddammit*! The . . .' Gebhardt halted when he realized the position in which he found himself. He couldn't continue the fiction of not having already searched the hotel rooms and the helicopter if he insisted on now searching the ranch.

'I said, *leave it*.' Kezler was bearing down hard on the Chief. Mayors do that sort of thing in the States. He squeezed my biceps and shone his teeth at me. 'When you get your passport back,' he said, 'go and collect your baggage. You won't be bothered again.'

After he had left the office, Gebhardt asked me to sit down. Then he lit a fresh cigar and busied his eyes and hands with a folder of papers.

I decided to have a mild go at him. 'What sort of narcotics am I alleged to be smuggling, Chief?'

He looked up from his papers. 'It didn't say.'

'Then how did you know what to look for?'

'That isn't diffic . . .' He stopped, realizing the trap he was falling into.

'It's all right,' I said. 'I'm not objecting. Sometimes justice isn't best served by sticking to the rule book.'

He regarded me coldly for quite a time, licking the end of his cigar. 'You slay me,' he growled at last. 'Don't do me no favours.'

'I wasn't intending to. It was a passing thought and I felt sorry for you.' I stopped him diving back among his papers. 'Do you have two men driving round in a big brown Pontiac? One looking like a third-rate Geronimo; the other, a fat little lady-killer with a caterpillar moustache.'

'They don't belong to me,' he said carelessly. 'They sound a couple of broken-down goons. Why ask?'

'They followed me from the airport.' I looked at my watch. It seemed likely I was being detained for some reason. 'Is your lieutenant going to be long copying my passport?'

He didn't bother to answer. He lifted the telephone and made an inside call to one of his subordinates about a training programme. I smoked another cigarette.

Presently, Sowerby came back with my passport. He received a nod of agreement from Gebhardt who was still talking and handed it to me. 'You want a ride back to the hotel?' he asked ungraciously.

'No,' I said. 'I'll walk.'

That made me a more suspicious character than ever. Nobody ever walked anywhere in Shiloh City. Not unless he was a bum.

9

My car was still outside the hotel. Despite Sowerby's assurances, there was a yellow ticket held to the windscreen by one of the wiper blades.

The night was warm and I was moist from the walk. It hadn't been far—three blocks—but it had given me the opportunity of thinking over events. I was being pressured by a Mr Big all right. So much was certain. That I had no idea of his identity was equally certain. He would have that advantage over me. I had only this. That he wouldn't know I wasn't a helpless sheep waiting to have my throat cut. That I had the will, the teeth and the ability to use them.

I collected the keys from the Night Desk Clerk and took the lift to the fifth floor. Unlocking the door to my room, I felt for the wall-switch and snapped it on. Nothing happened. I stepped further into the room to investigate. This was asking for trouble and I got it.

There was a rustle of sound behind me and a ring of cold metal pressed against my neck: in the right place, if fired, to sever my vertebrae and take my tongue and lower jaw with it.

'Don't move, man,' a voice whispered. 'Don't even look round.'

The door closed softly and we were in almost total blackness. The only light came from a crack in the window curtains. Through it shone the glow from a red neon sign. It was enough for me to see the dim bulk of a second man in front of me.

A hand patted over my jacket until it found the pistol and pulled it out from my waistband.

'Sit down,' a voice said, pushing me with the gun-barrel into a chair. I sat and peered myopically at my visitors.

In the deep gloom they were little more than solid shadows but I saw one was tall; the other short and fat. The tall one gave off a smell of violet hair oil and peppermint chewing-gum. The short one had bad breath. I didn't need to see their faces to know they were my friends in the brown Pontiac. Friends? I remembered the nihilistic mouth of the taller man and began to fret.

'If you want money,' I said into the darkness, 'I haven't got any. Only credit cards.'

'We're just waiting,' the Geronimo-type thug said. He sat near me, his gun pointing at my belly.

The short thug sat on my other side and breathed foetid air over me.

'May I smoke?' I asked, wanting to see their faces. Men without faces are difficult to assess.

'No.' Geronimo was making smacking noises as he chewed his gum.

Shorty scratched himself low down. I decided I didn't like him at all. Geronimo I could stand. He was just plain, ordinarily nasty.

'You're sure it's me you want?' I asked.

'We're sure.' There was a comfortable self-satisfaction in his voice.

'If you shoot that thing, you'll have the house detective banging on the door.'

'Save it. *You* wouldn't hear it.'

'What are we waiting for?'

'A telephone call.'

'For me?'

'No.' Words came sparingly from Geronimo; reluctant verbal teeth being pulled by a hesitant dentist.

I could see a fraction better now. Not much, but enough for the furniture, the pictures on the walls, the white telephone on the desk near the window, to take identifiable shape.

'Do you know my friend Gost?' I asked.

'Ugh?' he answered blankly.

'O'Brien?' It seemed worth putting out feelers.

Geronimo moved restlessly. 'Why don't you sit nice and quiet, man. Just so I don't have to bust you one.'

We were nice and quiet for a few minutes while I died for a smoke. 'Can I have one of my cigarettes?' I asked finally.

Shorty, my smelly *bête noire*, came to my rescue, shaming my hasty judgement of him. 'Let him have one,' he said in a high-pitched voice.

Geronimo said, 'Which pocket?'

I pointed to it and Shorty leaned across and took out my case and lighter. That close, his breath was asphyxiatingly foul. He rose and walked soundlessly to a corner of the room.

With his face concealed by the parchment shade of a reading lamp he lit the cigarette, shielding the flare of my lighter with cupped hands.

He returned the smoke to me and I shuddered. The end was damp but I thought it politic not to object.

'You're a limey, aincha?' he asked.

'I believe so.'

'My old man came from Liverpool.' He said it as if it made us first cousins.

'You should keep it a secret,' I advised him. 'It's not considered a social cachet in England.' He didn't understand that completely but what he understood he didn't very much like.

The two men were professionals to the marrow. Taking no chances and giving none. Hatchet-men, enforcers: doing their job without passion or pity. They were keeping me here while something happened. To Ingrid, I suspected. That began to eat away at the edges of my composure. I started to shake and a cold destructive rage built up inside me. All the worse because I suspected it would prove impotent.

I dropped the cigarette on the carpet and ground it out with the sole of my shoe. So far, things had been fairly civilized. Then I stood and said, 'I'd like to see you two bastards stuffed with a forty-foot cactus.'

Even this vulgarity seemed better than sitting around waiting. At least, I thought so until Geronimo leaned forward and, quick as a cobra with migraine, hit me on the cheekbone with the barrel of his gun.

It wasn't hard enough to crack the bone but it knocked me back stunned into the chair. I didn't think there was any animosity about the blow. Just something he felt he had to do: an unthinking cruelty that would get him killed one day.

When I had shaken the flashes of light from my brain, I saw the barrel was back pointing at my belly. I didn't say anything. Even in the twilight of the room he could see, if he had the wit to recognize it, what I would do to him when he was separated from his gun. Or I had mine.

Shorty tutted to himself. I presumed over my bad manners. The cigarette had, to him, been the equivalent of my eating his salt.

I nursed my aching face and we sat in silence in the crawling tension for what seemed hours. It was, in fact, a little over thirty minutes. Then the telephone rang with startling suddenness.

Shorty answered it, moving silently with his fat cat waddle. 'Yes? . . . yes, it is . . . yeah, right away . . . no . . . no, nothing at all.'

Geronimo gestured with his gun. 'On your feet,' he ordered. He took my pistol from his pocket and tossed it to Shorty. The fat thug must have had cat's eyes too, for he caught it neatly.

'Unload it,' Geronimo said.

Shorty unclipped the magazine and tossed the empty pistol on to the bed. The magazine, he kept in his hand.

'In the bathroom,' Geronimo ordered.

I walked slowly, my mind working frantically, certain I was going to get a bullet in the back. The muzzle of the gun jabbed at my neck, herding me along.

Once in, he removed the key from the lock and shut the door on me, securing it from the outside. My breath expelled slowly and I moved away from the door. It wasn't too late for either of them to be bloody-minded and spray bullets through the panelling. I didn't really believe they would. The rank and file of the Syndicate were as disciplined as soldiers. But there is always the exception.

When I heard the outer door close, I depressed the wall-switch. The light came on and I searched for a means to escape. The bathroom door opened inwards so I was denied the simplicity of the sharp kick on the lock, forcing the tongue from its socket.

I opened the window. There was a narrow ledge beneath. I thought I might, given some of the characteristics of a house-fly, just make it round the corner of the brickwork to the window of my room. If I didn't, a fall from the fifth floor could do no less than fracture my spine.

I lit a cigarette with unsteady hands and hauled myself out on to the ledge. Without looking down at the dark street, I shuffled my way along the face of the building. Negotiating the angle of the corner was the more horrifying, teetering on my toes and certain I would pitch backwards into space.

None of the people below noticed me. For all the attention

I received, I might have been on the north face of the Eiger in a blinding snowstorm. There were moments when I almost wished I was.

When I finally reached the window I found it unfastened and was able to climb in. Although I thought otherwise, I hadn't been long. The cigarette I held between my lips was still less than half consumed. I was trembling from the sheer muscular effort of holding on to not much more than cement pimples with my fingertips.

Unlocking the bathroom door and allowing the light to pour in, I located the lamp bulbs on the bed. When I had screwed them back into their sockets and switched them on, I retrieved my pistol and reloaded it with the magazine I found discarded near the outer door.

I poured myself an alcoholic's idea of a large whisky and lifted the telephone, dialling the number of the ranch. There was no answer. The electric impulses sounding in my ear echoed the far loneliness of a bell ringing in an empty room. I tried twice more and replaced the handset.

I checked the drawers and cupboards. Their contents possessed the indefinable stigmata of having been touched by alien hands. Chief Gebhardt hadn't believed in allowing grass to grow beneath his feet.

Completing the packing of my cases, I entered Ingrid's room and collected hers. Although I could not judge, I had no doubt her room had been searched also.

When I handed the keys back to the desk clerk and asked him to keep the rooms during my temporary absence, he hesitated. Then he said, 'Pardon me, sir. A man asked for you.'

'Oh? When?'

He looked at the clock on the wall. It showed eleven o'clock. 'About twenty after ten. He said he was a friend.' His rimless glasses glinted and his moon face looked worried.

'What did he want?'

'He asked if you were in. I said I thought you were, not saying definitely. I asked should I ring your room. He said, no. He would rather I didn't. He just wanted to know.'

'What did he look like?'

The clerk put his fingers on his chin. 'He had a small beard and a moustache.'

'Thank you. I'm glad you told me.'

He hesitated again. Then he took a five-dollar bill from under the desk. 'He gave me this. Not to say anything. What should I do with it?'

'Keep it,' I said, 'and add these to it.' I gave him ten dollars and the ranch telephone number. 'He's not my friend and if he calls again, let me know at once. You can reach me at that number. In any case, find out what you can about him. If he comes again, stall him. Don't tell him I'm not at the hotel.'

As he was folding away his money, I asked casually, 'Have I had any other callers?'

He looked up at me in surprise. 'No, sir.'

'Not a tall man with an Indian face? Or a short, fat one with a moustache?'

His expression was blank. 'No, *sir*,' he assured me. 'I would have seen them.'

That could have been true had they come in through the basement garage.

I was possessed of a dark foreboding as the bell-hop loaded the luggage into the car. The Paymaster was horribly active. He had either taken or killed Ingrid while Geronimo and his evil-smelling colleague held me immobile. O'Brien, snuffling always at my heels, posed an unknown threat. I didn't know whom I could trust. I began to feel I was ill-advised in refusing Charles's offer of assistance. The water was lapping my chin and rising fast.

*

I drove the Chevrolet hard along the highway to the ranch, its two beams of brilliant white cutting into the hot, insect-filled night. When I turned on to the dirt access road, I switched out the lights. The moon was bright enough to show me the bends and potholes I had to negotiate. If anyone was watching from inside the ranch, they had seen my approach long before my arrival. I didn't believe this a reason for further pinpointing my position by brashness.

I glided the car to a quiet stop in the deep blue shadow on the far side of the bunkhouse. Inching out of the seat, I left the door open to avoid noise. I removed my pistol from its holster and slipped the safety catch to the 'off' position.

Anything other than immediate survival was out of my mind. I was emotionless, conscious of only physical things and ninety-five per cent a hunting animal. I felt the pressure of the soles of my shoes on the pebbled sand, the roughness of the stock of the pistol and the curve of my forefinger on its trigger. The smell of crushed sage was in my nostrils.

My senses of vision and hearing were acute: I saw the barely perceptible movements of leaves against the night sky, the dust stirred by the gentle desert wind and the scaly whisper of a lizard's slither. I heard the creaking of timbers contracting in the cooling air. Small creatures made high-pitched mewings and squeakings as they lived in the tiny worlds of their own habitats.

I moved slowly, picking my steps, working my way from the bunkhouse to the inky shadows of the palms around the house, avoiding exposure under the cold blanched fire of the moon. I passed as a shadow myself through a passage into the inner courtyard where the water-drops from the fountain glittered like falling diamonds.

Here, I took off my shoes and crept ghost-footed through the corridors and rooms looming with dark masses of furniture and glistening with the lakes of polished floors. I swung doors open gently and stood back, apprehensive for the spurt of blue fire or the swing of knuckled fists into my face. I waited long minutes in the dead, unbreathing silence of an empty house.

Then, discarding the cowardly caution of fear, I pushed without concealment through the remaining rooms, snapping on the lights behind me.

There were no signs of violence and no indications that the rooms had been searched. I sat, staring glumly at a wall, a glass of whisky in my fist and a cigarette burning between my fingers. I thought, although not very usefully. I was no longer in control of the situation and events were overtaking me. It wasn't the best way of fighting a battle requiring purpose and initiative. I seemed to have run out of both.

The ringing of the telephone bell jerked me from my self-doubts and I leapt to answer it.

Her 'Roger?' was tentative, uncertain. 'We missed each other,' she said.

I don't know what I expected but it wasn't that. 'Are you all right?' I asked.

'Of course.' I detected a note of restraint.

'Then what do you mean?' I said irritably. '*We missed each other.*'

'I am back at the hotel.'

'You're *what*!' I exploded. 'How did you get there?'

'I took a cab.'

'Why? *Why*, Ingrid?'

'I found I wanted things from my room.' In the silence which followed, I heard faintly the clashing of moving metal. It had a deep musical resonance that was tantalizingly familiar but completely unidentifiable. It wasn't a noise I had heard in the hotel.

'That's silly,' I said, forcing myself to calmness. 'You had only to telephone me.'

'I did. I . . . I could not get a reply.'

All this was so stupid, so unlike Ingrid, that I knew she was under some constraint. I grunted like a man who long ago had given up trying to understand the vagaries of woman. 'All right,' I said, 'I'll come and get you. But for God's sake stay put for five minutes while I catch up with you.'

'I will wait,' she answered and then added. 'Did you meet Bill Gost in the bar?' She spoke slowly, emphasizing the words by a change of pace.

That shook me. It obviously needed an answer I didn't have. 'He never turned up,' I said cautiously.

'Oh, dear. You will have to work the contract out on your own.'

'*You* didn't see him? Bill, I mean.'

'No . . .' A hand was clearly clapped over the mouthpiece, muffling sound from the other end. Then, 'I have to go, Roger. I have left my bath running.' There was a click and the purring sound of a disconnection.

I recradled my receiver and went back to looking at the wall. What was she waffling about Gost for? Why call him 'Bill? And what was the significance of referring to a bar? I was certain of one thing if of nothing else: she was not going to be at the hotel. But somebody wanted *me* there; walking in starry-eyed with a happy, unsuspecting smile on my face. If they did, that somebody was going to get a surprise.

After unloading the luggage I got back into the car and headed straight for Shiloh City. My fear I had suspended like a library subscription. I was looking for trouble.

10

The desk clerk was reading the coloured cartoon strips from the following day's newspaper. You could tell the manager was in bed. He raised his eyebrows at my reappearance and reached for the room keys without being asked.

'You decided to come back, sir?' he said, putting his paper down on to his chair.

'I forgot something. Nobody's asked after me? Or called?'

He shook his head. 'No, sir. It's been a quiet night.'

I walked soft-footed along the carpeted corridor leading to our rooms. From beneath Ingrid's door there came only darkness. From beneath mine there was a crack of light. Before unlocking it, I cocked the pistol and held it ready in my left hand.

I swung the door open and stepped inside. Nobody said, 'Don't move,' to the back of my head or switched out the lights. I closed the door behind me and looked at my visitor.

She was sitting cross-legged on my bed and wasn't an hour over fifteen years old. She wore a wrist watch and a pair of white-spotted blue panties. She was otherwise naked. With her lipstick she had drawn designs and written words—not very nice ones—over her thin body. The young breasts and navel had come in for some heavy-handed gouache treatment in bright scarlet. Her large shiny blue eyes were glassy and unfocused. She was a pretty little thing with prominent cheekbones and freckles and long blonde hair.

She giggled in a mad sort of way that bristled my neck hairs. 'My,' she said in a slurred voice, 'you look like a Viking skirt-lifter with a sun tan. Are you going to shoot me?'

I walked to the bathroom and checked it. When I saw there was nobody waiting in there, I put my pistol away. I turned back to the girl. 'Aren't you in the wrong bed?'

'Nope, I don't think so.' She tilted her head at me. 'You one of these guys needing a hunk of pussy?'

'I don't believe so.'

'Brother,' she said, 'I think you do.' She hooked her thumb in the waist of the pants and snapped the elastic against her stomach.

'Suppose you get dressed and buzz off back to wherever you came from.' I was short with her, not liking the situation at all.

She peered at me from beneath the fringe of her hair. 'Say, what sort of a phoney accent've you got?' Then she stuck her thumb in her mouth. 'You're British aren't you?'

'I'm from Hoboken, New York.'

'*Hoboken*,' she corrected my mispronunciation of it. 'You're a limey all right. Gee, I've never been laid by a limey.'

She was hopped up to her pencilled-on eyebrows; a pathetic, manipulated little doll of a creature. I felt both sorry for her and angry. 'What are you doing here? Who sent you?'

'Wassamatter?' She was belligerent now. 'You don't want it?'

'No. You look to me as if you're playing hookey from Junior Grade High School.'

She pouted at me. '———— you,' she said. 'Are you queer?'

'Who set you up for this? How did you get in here?' There had been no key in the lock.

Instead of answering, she fell backwards on to the sheets and arched her body, slipping off the pants in one smooth motion and flinging them at me. She'd certainly practised it an awful lot for that kind of dexterity. 'Come on, mister,' she coaxed. 'It's ready and waiting for you.'

I went towards her and caught hold of one thin wrist, pulling her unexpectedly from the bed. Then I picked her up in my arms—for one moment the warm, smooth-fleshed body seemed totally desirable—and carried her into the bathroom, opening the door with a kick of my shoe.

She was wriggling like a greased eel, covering my jacket and shirt with the lipstick from her body. Her obscenities were low-grade gutter as she realized my purpose and she slashed out with her fingernails.

I propped her in a corner of the shower and angled the spray towards her, turning on the cold water tap. 'Cool down, you hot-assed little bitch,' I snapped at her. 'You're wasting your time.'

She spat at me and I slid shut the glass screen. Seen through the fluted glass her body was a rippled, undulating flesh-pink under the splashing water. She screamed her filth against the

94

muffling glass and hammered on it with her small fists. I held the screen secure until she ceased and I saw her turning on the hot water. Then I left her closing the bathroom door behind me.

Back in my room, I thought furiously. I was possessed of a naked and drugged nymphomaniac juvenile, a lipstick-covered jacket and shirt and no foreseeable defence to a charge of Contributing to the Delinquency of a Minor. Once in Gebhardt's hands on such an indictment and I wouldn't see daylight for weeks.

Timing in a set-up like this was important. I had to be discovered *flagrante delicto*. I imagined the squad car was even then on its way.

Then, shockingly, from the bathroom I heard a sharp *chuf! chuf! chuf!* and the sound of breaking glass. The scream that followed was thin and wavery and altogether tragic.

Pistol in hand, I burst through the door. Gost was standing with his back to an open window, horrified disbelief bulging his yellow eyes. The gun in his hand had a silencer screwed to its barrel and a tiny spiral of blue smoke came from it.

Lying in the shards of broken glass and half out of the shower was the wet, shining body of the girl. Water was beating into her open mouth.

Mouthing incoherencies, Gost swung his gun in an arc towards me. Mine was already pointing at him and I snatched at the trigger. It jumped in my hand with a vicious crack and I saw the bullet dimple the stuff of his trousers, hitting him in the stomach near his right hip.

Diving sideways, I crashed behind the partition dividing the lavatory closet from the bathroom. Gost's gun went *chuf! chuf!* again, clipping the heel of my shoe and jerking my foot.

Wedged helplessly between pedestal and wall, I waited with my pistol aimed where I thought his head would appear. I *wanted* to kill him. I wanted a bullet to liquidize the matter of his vicious, murderous brain.

The window banged and I heard the clatter of his descent on the iron fire escape outside. By the time I had wriggled free from the closet and opened the window, he had gone.

I returned to the girl and turned off the shower taps. The water swirling down the drain was pink and frothy. There were three purple-rimmed holes grouped round the girl's navel and gashes in her back from falling through the glass screen.

There was a fugitive shadow of life left in her. As I lifted her and carried her back to the bed, her eyes opened and I saw in them terror of me and her incomprehension of approaching death. 'Shh .. shu-ushh ... shu ... shu ...', she gasped and died.

I laid her gently on the bed and straightened her long wet hair. Then I pulled the blue silk cover over her. Time was running out on me and I snapped the lights off, opening the outer door slowly. I would have preferred the fire escape but the thought of mad-dog Gost waiting with his gun cocked was a chilling one. Locking the door behind me, I walked towards the stairs. Nobody ever used them by choice and if ever I wanted aloneness it was now.

As I passed the lift shaft, I saw the pointer above the doors indicating the approach of the cage. I dodged behind the ground-length curtains of a window and waited, my thalamus triggering off alarms.

The lift stopped and the cage opened quietly. Three men came out. One was Lieutenant Sowerby, grim and purposeful. One was obviously another policeman. The third was hatless and carried a key. He couldn't be anyone but the house detective. They halted outside the door to my room, none speaking but listening with heads tilted sideways to the wooden panels.

The original set-up for an offence under the Morals Code was now a pallid thing against the enormity of murder. It wasn't worth stopping to point out that the girl had three bullet holes in her stomach against the one shot fired from my pistol. These ambiguities took time to rationalize and I hadn't the time to spare. Somewhere, Ingrid was in danger and I had to find her.

Sowerby nodded to the house detective who inserted his key noiselessly in the lock. This was the *flagrante delicto* part and even in my own extremity I felt sorry for Sowerby and the unexpected troubles he was about to inherit.

When the door swung open and they burst in with guns in their hands, I ran for it. Taking the carpeted stairs in huge soundless bounds, I reached the foyer and paused. The desk clerk was standing near the lift shaft listening, a smug smile of anticipation on his face. When he saw me, a look of terror muddied his eyes and he dived behind the desk, his thumb prodding for the alarm button.

He never made it by a yard. I held him securely by the lapels of his linen jacket, screwing his collar and tie up under his chin and pushing him hard against the edge of the desk.

'You twisting, double-crossing little bastard,' I growled into his horror-stricken face. 'You knew all the time. Those two thugs, the girl . . .'

The answer was in his eyes. I snatched his spectacles from his nose, tossed them into the filing tray and hit him full in the centre of his moon face. The blow knocked him sideways along the desk to fall flat like a disarticulated dummy. It was about time I hit somebody. If only to reassure myself I could.

I left him there, bleeding quietly on to the hotel's carpet. Then I lifted the telephones from their cradles and pulled plugs from sockets on the switchboard.

Outside, it surprised me that no uniformed patrolman stood guarding my car with a big revolver. Sowerby wasn't so efficient after all. I forced myself to walk casually to it, expecting any second to hear the shouts and sounds of pursuit.

I had slipped into the driver's seat and inserted the key into the ignition before I became aware of the dark bulk behind me and the voice of Gost. 'It's pointing at your head, you————' he rasped, 'and I only want one goddam reason to open it up with a bullet.' He meant it all right. Desperation underlined his resolution in the way he said it.

Even in the dark interior of the car, his paleness was evident. The hand not holding the gun was clutched over his stomach. The fingers had splotches of blood on them. He looked sick and, once again, I thought pathetic. 'Move,' he ordered.

I started the car and put her in gear. 'Where?'

'To my wife.'

I thought this over as we moved along the street, gathering speed. 'And I know where she is?'

'You'd better,' he said grimly. 'If you don't, you're dead.'

'I do, of course,' I answered confidently. 'She's at the ranch.'

'Ranch?'

'El Rancho Madrito. Out near Painted Rock.'

'Is she on her own?'

I hesitated, not certain what was best to say. 'Yes.'

'O.K.,' he said. He had been drinking whisky and the fumes flowed over me. 'Go to the airfield.'

I turned at the next junction to join the freeway. He pressed the ring of the silencer on the bone at the back of my ear.

'Give me your shooter,' he ordered. 'And do it slowly.'

I gave it to him. Slowly, like he said; careful as I did so that my movements should not be misinterpreted.

Death was in the car like a black fog. It lay in the baleful eyes watching me so intently. Only Gost's assumption that I could take him to Ingrid stopped his shooting me out of hand. He had made one mistake in killing the girl. He was the type of man who would ensure he didn't make a second.

'Why the airfield?' I asked, keeping my eyes on both the almost deserted street and rear view mirror. I was expecting the eruption of sirens and flashing red lights behind me.

'For Christ's sake!' he said contemptuously. 'The cops. I saw them go in. They'll be swarming like hornets when they find that dame in your bathroom. Setting up road-blocks, checking everywhere. So, we'll fly.'

'You seem well-informed about me.'

His contempt kept him silent.

'Where are we flying?' I persisted.

'To that ranch of yours. *You bastard!*' he burst out. 'Did you have to screw her as well as my wife?'

'You wouldn't believe me if I told you.'

'No, I wouldn't. So don't bother.' The breath of a groan escaped from him. 'You've got an instrument rating for that chopper of yours?'

'Yes.' The houses were beginning to thin, rows of shadowed orange and grapefruit trees taking their place. We were nearing the airport.

'It's got a night landing light?'

'Yes.'

'Fuelled up?'

'Yes.'

He tapped the side of my throat with the gun. 'Listen, buster, and listen good. Sometime I'm going to kill you, so do exactly as I say. If you don't, it'll be that much sooner, that much more painful. Understand?'

'Yes,' I said. He seemed not to leave me the option of any other answer.

He was stupid. Nobody but an idiot would have made the tactical, psychological error of telling me I was going to be killed; full stop. Of leaving me no hope; underlining I had nothing to lose and everything to gain. It is hope that palsies the will, not fear. Fear galvanizes. It pumped cold resolve and anger into me from my adrenals. I saw everything with a stark clarity and inside my nervous system I felt coiled like a spring for bloody action. The urge to destroy him prickled the hair on my head, compressing my fingers savagely around the steering-wheel rim.

In silence I drove through the gates of the Heliport, clearing take-off with Control from the Night Guards' office. Gost remained quiet in the back of the car while I produced my identification papers but it was the quietness of waiting death.

The Heliport was ancillary to the Airport. It existed in the shadows of the huge metal birds thundering over the long cement runways, invisible now in the darkness but for the strings of yellow and red guide lights outlining them.

Gost was my second shadow as I parked the car on the grass apron and got out. While I unhooked the tethering wires and removed the control locks from the helicopter, he watched me.

He had been efficiently trained by the Army. He stood near enough to kill or disable me with the first bullet but not close enough for me to take the gun away from him. The muzzle of it, concealed always by the shadow of his body, followed me unwaveringly.

In the cabin, he said, 'No tricks. I know what you've got to do. I've done it all myself.' His hand was still holding his stomach and blood seeped through the material of his trousers. 'Dust your ass, buster,' he rasped. 'We haven't got all night.'

Clipping on our throat microphones, I told Control I wanted clearance for Sky Harbor Heliport at Phoenix. It was as good a destination as any other. Control gave me a flight path of 048° at 1000 feet and I started the rotors moving.

Gost followed my engine check with intent eyes. I remembered he had flown helicopters in Vietnam. He was briefing himself to take over the flying after he'd killed me.

Everything he did put his purpose into capital letters.

At lift-off, the airport tilted and fell away sharply and the silvered desert with its hard black shadows spread wider below us. The moon, its huge white disc flooding light into the cabin, etched lines and craters on Gost's coarse-grained face and frosted his hair. His expression was harsh and set for violence.

I swung the helicopter on to her compass course and pushed the stick forward, heading for the dark mass of Painted Rock. The blue glow from the dials of the instrument panel made the gun in his hand shine cobalt. It nudged at the concentration of my flying, not allowing me to forget his menace.

I had taken a ball pen from my breast pocket to mark my map. I retained it concealed in my left hand, flat against the throttle grip of the collective-pitch lever I was holding. I meant to kill him with it, having already chosen the exact spot on his throat where a stab was most likely to sever the carotid artery. All I had to do was to kick violently on the rudder and punch the pen backwards as the skidding of the aircraft put him off balance. I could imagine the spurting of blood over the perspex bowl; the look that must come into his eyes at being killed by such a ridiculous weapon.

I swallowed at a suddenly dry throat, also imagining his dying forefinger pulling the trigger in a final paroxysm and taking me with him. It was a danger I had to face.

He said, 'I killed that dame, didn't I?'

'Yes. You thought it was your wife?'

He made a noise in his back teeth that vibrated my earphones but gave no answer.

'I don't think your wife deserves that.'

'Shut up,' he grunted, 'or I'll shoot your ————— balls off. You ————— —————.' He hated me as much as one man can ever hate another.

I shrugged. Words were nothing: they bounced off me like rubber raindrops. 'You might be right at that,' I said. 'Were you involved in the heroin smuggling?'

He had calmed down. 'I used to be. Then I became hot with Narcotics Bureau. Ingrid stood in for me. For *me*.' His face twitched with what I hoped was pain. 'Didn't think the bitch would do this to me,' he mumbled, more to himself than to me. 'But *why*? You ain't nothing. A goddam blondie Britisher she used.' He wagged his head. The shadow of the canopy strut threw a bar across his face and the whites of his eyes sparkled with what I thought improbable tears. 'She sure took you for a ride, buster. Your *last* ride.'

The palms of my hands were slippery with sweat and I wiped them on my thighs, concerned that the pen might slide free during the final stroke.

He grinned at me, his thick lips peeling back from his teeth, his hair dropping over his forehead. 'I put the skids under you in L.A. I thought the bastards'd knock you off for sure. Never mind. This is better.'

'I'm also sorry I didn't allow myself to be electrocuted,' I said sardonically.

He bared his teeth again. 'You should have fried,' he growled. 'Did you see it?'

I shrugged. 'It wasn't so good.'

The black bulk of Painted Rock was now ahead, its peak outlined against the cyanosed sky. In a few minutes one of us was going to be dead. Given bad luck on my part, both of us.

Another groan came from him as he stirred in his seat. His intestines must have been in a dreadful mess. Possibly the bullet had hit the hipbone and slivered into fragments, slicing multiple wounds in his belly. He was leaking blood badly and, below the waist, the trousers were jellied black.

'You bastard,' he said painfully. 'You shot me.' It was something he found difficulty in accepting. No doubt he thought I should have hit him with a folded copy of *The Times*. 'Lucky . . . just goddam lucky . . .'

The flesh of his finger tightened as he pulled it harder round the curve of the trigger. He was a fraction of a second away from being stabbed with my pen. Then he relaxed and said, 'No. Give me some dual first.'

I let my breath out slowly. 'You've qualified on V.T.O.L.?'

He glared at me, his topaz eyes glinting. 'Just show me. Give me the handling characteristics and then shut up.' Another groan ripped out from his chest, some of the violence of his personality going with it. He leaned forward, peering down at the desert, forgetting his instructions to me. 'Where is it?' he croaked. 'Where's that ranch of yours?'

'On the other side of the peak,' I lied. Pulling hard on the collective, I lifted the helicopter up, centring the stick and maintaining climb without forward motion.

'Wha's matter. What're you doing?' He was slumped in his seat, only the lap belt holding him from tumbling sideways. He hiccupped and a thin runnel of blood spilled from the corner of his mouth.

'I'm taking her up to jump the peak,' I said. I gave the engine maximum throttle and the cockpit shuddered as the rotors thrashed the thinning air above us.

'S'nough,' he said sharply. 'S'nough, you bastard. Take her down.' For the first time the muzzle of his gun wobbled in its implacable regard of me.

I looked into his eyes and took a deep breath. 'If you shoot me, Gost, we'll both die. You're in no state to fly this.' My worst fear was that he would believe himself mortally wounded and finish me off as an *hors-d'oeuvre* to his own death. I couldn't gauge the extent of his injury but his reaction to it was bad. His pallor had a leaden tinge to it and much of the fierceness had gone with his blood.

At maximum hover we began to wallow badly, teetering drunkenly over the gulf of darkness beneath. Slowly I took my hand from the collective. I held the pen firmly in my curled fingers, exposing its pointed end by pushing the cap of it with my hooked thumb, holding it poised.

'I'll shoot . . . I'll shoot your . . .' He made an agonized mooing noise and tore at his collar with scratching fingernails. The back of his hand was shiny with blood. Liquid sounds came from beneath him. The gun was now pointing at his own foot. I could kill him any time I wanted to.

But this great ox of a man with his unbending hatreds needed no violence from me. Life was draining through the hole in his stomach, the coming darkness paralyzing his will. His eyelids drooped and I saw him convulse as the dying mind ordered his finger to pull the trigger. Then he shuddered and his body relaxed, a sigh coming from his mouth.

I reached sideways and took the gun from the nerveless fingers. He snored and twisted restlessly in his seat.

I returned to the controls and reduced power, dropping to my flight-path altitude. Having escaped Gost, I wouldn't relish the irony of being fragmented by a jet liner using the traffic pattern.

At some point during the descent, Gost died. When I looked at him and felt for his pulse, I saw his feet were in the pool of blood that had drained his flesh paper-white.

Ingrid really was a widow now.

While I hovered over the ranch, I chewed at my problems. I was saddled with the body of a man I had shot. Back in Shiloh City was the girl he had killed. So *I* said. But in *my* hotel room and, without question, laid to the door of my villainy. The reasons supporting my innocence sounded fairly convincing the way I told them to myself. I wasn't so sure they would to, say, Chief Gebhardt or Lieutenant Sowerby.

I was in a trap. Not of my own making, but one to which I had contributed by my zeal for total involvement. Of all the problems I had, the disposal of Gost and his gun bulked the largest and most immediate. I switched on the reading lamp over the instrument panel and unfolded my navigational map. I searched for and found the brown shading of the Little Horn Mountains. They were less than forty miles away north-west of my present position. In their rocky wastes, on the map, I located Virgin Peak, towering 3,000 feet above the surrounding desert. It would do for the purpose I had in mind. Landing might be tricky but I was in no position to exercise a choice. What I had to do had to be done unobserved.

I pencilled in a rough vector and set my compass on a bearing of 330°. It should be accurate enough. I would see and recognize the whale-shaped bulk of the range long before I ran into it. The map showed a stream running from its flank and this was important.

I clipped the folded map on to my knee-pad and swung the helicopter around in a swooping turn on to its new bearing. This lolled Gost's head over on to the seat squab and I saw his chin had dropped, exposing his tongue. The once-fierce eyes were dull yellow marbles. When I tried to think of something good about him I failed. He didn't honestly seem much of a loss.

I crossed high over the molten-pewter Gila River, keeping the blazing cluster of lights that was Shiloh City on my starboard side. The moon was falling down out of the sky but still bright enough to wash the landscape with its own lividity.

In twenty minutes I was skirting the illuminated side of the pine-covered flanks of the peak. I slowed the helicopter down to the leisurely flap of a cruising buzzard and scanned the rugged terrain for a level clearing suitable for landing.

When I saw the crescent of shadow near the summit of the peak I hovered and squinted through the perspex. It was a crater two or three hundred yards across. The sloping sides were covered with pines and rough scrub; its bottom, boulder-littered but reasonably flat, would provide a landing-pad of sorts.

I rode the helicopter just below the crater's inside rim and flicked on the nose landing light, traversing the interior with the sizzling beam. Finally satisfied, I settled her in position and dropped with my fingers crossed. The bar of downward-pointing light shortened until I felt the slight jar of impact. I cut the motor, sliding sideways on loose shale. The slowing rotors were whistling within feet of a skeleton trunk of a dead pine but the tilt of the aircraft was within permissible limits. Releasing myself from the lap belt, I opened the door and dismounted.

When I had breathed in enough of the fresh air, I lit a cigarette and looked around me. The walls of the crater rose above me like the sides of a bowl. I could only be observed from the dark jets which passed above and blotted out the stars, their navigation lights winking red and green.

I climbed back into the cabin and unstrapped Gost, lowering him from it as carefully as I could half-way out, I was forced by his weight to release him and he dropped with a thump to the ground. I laid him neatly under the fuselage, first searching his clothing and retrieving my pistol from one of his pockets.

I cleaned it and reloaded the magazine, putting it back in my waistband. I didn't like guns and I was sorry I had killed Gost with it. I had all the British policeman's *Angst* about carrying one. Even acknowledging that without it I would now be wandering the shadows in the place of Gost.

Then, huddled in the cockpit, I waited for the dawn. There was an immense outer-space silence at this altitude and it was a place in which to think solemn thoughts. But all I did was to worry and fret and kiln-dry my throat with endless cigarettes.

I watched two small blotched geckoes running over the

inside of the perspex bowl above my head, hunting insects with high-pitched, industrious squeaks. Opening the window to chase them out I heard a coyote howling, only just a shade more mournful than the rumbling of my famished stomach. I had eaten nothing for fourteen hours.

Soon the moon dropped behind the rim of the crater and the darkness grew velvet-black and more melancholy. I was the only man in the world and Gost, a formless shape near the starboard landing wheel, my familiar.

Dawn came at last with an arpeggio of distant shrieks from some sort of a desert owl. Gost's body began to take on shape, his face assuming the pallor of bleached leather. There were small coloured snails crawling on his flesh.

Outside the cabin I shivered in the cold, my breath smoking in the clear air. When it was light enough, I started moving rocks. I had no digging tools and the earth was too flinty for anything less than a pick.

Gost required burying for a number of reasons. He had a bullet from my pistol in his belly that provided evidence of a connection between us. His gun linked him with the murder of the girl at the hotel and thus, inescapably, with me. I could, given a cement stomach and a pair of thick rubber gloves, have dug the bullet out of him. But I had always possessed a rising gorge at the thought of handling dead flesh. So I decided against it. In one of my more bitter moments, straining at the carrying of rocks, I thought to leave him unburied; changing my mind on considering he might thus poison any unfortunate vulture chancing on him.

When I had fashioned a shallow trough, I dragged him to it, put his gun between his legs and covered him with boulders. There was some pity in me at this finality but also a sense of justice done. I didn't do anything mawkish like saying a prayer for a man who had tried to kill me. I don't think it would have done him any good had I done so.

While I sweated over the burying of him, the sun had risen above the crater, a brassy ball shimmering in its own heat waves.

I climbed up through the pines to the rim and looked for the watercourse shown on the map. I identified it by the brighter greenness along its path.

Returning to the helicopter, I unbolted Gost's seat from its moorings and removed the rubber strip on to which he had bled. I carried both down the slope to the stream, cursing as my shoes slid on loose stones and flies stung my sweating flesh. With some rag I scrubbed the congealed blood from them in the cold water. Although the plastic covering of the seat washed clean, I saw that blood had penetrated the seams and soaked the foam rubber interior.

Labouring back to the crater with my load, I left the seat on the ground while I replaced it with one removed from the rear. Then I tied the soiled seat to it with cord, leaving it hanging out through the open door.

When I finally lifted off, the sun was gold-bright and baking out perfume from the mat of pine-needles on the floor of the crater. I followed the watercourse down the mountainside until it ran into a narrow canyon, too barren and rocky to attract casual visits.

Over it, I put the aircraft into hover and opened out the blade of my pocket-knife. I reached across the cabin and sliced the cord, allowing the blood-soaked seat to tumble into the canyon. As I closed the door, I saw it rebound once and then vanish into a jumble of boulders.

If found, it would mean nothing and could never be associated with a man named Gost. A man who had ceased to exist some hours ago.

11

I circled the ranch buildings a shade above palm-tree height before deciding to land. The cabaña was shuttered and apparently deserted. No car with POLICE DEPARTMENT painted on it stood waiting on the front step.

It was just as well there wasn't. I desperately needed a bath, a shave, a change of clothing and some food. Facing what promised to be a scorching and desperate day was bad enough in itself. To do so in my filthy, starving state was impossible.

Letting the helicopter down on to the drive in a storm of whipped-up dust, I climbed bone-wearily out of the cockpit. Fumbling the key into the door I jerked like a galvanized frog when the voice behind me said, 'Good morning, son.'

To my fatigued eyes, the sheriff was ten feet tall and had materialized from the stony soil. He was Wyatt Earp watching me from behind a Dodge City moustache, his pale grey eyes pinning me to paralysis.

Although the revolver with the telescopic sight was still snug in its holster, his hand hovered too close to it for me to think of doing anything but stand still. Slung over one bony shoulder was the Hasselblad and my eyes riveted to it.

I said, 'You hid your car in a gopher's hole?' and waited, poised with the door key between finger and thumb.

'It's in your garage, son,' he replied. He made it sound as if I'd begrudged his car the convenience. More geniality showed through the moustache than had on his previous visit. 'I used a tooth pick. Didn't think you'd come down otherwise.' He nodded at the key in my hand. 'Open her up and let's both get in out of the sun.'

He followed me in, not taking off his big hat. It rode four-square on his forehead and suggested a massive puritanism.

On the floor, inside the door, lay a white envelope. I picked it up and said, 'Excuse me,' to the sheriff. He sat on one of the settees and took out and lit a cigarette. The camera he un-hitched and put at his side.

The envelope, unaddressed, was also unsealed. It contained a sheet of paper, a small key and a flashlight Polaroid photograph of Ingrid. She was lying on a bed with wrists handcuffed, her head bowed to avoid the intrusive stare of the camera lens. She looked unharmed but dejected and lost.

The message was as inelegant as the ill-formed capitals in which it was printed. '*WE GOT YOUR GIRL. PUT STUFF IN LOCKER # 32 AT RAILROAD DEPOT BEFORE 6. NO TRICKS OR SHE DIES.*'

I put the articles back in the envelope, my face expressionless, not reflecting the chill I felt in my stomach.

The sheriff was polishing dust from his cowboy boots with a red handkerchief. 'Trouble, son?' he asked.

'Not unless you brought it with you.'

He was momentarily startled. Then he said, '*I* haven't brought any, son. But it was sure on your porch an hour ago.'

I waited, slipping the envelope into my hip-pocket.

He continued. 'Lieutenant Sowerby from the City Police Department. I passed him on the way here.' He regarded my stained clothing from under the stiff brim of his hat. 'I reckon it was kind of lucky you two didn't meet. What is it, son? Blood? Woman's war paint? What have you been up to?'

'Nothing I can't . . .'

He held up a restraining hand, although his eyes were inquisitive. 'No. Perhaps you'd better not. What I don't know I can't do nothin' about.'

'You mean you haven't come to arrest me?'

He blew smoke up to the ceiling. 'I got no rightful jurisdiction in Shiloh. So don't embarrass me by makin' any confessions.'

'It's a social call, then?' I scratched the stubble of the day's new whiskers. 'If it is, do you mind if I get cleaned and fed?'

'It ain't a social call, son, but I'm not in a hurry. You just go on and pretty up.'

'Make yourself at home,' I said. 'There's some liquor in the bar over there.'

When I'd loofah'd my skin to an abraded pinkness, I changed into crisp underclothing and a linen suit. The bedroom showed unmistakable signs of a thorough search.

I went into the kitchen and opened some of Gribble's tins of food. They could have contained stewed camel for all I cared. I was just hungry. 'You want some coffee?' I called out to

Seamark. 'I'm about to cook some up.'

He was still on the settee; not drinking, just sucking away at his cigarettes, filtering them through his moustache. 'Yes,' he said. 'You need some help?'

'No. It's within my capabilities.' In between eating, I poured black coffee beans into the grinder and switched it on. Then, tipping the fragrant grains into the electric percolator, I quickly brushed the grinder clean of coffee and filled it with sugar. Reducing this to a fine talc-like powder, I repeated the process until I had half-a-pound of it. I spooned it into the plastic bags I had ready, sealed them with tape and distributed them about my clothing.

The pot stopped bubbling and I poured two cups of coffee. I hoped Seamark was sufficiently undomesticated not to appreciate the significance of the extra grinding he must have heard.

If he had, he said nothing except, 'Thank you, son,' for the coffee I handed to him. Standing that near him, it was mildly disconcerting to discover he smelt of body and shaving lotions. He seemed so eminently the quintessence of saddle soap and horse manure.

I sat in a chair after accepting one of his cigarettes. 'I think I'd better fill you in on one or two details, Sheriff,' I said. 'As you've guessed, I'm a pretty bad smell in the nostrils of the Police Department. But, whatever you've heard, it isn't true.'

The coffee was making heavy weather of getting past his moustache and I wondered why he wore such an anachronism. Perhaps the Indian women liked it. Behind it, he seemed a decent, civilized human being. 'I'm not sittin' in judgement,' he answered. 'And I'm not working for the City Police Department.'

'I need a friend, Sheriff.'

'From what I've heard, you do. You're sure as all hell makin' a heap of enemies.'

'Someone doesn't love me, that's certain.' I looked puzzled. 'I'd give a lot to know why.'

'I wouldn't know, son, but I'll give you some advice. Out here ain't the same as in London, England. If somebody's got you by the short and curlies, you maybe ought to be wise and co-operate.' He was looking me over with his pale eyes, reading between the lines of my reluctance to communicate. 'Perhaps you'd better just say what gives,' he said finally. 'I may be able to help.'

'It's simple enough, Sheriff. I had a telephone call from Mrs Hansson last night. She asked me to pick her up at the hotel. The Thunderbird at Shiloh. I think she was under some sort of duress. I have a room there myself and I'd just left. When I got to it, I found a girl in my bed.' Naïveté wasn't in my line but I did my best. 'Believe me, Sheriff, I'd never seen her before in my life. She was planted there by somebody. I think, to blackmail me.' I wrinkled my forehead. 'But why? Why me?'

Seamark pursed his lips. 'It happens, son. There's always some guy out to make a fast buck. But that wasn't all?'

I smiled uncertainly. 'I'm no man for casual fornication. I put her in the bathroom to cool off. Then I heard a gun. I ran in and found her dead.'

The policeman in him asserted itself. 'Come on, son. Be explicit. Who did it?'

'I don't know. A man I hadn't seen before.'

'He was twelve feet tall and wore purple galluses?' he suggested mildly.

'I'm sorry, Sheriff.' I gave him a bowdlerized description of Gost. Saying I knew would raise all sorts of complications and side issues.

'It's a wicked world, son. I wonder why he should do that?'

'He could have thought it was his wife.'

He regarded me sadly. 'You were screwing that nice Mrs Hansson?' He sounded as strait-laced as Gebhardt.

I shrugged. 'It doesn't mean anything these days, Sheriff. It's always on somebody's menu.'

He didn't think much of that observation but let it go by. 'Where was Mrs Hansson?'

'I don't know. Not at the hotel.'

'What happened when you found the girl?'

'The man shot at me and I shot back at him. We both missed and he went out the window.'

'And you ran for it?'

'Sowerby was leading a posse to my room. It was bad enough before. Having a girl in my bedroom, I mean. She was only a child. Having her shot dead there was really serious.'

He thought that over, no doubt fitting it in with what he already knew. 'I ain't much of a lawman, son,' he said modestly, 'seein' I was only a coyote hunter before. But you don't add up to bein' a killer to me.'

'Thank you, Sheriff. I wish I could be as sure of the opinion of Chief Gebhardt.'

He hooked one of his thin legs over the other and pulled down on the brim of his hat. 'It ain't no good pretending you ain't wanted by the law, son.'

'Are you going to hand me over?'

He shook his head, sucking in his rawboned cheeks. 'Nope. I hope it don't cost me my star, but I ain't. I guess you got to trust somebody in this life.'

I cleared my throat. There didn't seem much I could say.

'That note,' he said. 'I was watchin' your eyes. It spelled trouble, didn't it?'

'Yes,' I admitted.

'But you ain't goin' to tell me.'

'I'm sorry. It would strain your oath of office.'

He looked down at the polished star on his shirt. 'Yep. I guess it might,' he said dryly. 'So don't.' His face was serious. 'I told you before, son. If somebody *has* got his fingers in your short and curlies, don't struggle too hard. Relax a bit, son. If a woman gets her titties caught up in a wringer, she don't pull. She gives.'

'Your analogies are excruciatingly clear, Sheriff. What am I to give?'

'I don't know. All I know is that if you're in trouble, do what the letter says, son. Whatever it is.'

'I'll think about it.'

'Yep, son, do. Anything's better'n a hole in the head. I want you to remember that.'

'I will.'

'You've got somethin' somebody wants?'

'Yes. You said you'd help me?'

'This side of the law, son.'

'Would you try and locate Mrs Hansson for me?' I offered him a cigarette and he took it.

'I guess I can do that for you. Shiloh's a mite dangerous for you to be seen visitin'.'

'It isn't that. I don't know my way around.'

The slate eyes were searching mine. 'You think she's in trouble?'

'I'm sure.'

Pulling his hat more firmly over his eyebrows, he came to a sudden decision. 'I'll make some inquiries for you, son. I got enough pull, know enough folks, to pick up information.'

The man's kindliness touched me. 'It won't embarrass you with Gebhardt?'

A shadow crossed his face. 'Don't fret about that, son. There ain't no possibility of that.'

'It's kind of you, Sheriff,' I said. 'One day, perhaps, I'll have the pleasure of buying you a drink in Charlie's Bar.'

'Charlie's Bar?' he said blankly. Then he shook his head. 'I don't drink, son. I thought you knew.'

'I'm sorry.'

'It don't matter. What about the feller who shot the girl?'

I pulled the corners of my mouth down. '*I* didn't do it and the evidence at the scene can't do anything but clear me. It's just that I can't afford to be inside explaining while somebody holds Mrs Hansson.'

'That sounds reasonable. Anything else, son?'

'There are two men.' I hesitated. 'They pushed me around in the hotel. Before I received the call from Mrs Hansson.' I described them to him and told of what they had done. 'I don't think there's any doubt they're connected with her disappearance.'

He was thoughtful. 'They sound a mite familiar to me, son. I'll go back to the office and look up the records and teletypes.' He suddenly tossed the camera at me and I caught it. 'There y'are,' he said. 'Is that what all the frettin' was about?'

The casing had received a battering from the thousand-feet drop. The lens turret was twisted sideways and the ground-glass viewer smashed. It was smeared with green where it had hit a cactus. Structurally, it was intact.

'It's the one,' I said. 'Shall I hold on to it?'

'Better check it, son. It was loaded?'

I thumbed back the lever. It worked without obstruction. 'Yes. It seems all right. I'd better leave it for her to check.'

'Yep.' He cocked his head at me. 'You didn't ask me how I

found it.'

'I'm surprised,' I admitted. 'Pleased, of course.'

'It wasn't anywhere near where you said, son,' he said reproachfully. 'Knowin' every inch of the territory helped. But *you* didn't.'

'I'm sorry,' I said. 'I was having trouble with the flying at the time. Was I far out?'

'Far enough. I could see the lady wanted it back so I spent some time at it.' He dismissed the camera. 'You can't stay here,' he pointed out. 'Sowerby'll be out here again. And mighty soon.'

I looked at my watch. It was almost ten o'clock. 'I'll have to take to the hills. Or buy myself a false beard.'

Seamark stood and hitched his gunbelt. 'Come outside a minute, son.'

I followed him on to the patio and stood by his side. The sun was pounding the sandy earth, bouncing its heat back in humid waves. Clouds—looking for somewhere to rain—were sailing in from the far range of mountains.

He pointed across the waste of cacti to Painted Rock. 'A friend of mine's got a huntin' lodge up there on the south saddle,' he said, wiping sweat from his face with the handkerchief on which he had polished his boots. 'It ain't visible from the trail but you'll see it easy from that chopper of yours.'

'It can be reached with a car?'

'Yep. So keep the chopper hid.'

'You're saying I can use the lodge?'

'The key's under a rock near the water barrel.' His face was anxious. 'I'm trustin' you, son,' he cautioned me. 'You ain't got the makin's of a gabby man.'

'No,' I assured him.

'If things boil over I'll have to arrest you.'

'I understand. I wouldn't cause any trouble.'

He chewed at his thumb. 'Don't ever do that, son. I can be a mighty mean man at times.'

'I hope you don't think me ungrateful, but I've got to go to Shiloh first.'

'Aaah!' He looked sad. 'By the sound of it I'd be wastin' my time objecting.'

'It's something I've got to do.'

'Nothing I can do for you, son?'

'I'm sorry. Your star wouldn't stomach it.'

'You goin' in the chopper?'

'I thought I'd fly her in so far and hitch a lift. I can pick her up later.'

'You know Mohawk Creek?' he asked.

'Yes.'

'I'll be there at noon. Land your chopper in the wash near the cottonwoods and I'll ferry you to Shiloh. Then you can find your own way back.' He flipped the brim of his hat and screwed his boot on the cigarette butt he dropped to the patio. 'Take some food and blankets with you,' he said. 'It gets a mite chilly up there. And if I forget to tell you, mind out for bear.'

I watched the dust his car wheels churned up until he reached the metalled highway. Then I returned to the room we had just left.

As I anticipated, the ranch had been searched. Even the paintings on the walls had been lifted and their backs examined. I looked at the brass tongue of the outer lock. There were no scratches on it. Whoever opened the door had done so with a duplicate key or a strip of mica.

Fearing the return of Sowerby, I packed a few tins of food and bottles of wine in a box and collected blankets and pillows from a bed. I stacked these in the space left by the missing seat of the helicopter. I added to them our travelling cases, filling a sponge bag with a battery shaver and some toilet things, locking the door behind me when I left.

I lifted off to a height of twenty feet and kept her there, following the sinuosities of a dried-up river bed towards Shiloh. It was unlikely I would be seen through the screening of saguaro cacti and cottonwood trees. The cabin was a heated glasshouse and I sweated, squinting through my tinted glasses against the reflected glare of the bright sun on the perspex bowl.

When I reached the open desert I dropped lower, skimming the stony soil, weaving between the thorny scrub and rocky outcrops. Birds flew up in my path and once I saw a small herd of venturesome peccaries trotting briskly into the undergrowth.

Mohawk Creek was a spit of dry sand in a declivity of red

stratified rock. I dropped on to the sand in a staccato racketing of richocheted engine noises and cut the ignition.

The creek lay a mile or so outside Shiloh. Between the two rose a mound of rocky ground. There was nothing in the creek itself to suggest anyone would want to be there and I felt secure.

Before leaving the oven-hot cabin, I opened the First Aid Box and took from it one of the tear gas projectors. Clipped in my breast pocket, it resembled a stubby fountain pen. The gas, discharged into the eyes, would stun and disable a man for fifteen minutes or more. It seemed more civilized, less noisy than using a gun.

I sat in the dappled shade of a cottonwood and smoked. I had half-an-hour to wait and in that time I gnawed and worried at my problems. I pulled the photograph from the envelope and studied it carefully. Ingrid was dressed as I had last seen her. The bed told me nothing. Behind it was a large window. The curtains, partly drawn, were decorated with a pattern of stylized pineapples. Through the window opening, I could identify the railing of a balcony and the neon tube letters LGRENS DRU. The picture had been taken at night.

I re-read the demand note. It told me little more than I already knew. The crudity of the lettering was an obvious disguise; the threat simple and forthright.

Seamark arrived punctually at noon, his huge battleship of a car bouncing on the rough dirt road. It was not his official vehicle. I put my jacket on and scrambled up the creek bank. He pushed open the door and I climbed in.

'All right, son?' he asked. 'No troubles?'

'Not yet.' I nodded at Painted Rock. Its jagged summit was scraping the bellies of overflying clouds. Some of the white mist flowed down the flanks of the mountain. 'I'll have to get my car. I can't land on a mountain in that.'

'No more can you get your car, son. There's a stake-out on it at the airfield. Sowerby's got Shiloh sewn up on you.'

'I'll hire one. What's the going like up there?'

'Rough. But passable. Watch your suspension and don't get too close to the edge. There're some mighty scarifying drops near the lodge.'

He didn't say much else but concentrated on getting along

the track without holing the sump on a rock. I got no more homespun philosophies about bosoms being trapped in moving machinery. He contented himself with puffing out the fringe of his outrageous moustache and blinking his wise old eyes at the shifting pattern of sunlight and shadows. He was plainly worried and I felt guilty.

When he dropped me in a street at the back of the Greyhound Bus Terminal, he said, 'Watch it, son, and keep off the main drag.' I watched him until his dusty car was lost in the river of midday traffic.

*

Entering the first menswear shop I saw, I bought a blue linen hat with a wide brim. It wasn't me. But then, I didn't want it to be.

Feeling more of an anonymity under its shadow, my eyes screened from the vulgar gaze by impenetrable sunglasses, I sought for and entered a Walgren's Drug Store. In one of the telephone booths, I searched the pages of the local directory under P and found the entry PAUL'S BAR, Jefferson Street.

I left the booth and asked the starched-white counter clerk, 'Where's Jefferson Street, please?'

He jerked a thumb towards the back of the premises. 'The other side of the block.'

'You know Paul's Bar?'

'I know it.' He was ladling chocolate syrup on to a heap of pink icecream for a spotty youth in spectacles and a bow tie.

I waited until he completed what he obviously considered a gastronomic *chef-d'oeuvre*. 'What goes on there?' I asked.

'I wouldn't know. Not being able to afford to go.'

'It's more than a bar?'

'Yeah.' He looked around him, checking the place for F.B.I. agents and Russian spies. 'It's a gambling joint. Very toney.'

I bought a Coca Cola, drank it and gave the clerk a tip. Back in the booth I got my small change out and dialled Gribble.

'Rog!' he cried. 'Are you all right?'

'Battered. A little bloody. But unbowed.'

'Serious, Rog. What the hell's going on?'

'You tell me.'

'The cops have been living on my door-sill.'

'What for, Newt?'

'*What for?* Are you kidding? They were belly-aching about a female being shot up in your hotel room. The room *I* reserved for you, Rog,' he said. 'I'm *serious*. I can't have the business involved in police trouble.'

'*I'm* serious too, Newt. I had nothing to do with that girl.'

'They don't seem to agree with you.'

'Which is why I'm staying under cover. Trust me, Newt,' I coaxed. 'I want only to do one or two things and I promise it'll all be cleared up. Which police were after me?'

'A Phoenix Homicide detail. They dragged me out of bed in the middle of the night. Acting for the Shiloh City Police they said. Wanted to know where you were supposed to be. What made you tick. Had I a photograph of you. The lot!' Gribble was irritable. 'Then this morning the Sheriff of Caliente County phoned me. Said he had a camera. A *camera*! Christ, Rog!' he burst out, 'why don't you stick to fornicating.' He didn't use that exact word. 'Like a good old American citizen.'

'I tried to,' I said, 'but it all got out of hand. Like a friend of mine has already pointed out; somebody's got me by the short and curlies.'

'Why, Rog? Why you?'

'I seem to be the type things happen to.' I pushed this uninformative chit-chat to one side. 'Newt. Do you know Paul's Bar here in Shiloh?'

'By repute, yes.' Like the counter clerk, he sounded very cautious. 'It's a gaming-house for well-heeled hoodlums and shady politicoes.'

'Who is Paul? Or is that just a name?'

'A name. Nobody knows who's really at the back of it. But whoever it is, he's well in with City Hall.' He paused. 'You haven't tangled with him, I trust?'

'Not willingly, Newt. Will you stall everybody off as much as possible?'

'Short of getting myself indicted, I will. Where can I connect with you?'

'For your ears only, Newt. A hunting lodge on the south side of Painted Rock.'

'On your own?'

'Not if I can avoid it. I've got to go . . .' I disconnected by pressing the studs with my forefinger. I lit a cigarette, checked on the number of Paul's Bar, pushed in a coin and dialled.

A respectful voice at the other end said, 'Paul's Bar at your service.'

I put on what I thought to be a mid-western accent, laced with alcohol. 'What time you op'n, bud?'

'You *are* a member, sir?'

'Do I have to be? To lose a few lousy bucks?' I said it aggressively.

He was still polite. 'It helps, sir. An introduction by a member would be sufficient.'

In the background I heard the musical clashing of moving metal parts. It was the reason for my call and identified now as the sound of money being lost in gaming machines.

'All right, bud,' I said. 'Thanks for nothin'. I'll go lose my money someplace else.'

Outside, I turned the corner of the drugstore into a bisecting street and bought a *Shiloh City Globe* from a newsstand. I crossed the street and from behind the newspaper studied the frontage of Paul's Bar. It was located in the same block as the drugstore, being held apart by a narrow, rubbish-filled alley.

I returned to my original position through a press of moving, horn-blaring vehicles. A prowling police car made me catch my breath but its wheels missed my toes by inches without either the driver or his observer looking at me.

Entering the alley, I leaned against the wall with the spread paper masking my face. I wasn't able to see the Walgren's neon sign from where I stood but I saw a balconied window on the second floor from where it could. There was a pineapple motif on the visible strips of curtain. An iron fire escape zig-zagged up the wall of the building, rising from a huddle of card boxes and overflowing bins, leaving an eight-foot gap at ground level.

Although it missed the window with the pineapple curtains, a decorative ledge ran to it. Access should present no difficulties to a man whose soul bore already the stigmata of a similar climb.

Leaving the wall, I crossed to the other side of the alley. I leaned on the handle of a door marked PRIVATE. It remained solid and unmovable. There was no easy way in there.

Abandoning the alley, I searched for and found a used car lot, renting a Chrysler Station Wagon on the strength of one of my credit cards. Then I went shopping, buying a short aluminium ladder, a well-worn leather grip complete with wrenches and cutters, a coil of copper wire, a green boiler suit, a baseball cap with a jutting peak and a bottle of black shoe dye.

It was past noon when I finished and I ate a salami sandwich meal in a back street diner. Returning to the parked station wagon and using the shoe dye, I printed STANDARD TELEPHONES in big, thick letters on the back of the boiler suit.

When it had dried, I put it on over my suit and pulled the baseball cap down on my blond hair. The end result was comparable to being in a Turkish Bath with hot-water bottles. I rolled my linen hat into a tight cylinder, concealing it in a side pocket. Then I checked my pistol and aerosol of tear gas, hooked the sunglasses on my nose and reckoned I was in business: safe from everybody but a union official.

Dropping the Chrysler near an intersection with Jefferson Street and locking it securely, I walked purposefully to the alley. The leather grip and coil of wire I held in one hand. The ladder I slung over my shoulder. I ran with sweat and thanked God I hadn't to work for my living.

Passing the front of Paul's Bar, I saw Geronimo's metallic brown car broiling on the hot tar of the street. It was nice to know I was doing something right.

In the alley, I propped the ladder against the wall and easily hauled myself up on the lower steps of the fire escape. I made no unnecessary noise but neither did I act furtively. I was a paid-up union member coming to fix a telephone.

Reaching the second floor staging, I put down the grip and the coil of wire. The ledge on which I proposed walking was a comforting six inches or so wide. Opening the middle button of my boiler suit, I eased the pistol in its holster, cocking it as I did so. I tested the aerosol by squirting it across the alley. It gave off a powerful hissing noise like boiling steam.

Then I put my face to the brownstone wall and shuffled along the ledge, palms flat against the cement, their adhesion seemingly dependent on the perspiration I was leaking. I was a green tree frog spread-eagled on a brown precipice. Screened from the entrance to the alley by the latticework of the fire escape, I was still exposed to any unkind observer from one of the windows. Sweat poured from my straining body as it suffocated in its cocoon of multi-layered linen and cotton and heat reflected on to me from the baking wall.

When at last I reached the balcony I paused, allowing the tension in my legs to run down. No sounds came through the open window. I eased myself over the rail and stood soft-breathing on the tiling, hidden from inside by the architrave. Holding the pistol in one hand and the aerosol in the other, I edged an eye around the curtain. This was the most dangerous manoeuvre of the whole operation.

Ingrid was seated in an easy chair, reading a paperback. She smoked a cigarette and looked unutterably bored. No longer handcuffed, she sat sideways to my window.

Opposite her a man lay sprawled in another chair, a *Shiloh City Globe* spread over his face. His fawn-trousered legs stuck straight out, the shoeless feet heels-down on a stool. The steady rise and fall of his chest suggested deep sleep. He could be Geronimo. If he was, the newspaper covering him could only be an improvement.

When Ingrid raised her eyes and saw me she started, the book on her lap dropping to the floor with a quiet thud. Then she recognized me behind the sweat, the green boiler suit and the baseball cap.

I put the barrel of the pistol against my lips and shook my head warningly.

She leaned stiffly back in the chair, her eyes steady on mine, the fingers of her free hand pressed hard into the stuff of the padded arm. The other held her cigarette in mid-air.

Disengaging my eyes from hers, I gently, very slowly, lifted the window frame. I was as noiseless as a shadow. My regard was now fixed like a steel rod on the man in the chair. I lifted a leg over the sill and stepped into the room. Time stood still. The fastest moving things in my personal universe were the beadlets of sweat trickling down the furrow of my spine.

With the pistol aimed at the man's belly and my thumb on the button of the aerosol, I moved in slow motion across the carpet. Step followed step in a dream-like sequence until I stood above him. Near enough to smell the stink on his body to see a vein pulsing in the segment of chest exposed through his open shirt, to read that Brooklyn Boy won the 3.30 from a field of eleven at Shiloh Park the previous day. The hairy fingers intertwined across his flat stomach were twitching.

I had a sudden irrational horror that he was watching me through the newspaper, his eyes wide open, a triumphant smile on his nihilistic mouth.

Ingrid's stare was almost cataleptic and she hardly breathed. The cigarette burning between her fingers sent up a tremulous spiral of blue smoke.

I hooked the pistol barrel under the paper and slowly lifted it. As it slid sideways, exposing the Indian face of Geronimo, so his eyelids snapped open, awareness sharpening his features.

I said, 'Good afternoon,' and gave him a three-second burst of gas. It blotted vision from the chocolate-brown irises and he screamed hoarsely from deep down in his throat. His hands flew up and he dug the heels of them convulsively into his eye sockets.

Putting the muzzle of the pistol to his forehead, I pushed him back in the chair. If he couldn't see it, he could feel it. 'I'll kill you if you move,' I said. I took his gun from beneath his armpit and pushed it under Ingrid's chair.

Geronimo was stunned, blind and helpless and breathing in whooping gasps. He wasn't going to be operational for some time.

'There's nobody else?' I asked Ingrid.

She rose from the chair, white as bone under her tan, dropping her cigarette 'No. Oh, *Roger*!'

I put an arm around her waist and kissed her lightly on the forehead. 'Sorry about the delay. I met a man.'

Geronimo's necktie lay on the carpet at the side of him. I used it to tie the sweaty wrists together and then gagged him by knotting his handkerchief between his teeth. It was a very dirty and disgusting handkerchief but that seemed his own bad luck. I picked up his shoes and dropped them into the alley. Then I unlocked the door with a key I took from his trousers pocket. He moaned softly to himself, his eye sockets a swollen jelly of red inflammation. I thought it unfortunate that in an hour or so he would be back to his normal bloody-minded self.

'Is there a back way out?' I asked Ingrid. She wore the same sand-coloured dress. It was creased now with smears of dirt on it. A button was unfastened, showing her brassiere and her navel. It was fitting that Geronimo was eyeless.

'Yes,' she said sadly, 'but we will not make it.'

'We will.' I showed more confidence than the circumstances justified. 'You lead the way. I'll hide behind your skirts.'

She laughed shakily. 'Where did you get those incredible clothes? You are not my Roger any more.'

Opening the door, I said, 'I'm worried about Shorty.' From below I could hear the metal crashing of machinery.

'Shorty?'

'A fat little man with curly hair and bad breath.'

'You mean Luigi?'

'If that's his name, yes. Where is he?'

'He went out to eat. He will be back soon.'

'Come on,' I urged her. 'We're on our way.'

My pistol was back in its pocket but I held the aerosol pen ready. We descended two flights of stairs before we met anybody. He was a waiter in a white coat carrying a tray. On it stood an uncapped bottle of beer, a bowl of ice cubes and a tumbler. When he saw Ingrid, he froze and his mouth opened to say, 'Hey!'

Even at ten feet and downhill, the jet was beautifully accurate. From over her shoulder it sprayed abrupt blindness into his eyes. He fell on his knees and put his face into cupped hands, the tray and its burden thumping down the remaining stairs.

I grasped Ingrid's wrist and ran, ignoring the noise we made. The door at the bottom was bolted and I spent heart-stopping seconds wrenching back the stiff bars securing it. The heat confined in the alley hit us like a wet sponge. I ripped off the boiler suit, scattering its buttons broadcast. Flinging the baseball cap after it, I unrolled my linen hat and clapped it on.

When we turned the corner into the street I pushed her into Walgren's Drug Store. 'Watch for me through the window. I'll be driving a cream and blue station wagon. A Chrysler. When I stop, jump in fast.'

There was no obvious activity from Paul's Bar as I passed it on the way back to Ingrid. Nor did anybody shoot at us as the Chrysler picked up speed under the urgent pressure of my foot and we headed for Mohawk Creek.

There was little point now in considering the bags of sugar in the pockets of my jacket. It probably avoided some unpleasant misunderstandings and they would remain the equivalent of a derringer up my shirt sleeve.

12

The clouds were still shrouding Painted Rock and I decided to leave the helicopter where she stood.

I worried about the pennant of ochre dust the Chrysler trailed from its rear as we climbed the winding road to the lodge. The air grew cooler and the saguaro and cholla gave way to scattered pines and outcrops of rock. The clouds hung above us, a grey-white woolly ceiling. Below, the ranch receded and shrank to the size of a shoe-box.

Finding the lodge was not easy. It lay hidden in the shelter of a small copse. The road by which we approached spiralled and looped the side of the mountain, each dizzying curve allowing a view of its tail beneath. Sometimes it skirted deep, brush-filled canyons.

The lodge looked as if Abraham Lincoln had slept there as a young man. The clapboarding of its sides was curled and bleached from years of simmering under fierce sunlight.

The interior was an entirely different matter, its two rooms constituting a well-feathered funkhole for tired businessmen. They had been furnished with the entertainment of women in mind. The only hunting the lodge would know was of the horizontal kind. The windows were cold steel-barred against casual trespass by desert tramps or hungry bears. The bed was pink and flouncy. There were already enough blankets on it for weathering out any blizzards the altitude might provide. The table and chairs in the living-room were handcarved American colonial and stood on plush carpeting. A polished brass lamp hung on chains in front of the huge stone fireplace.

Ingrid had been uncommunicative on the way up. After I unloaded the remaining luggage and the food and wine from the rear of the Chrysler, there was time to talk. And the need.

She sat on the table smoking one of my cigarettes, following my movements with wary eyes. A bar of sunlight, striking down through a hole in the clouds and into the window, suffused her skin to a warm cream. She had changed into a gold dress. She looked thinner and her hair was glossy with hard brushing. Her perfume reached out like a delicate finger, touching my emotions with her utter desirability.

'You are anxious to ask me questions, Roger,' she said.

I nodded, looking up from where I crouched unpacking the wine bottles. 'Some need asking. Like, for example, who took you away from the ranch?'

'Do you trust me?'

Thumping a bottle down on the carpet I stood, straightening my legs. 'Not enough to do without an answer.'

She wrinkled her forehead at my unsmiling expression. Uncertainty made her bite her lip. 'Please, Roger, do not joke.'

'I'm not joking.' My face remained stern. 'I asked, who took you away from the ranch?'

Her throat twitched in an involuntary swallow, the prelude to a lie. 'Mendoza. The man you blinded.'

'And Luigi?'

'Yes.'

'By force?'

'He pointed a gun at me.'

'I told you not to show yourself.'

She drew in deeply at her cigarette. 'I am sorry . . .' This was the second time I had caught her without a prepared story.

I shook my head. 'No,' I said in a hard voice. 'That won't do. You went voluntarily. But not with them. *Tell me*, Ingrid.'

She rubbed her palms together, making a dry rustling sound. 'I cannot, Roger. Really and truly I cannot. There are nasty things . . . things you must not know of or get involved with . . .'

Her opinion of my mentality was a minus one if she thought the fact of her kidnapping could be happily glossed over by these evasions. It irritated me. Even my role as a philandering playboy demanded more respect than this.

'I *am* involved with them.' I watched her eyes. 'Mendoza and Luigi have already paid me a visit. You didn't know?'

'Oh, no!' The truth of it was in her face.

'It's "Oh, yes!"' I said, 'and while you were being taken from the ranch. So you lied about them, didn't you?'

She twisted uncomfortably on the table. 'Please do not ask me.'

'Why the paradox? Kidnappees are not so usually uninformative: not so unforthcoming about who did it.'

'There are worse things than being kidnapped, Roger.

Things like ... like being dead ... being burned with acid ...'

'You *were* a prisoner, I suppose? Not just bait for me?'

'You know I was,' she retorted hotly. 'Did I not tell you where I was? Is not that how you found me?'

'I believe you on that,' I said, 'although it could still have been bait. So tell me who ordered the whole thing.'

'I cannot.'

Her stubbornness added to my irritation. 'That's stupid. Unless, of course, you are involved with him. Then it makes sense.'

'You frighten me, Roger. Your eyes are cruel.' She regarded me warily. 'Why are you so insistent?'

I picked out one of the bottles of red wine and popped the cork. I poured two glasses of it and put one of them on the table near her. She didn't touch it. Which was probably perceptive of her. It drank warm and harsh and should have stayed in its native California.

Her face was rigid with the storm brewing up inside. 'Roger,' she said. The knuckles of her fingers were white.

'Yes?'

'You did not answer my question.'

'No, I didn't. Insistency doesn't need explaining. It might be I don't like being made a fool.'

She frowned. 'I have just thought of something. You dropped the camera on purpose.' Angry puzzlement was in her voice. 'Of course, you *must* have.'

'Why would I want to do that?'

'Yes, why?'

'Because it was your daddy's?'

She thinned her lips.

'All right,' I said. 'Because of something in it perhaps?'

'So you *do* know!'

'It was difficult not to.'

'But *why*?'

Looking at myself from her viewpoint, I could see I was being plain bloody-minded. 'Perhaps I don't like filth. Or the people who batten on its sale.'

Her chin went up and I could sense a return to the two Afghan hounds on their gold-studded leashes. 'I am not ashamed. If I did not do it, someone else would.'

It was then I recruited myself back into the ranks of Charles's army from which I had temporarily gone absent without leave. 'That sort of sophistry is the stock-in-trade of pimps and whores.'

She blinked at that and I felt sorry for my harshness. 'Do you want to put me in a prison, Roger? Or have me killed?'

'Would it be undeserved?'

'But what business is it of yours?' Her eyes widened in comprehension. 'Of course. You *made* it your business. You lied to me, tricked me . . .'

'Oh? I thought it was you who had lied to me. Weren't you supposed to be meeting your sister? Mrs Karin Gost, isn't she? Or did I get her confused with you?'

Her eyes dropped to her thighs and she bit her bottom lip. 'I can explain . . .'

'Not to me you can't. It just makes me feel sorry for Gost.'

Pink patches were over her cheekbones, her eyes glittering. She was beautiful and wholly a Coptic arch-priestess. She almost spat at me. 'He wouldn't care what you feel. One day he will kill you.'

'If he does, you would never know where I've hidden your heroin.'

There was a silence in the room. A bird outside sang liquid notes, uncaring of the cross-purposes of *homo sapiens*. She pushed herself from the table, hope quickening her breathing. 'It is not in the camera?'

'You should be grateful it's not. The sheriff found it this morning.'

Her hand went over her mouth. 'He told you?'

'Better. He brought it to the ranch.' There was a further silence which the bird exploited with its singing.

'Oh, Roger! You have killed me! Everything you have done has. As certainly as if you had shot me.'

I looked down the length of her fine body. On the physical plane she was still suffocatingly tempting. 'Stop being hysterical. You overrate this unknown boss of yours. He's only a man.'

'A man! There are many men. Everywhere. All with guns. You cannot begin to know.' Her cheek twitched. 'You are dead too. Unless . . .'

'All right,' I said impatiently. 'Unless what?'

'Unless we return the heroin.'

'You are singularly naïve if you believe that. Only my knowledge of its whereabouts is keeping us alive.' I was nasty again. 'Then, of course, there's the matter of your courier's fee.'

'I will not let you hurt me, Roger. It is not the money. It is your life and mine.' She moved towards me, her eyes dark and lustrous, pushing her belly against mine. 'Where is it, Roger?'

I could feel the warm firmness of her thighs and pelvis. She was making the small movements known by women to provoke the male beast into standing on its hind legs and howling. Her perfume was nudging my desire for her. 'Don't waste it on me,' I growled. 'I'm not in season.'

'Anything,' she whispered, rubbing herself insistently on me. 'Anything you want.'

Her body was pressing the pistol into the flesh of my waist, serving to remind me I could no longer trust her. I put my fists on her arms and pushed her away. 'No. Once I might. Not now. I should have left you with Mendoza. You knew they were using you to trap me. To get the heroin back.'

'Yes. But not with my help.' She looked forlorn, rejected. 'I wanted you to help *me*.'

'You knew about the girl planted in my room?'

'Girl?' It was obvious she did not.

'All right,' I said. 'It doesn't matter.'

'*Please*, Roger. I mean nothing to you?'

'Not that much. I can't imagine a woman who would.' I was ice-cold with her. This was how it had to be. This was the bruising I had prophesied to Charles.

She was sad, defeated. 'What are we waiting for?'

'Darkness. So I can do a bit of hunting on my own account.'

'Hunting?' she echoed blankly.

I yelled at her. 'Do you think I'm a ————— lap dog to sit here with you, waiting for some murderous bastard to cut my liver out!' I saw her face and stopped. 'I'm sorry,' I said. 'But I don't want even you to think I'm a spineless ninny.'

'They'll find you.' Her courage was coming apart at the

seams.

'Mendoza and Luigi?' I made them sound like Micky Mouse and Brer Rabbit.

'Yes,' she said shivering. 'They will kill us both. Me first. Then you.' She picked up the glass of wine and went into the bedroom. Defeat sat like a black shawl on her shoulders.

I went outside to get away from her flabby pessimism. The clouds were breaking up and patches of blue showed through. The desert beneath my feet was blotched with yellow. The phallus of Painted Rock rose clear and unmisted into the sky.

A fallen pine lay on the edge of the escarpment and I sat on it. I could see the road snaking towards distant Phoenix on the far flank of the mountain and our route dropping down towards the ranch. Nothing moved there, no disturbed dust indicating the approach of a car. Shiloh City was hidden from me behind the shoulder of the jagged south slope. A soft wind moaned through the rocky pinnacles above the lodge, rattling the leaves of the aspens. It would be cold when the sun dropped.

Holding a cigarette in one hand, I picked with the other at loose bark from the rotting trunk. Feeling a smooth hardness wriggle beneath my fingers, I looked down and saw jointed legs and notched claws. My reaction was a second too slow to avoid the lightning stroke of pure agony piercing the base of my thumb. I cried out, startled and hurt.

The scorpion was straw-coloured with a bristled tail poised menacingly above its slender body. While I sucked at the tiny puncture made with the sting, it scuttled away beneath the bark. I made no effort to kill it. There was no malice in what it had done.

The sting of the small yellow scorpion can be fatal. I remembered this and the remembering of it touched me like a cold wind. The blood drained from the capillaries of my face as I walked slowly to the Chrysler. I remembered also that the venom of scorpions paralyzes the heart muscles. Violent exertion could only worsen its effect. I nursed myself along like an old man with a double hernia.

Opening the First Aid Pack, I gazed stupidly at the contents, not knowing Sal Volatile from a suspensory splint. My mind teetered on the edge of blind, unreasoning panic. Half-recollected medical mumbo-jumbo produced little coloured pictures of myself slashing a bloody cross in the flesh of my hand with a cauterized knife. I thanked God for the absence of a fire in which to heat the blade. I saw, anyway, that a blue vein throbbed jerkily beneath the seat of the sting. I was saved, at least, from self-mutilation.

Despair convinced me the poison was already doing its work. It seemed such a childish way to die. Stung by a two-inch creature I could normally crush beneath my shoe heel. There might be a certain dignity about dying by the claws of a tiger: there seemed none in this case.

I took out my handkerchief and knotted it around my biceps with fingers and teeth. Pushing a stick through the loop, I twisted it tight until the improvised tourniquet cut deeply into the flesh, bulging the veins and arteries above it. I began to feel sick.

Staggering to the front of the Chrysler, I lifted the bonnet cover, my fingers thick and unfeeling. With difficulty, I un-clipped the distributor cap, immobilizing the engine by removing the rotor arm.

I weaved on boneless legs towards the lodge, breathing asthmatically, iron bands compressing my chest. Black cob-webs crawled over my eyeballs, obscuring my vision. Although there was no swelling of the hand, the pain was intense and radiated up through my arm and shoulder muscles to my jaws.

Reaching the door, I unlatched it fumblingly and fell drunkenly through, the walls of the room toppling sideways on to me. The black cobwebs curtaining my eyes became thicker and I hurtled swiftly down into a deep, dark well of utter silence.

13

A disc of luminescence shimmered at the top of the well as I struggled in my long climb out of it. It wavered, broke into fragments and resolved itself into the anxious face of Ingrid.

'What is it, Roger? What happened?' Her voice was reedy and a long way off. My ear drums vibrated as if they had lost their tautness.

I identified the piece of dry cloth in my mouth as a tongue. 'Scorpion sting,' I said around it. 'Drink, please . . .'

I was in a sitting position on the floor with my shoulders flat against the wall. I felt I was tossing in a boat on a stormy sea. A blanket covered me to the waist. My shirt and trousers clung to my body like wet seaweed. I was dangerously vulnerable: a bull with a broken leg and hyenas howling in the distance.

The rotor arm was still clenched in one fist and while Ingrid poured wine into a glass I pushed it in the gap between wall planking and skirting behind me. Cocking my pistol—it seemed the size and weight of a 75-millimetre howitzer—I wedged it in beside the rotor arm. From my level the butt could be seen but not, I thought, from any other angle.

Ingrid knelt, holding the rim of the glass to my mouth, pouring the wine in. The vintage didn't matter. It was wet and that was all I wanted. 'More,' I croaked and drank another glassful. She left the bottle at my side.

The tourniquet was still strangling life from my arm, the flesh below it puffed and bloodless. I plucked feebly at it and Ingrid untwisted the stick, releasing the blood back into my veins. I sweated gently at the pain of it.

'How long?' I asked, managing to get my eyes in parallel.

'How long have you been unconscious?'

I nodded.

'Nearly an hour.' Her face was haunted by concern. 'I thought you were going to die. Are you better now?'

'Not much.' I put my palms flat on the carpet to steady myself as agony tore holes in my stomach. The wine hadn't been such a good idea. 'Leave me alone. Don't touch me.'

I didn't want her sympathy. Nor her further help. We were separately aligned now with our opposing parts to play. It didn't allow for a refiring of emotional ashes.

She stood, rebuffed, and her bottom lip trembled. 'I will be in the other room if you want me, Roger.'

My eyes were cold. It was something I couldn't disguise. 'Thank you for what you've done but I'm all right now. It was nothing. Just a sting.'

I let my head nod forward on to my chest. My awareness drifted off in wine fumes to a dark kind of sleep. The clinking of stone against stone jerked me back to consciousness and my goggling eyes, desperately focusing themselves, saw the door burst open and slam back into the wall.

Mendoza stood there, his knees bent, the gun in his hand searching a target. The muzzle found me on the floor and steadied on my stomach. He grunted in his stomach and said, 'Aaagh!' The odorous Luigi was immediately behind him, his gun also pointing at me.

Mendoza moved towards the bedroom. Ingrid, startled by their noisy entry, stood in the doorway, the colour bleached from her face by realized fear. He pushed her roughly to one side and checked the bedroom.

He returned and stood over me, looking down the ridge of his Apache's nose. He seemed to have survived scatheless the tear gas although he wore dark glasses. He stooped suddenly and hit me viciously on the mouth with the barrel of his gun. He snarled savage and incoherent words.

I slumped sideways and vomited wine and salami over the blanket and floor. Tears flooded my eyes from the choking paroxysms. I felt his hand searching my clothing; patting my body, legs and crutch for the gun he thought I carried. He grabbed my shoulder, heaving me sideways to ensure it was not under me.

'What's up with him?' he asked.

Ingrid said, 'He is very ill. He has been stung by a scorpion.'

He exposed his canines in a nihilistic sneer. 'The bastard. It should have been a rattlesnake.' Taking hold of my shirt in his big fist, he hauled me to a sitting position and smacked me back against the wall. Although my mouth felt swollen to large sausages of bruised flesh, the vomiting had cleared my head.

Sufficiently for me to be frightened.

He slapped my face hard. 'O.K. loverboy. Where is it?'

'I don't . . .' Another jolting slap knocked the back of my skull on the planking. There was blood in my mouth and I swallowed it.

'*Where?*' he barked at me. 'Where?' My head jerked sideways with each blow of his powerful arm. I leapt back into the friendly blackness of the well from which I had so recently climbed.

When I groaned and opened my eyes, I saw Ingrid seated in a chair with Mendoza standing over her. Luigi straddled the other chair backwards, his fat thighs straining the cloth of his trousers, his elbows on the table. His gun was aimed more or less in my direction. Both men had been drinking my wine.

Mendoza smiled a wolf's smile and walked briskly over to me. 'It's loverboy back with us,' he mocked. He stooped, close enough for me to see the black hairs in his nostrils and the sweat starting from the pores of his swarthy skin. Close enough to see myself reflected in duplicate in the lenses of his glasses. I looked a dreadful mess.

As he crouched, so the button of his tight-fitting brown jacket stretched and pulled creases in it. The shiny hole at the end of his gun was a few inches from my nose and the biggest thing in my view. He tapped me on the forehead with it. 'Loverboy,' he repeated. 'Little, poxy, yellow-haired loverboy.'

'You stink,' I said unwisely, 'Why don't you take a bath?'

This time he hit me in the right eye and I shouted in agony. I let my chin drop on to my shirt front, feigning unconsciousness.

Ingrid cried out, 'He is ill!'

Mendoza twisted his fingers in my hair and shook me. 'Button up,' he said, 'or I'll really bust you one.' He rattled my skull against the wall.

'Doctor,' I mumbled. 'Need doctor . . .'

'Bollocks to the doctor,' he grunted. 'Where's the stuff?' He beat time with my head as an accompaniment to his words.

'No.'

He looked around at Ingrid. 'You been shacking up with the dame?' he demanded.

I shook my head and tried to look as if the thought of it sickened me.

He straightened his legs, strode across to Ingrid and hit her cruelly on the face with the back of his hand. As she staggered backwards across the table and on to the floor, he watched my eyes.

I tried to struggle upright but fell back under the menace of the aimed guns and Mendoza's small tight smile. He *wanted* an excuse to kill me.

He kept his blank gaze on me but spoke to Luigi. 'Work her over,' he said coldly.

Luigi stuffed his gun back into its holster and took his jacket off. He grasped her by the front of her dress and pulled her upright. She looked at me then. Not at Luigi but me; in bewilderment and disbelief, her dark eyes enormous. One side of her face was blotched pink from Mendoza's blow.

Luigi drew back his arm and went to work on her. For all the emotion he showed, he might have been chopping wood to light a fire. It was just another job to him.

My breaking point was fast approaching. That I would be a dead man as soon as I disclosed the whereabouts of the heroin, I had little doubt. I tried to shut out the sounds of smacking flesh and Ingrid's terrified moaning. I closed my only operational eye and measured up the destruction of a woman's face against my life and probably her own.

Mendoza scraped a chair to my side and sat on it. He prodded the gun against my temple. 'Don't go to sleep, loverboy,' he whispered. 'We're doin' this for you.' He was enjoying every minute of it.

He prised my eyelid open with the barrel and, blinking, I saw her bloody face and accusing eyes. I turned my head and vomited. When I had finished, I cried, 'Stop it! I'll tell you.'

He jabbed the gun harder. 'Where?'

'In my jacket. In the bedroom.'

He licked his lips and breathed deeply. He must have been promised a commission on its recovery. 'Wrap it up, Luigi,' he said sharply. He unhooked his glasses and wiped his eyes with the back of a finger. They were red-rimmed, the whites bloated.

A sheen of sweat polished the forehead of the fat man and

his tight curls had become unsprung. He released his hold on Ingrid, allowing her to slither senseless to the floor.

Mendoza stood. He was already killing me in his mind's eye. 'Watch the bastard,' he ordered and went to the bedroom.

It was then that Luigi stopped being a professional for long enough. He moved to the table and poured himself a glass of the Californian wine. His gun, turned loosely in my direction, pointed at the floor.

When he turned back to me, looking heavy-lidded over the rim of the glass, my pistol was aimed at him. It was a short distance. Too short for even a man with only one eye to miss.

I dropped the blade sight on the barrel from his ashen face down past his hair-plastered chest and on to his belly. Then I lifted it halfway back again, swinging leftwards an inch to compensate for the parallax caused by my one-sided vision.

He must have seen his death in that remaining eye for he did several things at once. His disorganized cerebellum told him to dodge sideways, bring his gun up to an aiming position and shout to Mendoza. He did none of them successfully. I squeezed the trigger and the pistol jerked like a live thing, the bullet from it giving him an instant *angina pectoris*.

The gun he was holding banged aimlessly, sending a bullet ploughing into his thigh. He dropped the wine and his pink baby lips sucked in, the startled eyes vanishing into their sockets. His knees folded, dropping him into a praying position on the floor. He looked blindly at the puddle of wine on the carpet for a while. Then he toppled slowly forward on his face and lay motionless.

A painful quietness emanated from the bedroom. Mendoza would be weighing the situation and not liking it. The window was barred, the gaps too narrow to allow the escape of anyone but a starveling runt. The doorway remained and I was on the right side of that. Out of sight and with a pistol.

He called out, 'Luigi?' without too much hope in his voice.

I laughed as I licked my sausage lips. I felt light-headed, certain now that I was going to kill him. But it had to be soon. The floor shifted under me and my stomach rippled with nausea. If he caught me in a bout of vomiting, I was finished.

'Drop your gun,' he called out, 'or I'll shoot the dame.' From where she lay she would be visible to him. A tiny whimper came from her.

I didn't blame her. I hadn't been too far from it myself. 'Go ahead,' I called, managing a derisive laugh. 'See what it'll buy you.' I must have been delirious, for I added, 'I'm the fastest gun in Shiloh!'

In the silence that followed, I pushed the blanket from my legs and twisted my body soundlessly to a kneeling position, my eyes never leaving the bedroom door. Then, pistol in hand, I commenced to crawl slowly towards it. I thanked God Ingrid was not watching me. Mendoza could have followed my progress from the movements of her eyes.

When he called, 'O.K. loverboy, you've got two minutes,' I remained silent, concentrating on making no noise. I was weakening and the spasms of nausea were increasing in intensity.

Ingrid stirred on the floor. 'Roger,' she pleaded, looking at the place where I had been lying. 'Please do what he says. He will kill me.' Her voice broke. 'I do not want to die . . .'

Two shots cracked in quick succession and weakness came into my arms and legs. It sounded as if the bullets had hit the floor near her but I could not be sure. She made no move and remained silent. Not once did she look at me.

As I crawled past Luigi, I saw his eyelids flickering. Then they opened fully and he saw me. I froze and pointed the pistol at him but they were dull and unseeing and he closed them again. When I reached the side of the doorway leading to the bedroom, I propped myself against it and waited.

Then another shot rang out and Mendoza came through the door in a rush, stopping suddenly and swivelling his gun to where I had lain. I fired my pistol upwards and saw a little hole like an opened red eye appear beneath his jawbone. He went down heavier than a pole-axed steer, his gun bouncing on the carpet.

I drooped on my knees after him, vomiting painfully in whooping gasps. When I had finished, I hauled myself to my feet and wiped my face with a handkerchief. I felt like Death itself. I was weak and shaking, my forehead pimpled with cold sweat.

Ingrid stirred and groaned, raising her head and watching me with bitter eyes.

It was now a time for words, not guns. I turned Luigi over to lie face upwards. He was going fast, his fat face mauve from air starvation. His thigh bled a sticky blotch on to his trousers. His eyes opened and a cough choked from his baby-pink lips with a noise like an emptying waste-pipe. 'I'm dying,' he gasped.

'Yes, you are.' I took two cigarettes from my case and lit them both. 'You gave me a smoke once,' I reminded him, pushing one between his lips. 'It's all I owe you.'

The cigarette wobbled as he tried to draw on it and it fell from his mouth. I put it back. 'Who are you working for?' I asked.

He didn't answer. Instead, he said, 'A priest. Get me a priest.' His eyes widened and he cried out hoarsely, chopping it off abruptly as his head fell sideways. He shuddered violently and stopped breathing.

Ingrid had climbed upright and was holding herself steady by clutching the table. She stared numbly at the twitching Luigi. Her face was steak tartare and tomato ketchup. I felt no better than she looked. Both of us had been through the Syndicate's meat-grinder.

I laughed shakily. Being alive against all the odds needed a catharsis. At another time it would have been a woman. 'The winners,' I said. 'But appearances all against it.'

There was no response to my sorry witticism. 'You let them beat me,' she said accusingly.

Denial was pointless. 'So I did. I thought it better than being shot dead.' Uncocking the pistol, I reholstered it behind my waist band. 'It was all a matter of timing.'

'I would not have been beaten had you told them in the first place.'

'You'll survive,' I said curtly. 'You weren't crucified on your own.'

She turned to a wall mirror and pulled out her lower lip with her fingers. Over her shoulder, I saw reflected the purple cuts on the shiny pink skin and the lapping of blood along the edge of gum. Leech-like contusions made her jaw line lumpy. She had a watery bag under one disfigured eye. Given that she didn't believe Mendoza and Luigi were going to kill us, she had a point about my allowing her to be savaged.

While she brooded over the mess of her face, I collected the guns of the dead men. Bending down to do so produced a nausea in me. I removed both magazines and pocketed them, putting the guns on the table.

When I looked up, I saw her eyes watching me in the mirror. 'Will you give me the heroin now?' she asked. 'I heard you say where it was.'

'You still want your blood money? After all this?' I was groggy enough to be nasty.

She said impatiently, 'You are playing at being God again.'

'Tell me I'm wrong.'

She looked at me for a long time in silence, indecision flowing over her features like quicksilver. Then she shook her head. 'I wish I could trust you.'

'You've been saying that until it means nothing.'

'I was never more serious, Roger. You misunderstand everything I do.' She walked to me, standing close and cocking her head to one side.

'I doubt I have,' I replied. 'Anyway, you can't have it.'

She arched against me, her arms going under my jacket. Until I felt her grasping at the pistol in my waistband, I thought she was about to embrace me. Then I saw her eyes, unfriendly and hostile.

I stepped backwards and held her thin wrists. 'It's no good, Ingrid. That stuff in there is sugar.'

'*Liar!*' Her fingers were wriggling to escape.

Contemptuously I released her and turned away, not interested in convincing her.

I went outside to the rear of the lodge where the mountain grew upwards in a pile of jumbled grey rock. A tiny cataract sluiced from a mossy ledge above and vanished into a large hole. This fissure slanted down into a shadowed interior and seemed big enough to take a man. I dropped a boulder, listening to its clattering progress and final splash.

Ingrid was cleaning her face with tissues when I returned. Although puffed and bruised, the flesh was not badly cut. She ignored me.

Stifling my repugnance I searched Mendoza's clothing, removing his wallet and car keys. His Social Security card said he was Peter Clarence Mendoza. Killing a Geronimo, a

Mendoza, could be rationalized: killing a man called Peter Clarence was something else altogether.

I tossed the keys on to the table. 'When you're ready, take his car and go. Use the back trail towards Phoenix. I'm doing this because you helped me with Mendoza and Luigi. But I hope we don't meet again.' I wanted to go off somewhere and cry.

She lifted her head and regarded me mutely. Then she turned and went into the bedroom.

The fat man's wallet disclosed his identity as Luigi Zacchio. It contained a few dollar bills and photographs of some black-eyed children. I hadn't thought of him as a family man. It made the whole thing unreal. With his breath, he should have been a fly-spray salesman.

Grasping Mendoza's ankles, I dragged him along the floor and out through the door. He was as unwieldy as a dead mule and his head bumped on the stony ground. A plague of tiny black flies circled his upturned face and feasted on his mouth and tongue.

The sun was back at full strength and I sweated. It took me a long time and some hard hauling to get him to the fissure. In death, his Indian's face had lost none of its hard-planed savagery. His half-closed eyes watched my struggles with sardonic amusement.

I levered him up into the narrow cleft where the water hosed on him, darkening his jacket and turning his hair to lank ribbons. It is compulsively introspective to look at the face of a man who is about to leave the human race for oblivion. To me, Mendoza was an undisputed whole-cloth bastard and the manner of his going appropriate. But I was still civilized enough to feel for him.

As I hung on to his ankles, hesitating, I heard the growling of a prodded starter motor and then the squealing of tyres as the car took the first hairpin bend at increasing acceleration. I relaxed the muscles of my hands and Mendoza slithered away. Halfway out of sight he stuck, showing me the scratched soles of his shoes and a patch of pale ankle. Then he was gone in his long dive, the sullen splash of his entry into subterranean waters echoing up to me.

Luigi's going exhausted me. His body wobbled in its progress over the uneven soil, a bladder of fluids difficult to manoeuvre and handle. Head downwards in the fissure, he jammed. For one disorganized minute I had to shove with my foot on his fat backside, squeezing him through the constricting rock like toothpaste from a tube.

I consigned his jacket and the guns and wallets after him. Then I sat exhausted, my head between my knees. I saw Gost, Mendoza and Luigi in my fevered imagination, all neatly planted in the harsh rocky soil of Arizona. I prayed they wouldn't turn out to be dragon's teeth. For an ex-policeman with an admitted *Angst* for firearms, I was light years away from London and the Judges' Rules: from warning *Homo Sapiens Criminalis* it need not say anything unless it wished to; that anything it chose to say would be taken down in writing for its subsequent denial with all the authority of a paid-for mouthpiece.

Back in the empty lodge, I found the packets of sugar had been taken from the pockets of my jacket. I really hoped she knew what she was doing.

I stripped naked and ladled water from the butt on to my soiled skin, the coldness of it stinging the raw flesh of my face. I changed into a smooth tweed jacket, a solid red shirt and fawn twill trousers. I knotted on my Marlburian tie in much the same spirit as braver men have shaved to die. I wrapped my discarded clothing around a rock and made a last journey to the fissure.

After clearing the evidence of violence from the lodge, I packed my gear and refitted the rotor arm to the Chrysler. Finally, I cleaned and reloaded my pistol, burying the rag I used to do it.

The sun, low on the horizon, spilled indigo shadows into the desert from over the rim of mountains in the far distance. I shivered in the chilling air. I wasn't a whole man yet. Although the venom had been dissipated through my system, I could still suffer dizziness and weakening heat flushes. My lungs felt as if they had been pumped up with red-hot methane gas and suddenly deflated.

I climbed into the car and drove it gingerly down the slope of the clearing on to the road. By the time I reached the lower slopes, my confidence was almost itself again.

Then the windscreen shockingly splintered to complete opacity and, following it, I heard the rolling echoes of a shot. Before I could punch visibility into the glass, the car lurched, its nose dropping abruptly as we left the road with a bumping rush.

I was weightless inside a bouncing steel and leather coffin, the world a confusion of scraping metal and splintering glass. A broken spear of cactus stabbed through a window, stippling my arm and neck with a bristle of spines.

As the wounded, sliding vehicle settled on one side, stones rattled in its wake. I held on grimly to the bucking steering wheel while the door above me flew back on its hinges, letting in the blue sky, the bonnet cover snapping open like a shark's jaws. Then it jolted to a halt and lay quietly on its flank. There was a silence of water running from the radiator and the loud thudding of my over-worked heart.

I pulled at my legs and found them mousetrapped beneath the dashboard: not hurting but immovable. Nausea returned threefold, my mind slipping sideways on well-oiled runners. I waited for something else to happen. For the unseen gunman to shoot again.

I pulled out my pistol and waited. Time was an elasticated, rubberized ribbon of dreamy silk that stretched from me to nowhere. From the shadowed interior of the Chrysler, I saw the day turn orange as the sun slowly died.

A hundred years later, I heard the hum of an approaching engine and then the slamming of car doors. Purposeful feet crunched stones and I heard the deep rumble of official voices.

Sowerby's parti-coloured face, peering down through the opening in the ruptured metal, wore a crooked triumphant grin.

14

The windows of the room in which I sat were fitted with bright steel bars. Through them, from the outside darkness of Shiloh, came the smells of squeezed citrus fruits and frying hamburgers.

The bare walls were battleship grey, well-sluiced with a pungent disinfectant. In one of them was fitted a large see-through mirror. A metal table supported a workworn typewriter, a sheaf of flimsy paper and battered carbons. The legs of the table had torn holes in the blue linoleum. It wasn't a very comfortable room and wasn't meant to be.

Sowerby and his companion had levered me from the Chrysler without adding to my existing injuries. Brought to this room, the police doctor had tapped me over with the knuckle of his forefinger, looked into the retinas of my eyes and tutted his disapproval. The cactus spines embedded in my arm and neck he extracted without using a pain-killer, swabbing the punctures with a dab of wet cottonwool.

He questioned me closely about the size and colour of the offending scorpion. 'You could have died,' he reproved me as if I had done it on purpose. He thumbed the beefsteak flesh of my face. 'These weren't collected in the auto accident,' he said confidently.

'I fell over after the scorpion stung me.'

He didn't believe me but I wouldn't be the first liar he'd had as a patient. He asked for ten dollars, telling me I should go to bed and lay off liquor and women for a day or two.

Sowerby stood and watched, making sure I wasn't running anywhere. Not while he had anything to do with it. Now and again he touched the strawberry jam blotch on his face with the back of his hand. When the doctor had gone, he said, 'Fit?' It wasn't in him to be solicitous to a murderer. He was telling me to move.

His made-up mind went with the knitted tie and sharp navy blue suit he wore. He was a Police Officer-of-the-Year type, probably with 'Defend the Law: Defeat Crime' tattooed on his tail. I admired his implacable dourness but he rasped my sensibilities.

I preceded him meekly enough, limping a little. There is a time for walking softly and this was it.

Gebhardt sat buddha-bellied behind his desk, a brown pole of a cigar aimed at me from his tight-shut mouth. He nodded, giving me an appraising stare. His Dobermann Pinscher raised her hackles at me and bared her teeth.

Sowerby sat across the room; his hat on, his unwinking eyes rock-steady on me.

'Sit down, Mr Tallis,' Gebhardt said pleasantly enough. 'You and me got lots to talk about.'

Sitting opposite him, I pulled out my cigarettes and lit one. It felt thin between my swollen lips. 'Can we come to a conclusion about the girl first?' I asked. I knew enough about the art of interrogation to seize the initiative when I could.

Watching Gebhardt's eyes I guessed I wasn't the heavy suspect I might have been earlier. He removed the cigar and squinted along its length. 'A naked dame,' he said gummily, smacking his lips. 'Shot three times in the belly from zero range in your room. Then you high-tailing it down the stairs and committing a felonious assault on the desk clerk.' He showed me how white and scrubbed his dentures were. 'You take it from there.'

'A girl I'd never seen before in my life,' I said, 'shot by a man climbing through the bathroom window. As, no doubt, your scenes-of-crime men have already told you.'

'Go on,' he said.

'Shot with a forty-five automatic, I'd guess. You saw my pistol the last time I was in. The ballistics don't fit.'

'You wouldn't be the first man to own two guns.' He dropped a coil of cigar ash on the bitch's head.

I hooked an ankle on a knee and unlaced and removed my shoe. I slid it across the desk to him. 'You'll have found two odd bullet holes somewhere there,' I said. 'One of the bullets clipped my heel.'

He looked at the shoe without enthusiasm. 'Very interesting.' He pushed it back with one finger. 'If it proves anything. So why'd some other man shoot this dame?'

'If this was open-season for guessing,' I said cautiously, 'I'd say he thought she was Mrs Hansson.' I was grunting, putting the shoe back on.

'Aagh! *Le crime passionnel.*' His accent missed being Parisien by the width of the Atlantic but it wasn't bad. 'Where was she?'

'Back at the ranch. I was collecting our gear.' I looked at Sowerby. 'What were *you* searching for?'

He narrowed his eyes at me. 'What's that?'

'You searched the ranch-house.'

His nose got pinched and white, his mouth small. 'I don't know what you're talking about, fella.'

I was openly sceptical. 'You searched my hotel room and my helicopter. Both without the courtesy of a search warrant. Probably my car as well. What ethical paralysis stopped you short of the ranch?'

My sarcasm offended something of the F.B.I. Academy training in him for he stiffened with all the outrage of a man unjustly accused.

Gebhardt pulled me off his lieutenant's back. 'You know the man shooting the dame?'

'No,' I lied. 'I had only a second's glimpse of him. I was too busy dodging his bullets.'

'You shot at him?'

'I didn't get the opportunity.'

Sowerby's sneer was sour disbelief. 'You wouldn't have a description, naturally.'

I locked antagonisms with him. I didn't know why I felt as I did for, professionally, I was on his side. 'You want me to make one up? You were there. Why didn't *you* see him?' I turned to Gebhardt. 'That was about the rawest fix imaginable.'

He rumbled deep down behind his medal ribbons and SHILOH CITY POLICE CHIEF badge. That had hurt him. His beefy fists clenched and showed tendons and whitened knuckles. The red coloration of his jowls darkened. 'Tell 'im,' he ordered Sowerby in a harsh voice.

'I had a tip-off on the telephone,' the sandy man said reluctantly. 'Saying, go to room forty-two.'

'Alleging what?' I asked politely.

'Alleging you were shacking up with a minor.'

'All right. So it was something you wanted to believe. Like the other tip-off the Los Angeles police were supposed to have received.' When Sowerby didn't reply, I asked, 'Who was she?'

He looked at Gebhardt. Then he stood and filled a waxed paper cup with chilled water from a dispenser. Finished, he crushed the cup in his fingers and dropped it in the disposal bin. His eyes never left mine. 'She was a stripper from a Shiloh club,' he said. 'Name of Julie Aiken.'

'Paul's Bar?'

Their shying away from facts was almost visible. Gebhardt grunted. 'Are you satisfied now?'

'No, I'm not. It didn't come off but somebody tried hard. Went to an awful lot of trouble to have me fixed. Somebody,'— I stared arrogantly at Sowerby—'who might try again.'

'Watch your yap.' Sowerby's face was bone-hard.

Gebhardt rotated the stub of his cigar between his teeth. 'Tell me what the man was like.' He was getting irritated at the sniping going on between Sowerby and myself, working hard at keeping us from each other's throats.

'More than six feet in height. About the thirty to forty age group.' I gave the appearance of thoughtful recollection. 'Whitish hair. Athletic build. The gun he was using looked like a forty-five Army Colt. That's about all.'

He jotted this down with his pencil. 'Where did you go after you fled the hotel?'

'I hid up at Painted Rock.'

'Why, if you are innocent?'

I laughed incredulously. 'You expected me to hang around for Sowerby to put his little pinkie on?'

Gebhardt cleared his throat. 'Where's your chopper?'

'Parked out in Sheriff Seamark's territory. It was too obvious to fly, so I used a car.'

'You didn't use your own.' He was sweating at the armpits, the crisp khaki twill turning to limp cocoa brown.

'I rented one in Shiloh. Nobody seemed to be worrying much. How did you find me?'

'Lieutenant Sowerby was waiting at the ranch. He saw you coming down the creek road.' He regarded me distrustfully. 'How'd you come to groundloop your car?'

Sowerby intervened. 'I heard a shot.'

'*I* didn't. I misjudged a bend and slid over.'

'There was a bullet hole in the roof,' Gebhardt said, '*and* in the windshield.'

I couldn't think of an answer to this.

'The Chief asked you a question, Tallis,' Sowerby rasped.

'Oh? I thought he was stating a fact.'

'Who shot at you?' Gebhardt asked mildly. His manner suggested I had misjudged him on first acquaintance.

'If somebody fired at me, I didn't know it. So I wouldn't know who. Or why.'

They chewed that over in silence and, surprisingly, swallowed it.

'Where is Mrs Hansson now?' Gebhardt asked.

'I don't know.' I could say this without blinking. 'I never saw her after I ran from the hotel.'

Sowerby changed the pace. 'Why did you clout the desk clerk?'

'Because he knew the girl had been planted in my room. Or was that an unwarranted conclusion?'

'How would he?'

'The room door was locked.'

Gebhardt said, 'I see what you mean. We'll go to work on him.'

'You mean he's still there? Waiting to be questioned?'

The two men exchanged glances, neither answering.

'There's been a lot of talk about narcotics.' Gebhardt blew cigar smoke absently at a fly scraping its back legs together on his blotter. Had it been able to cough, it looked as if it would have done so.

'Not by me. Only by you and Sowerby.'

'One thing you are not, Tallis,' Gebhardt said roughly, 'and that is the goddam blue-eyed moron you think you're kiddin' me you are.'

I smiled and shrugged non-committally.

'Would Sheriff Seamark think you are?' he pressed, turning down the corners of his mouth.

'I found him a reasonable man,' I said carefully. 'Willing to listen.' I screwed my cigarette out. It tasted of burning rubber.

Gebhardt spat out a brown fragment of tobacco leaf. I could interpret it as his opinion of Seamark only if I chose to. 'I'm serious,' he said, 'and warning you. Somethin' nasty's going to happen to you if you don't watch out. Specially if you stick your ass in where it ain't wanted.'

'You are satisfied I didn't entice this stripper into my room and then shoot her for the hell of it?'

'A man was seen climbing down the fire escape about that time. He had grey hair.'

'You are satisfied then?'

'I didn't say that. A cop's never satisfied. And he can always change his mind.'

He didn't ring true. He wasn't pushing me hard enough and he seemed to be waiting. 'These narcotics,' he continued. 'You sure you don't want to tell me something?'

Sowerby stirred protestingly in his chair. I obviously wasn't bleeding enough for his liking.

'I'm sorry,' I said. 'There isn't anything I can tell you. All I want to do is to sell real estate.'

Gebhardt's cheek twitched and he scowled at the ceiling. He reached a fat paw into a wire tray and fished out a teletype message form. 'The Department of Justice in Washington's taking an interest in you,' he said. 'Illegal entry . . .'

'Oh, balls,' I interrupted him. 'I've got a visa.'

'Not to traffic in horse, you ain't.' He glared at me. 'Listen,' he said, 'and listen good. Washington's askin' if we have evidence to support a charge of illegal entry. If we have, there'll be an order signed and you're out. Some guy's been lobbying in the Senate and bein' listened to.' He slapped the form back into the tray. 'When you get top brass shovin' at us little folks, somethin's got to give.'

'You aren't telling me who should be so interested?'

He was contemptuous. 'You wouldn't think I'd *know*, would you? Or that I'd tell you if I did?'

There was a knock at the door and it opened. A capless patrolman looked around it. 'He's on the way,' he said.

The effect on Gebhardt was electric. He rose from his seat, a squat, barrel-bellied man of brutal menace. He grasped me unexpectedly by my shirt collar and tie and yanked me upright, ripping the shirt with the violence of it. His fingers curry-combed through my hair and he slapped me backhanded across my astonished face.

I staggered backwards on my heels into the enfolding arms of Sowerby. I lashed out futilely with my feet.

Gebhardt was an apoplectic crimson and yelling at me. '*Punk!* You goddam smarmy lyin' punk! I'll beat it outa you with these two fists.'

Sowerby was as strong and wiry as a polecat and he held me in a sinewy embrace.

The door opened. '*Chief Gebhardt!*' Mayor Kezler was angry as he took in the picture of my discomfiture. 'I had thought you above this sort of brutality.'

Sowerby released me abruptly. The torn shirt and disordered hair went well with my already battered features. Although Gebhardt's slap had been light, I appeared to be the living proof that Shiloh possessed a keen and energetic Police Department. I rested the palms of my hands on the desk and hunched my shoulders in seeming dejection.

In that position, I could read upside-down the teletype message form. It was an F.B.I. Field Office warning about the fraudulent cheque-pushing activities of one Mrs Marian Norma Peters. Gebhardt was, indeed, a trier.

'I'm waiting, Chief,' Kezler said coldly, 'for an explanation.' His dark suit was impeccably pressed, his linen crisp and white. All the bits and pieces of his jewellery were gold and gleamed richly as he moved.

Gebhardt moved his weight from one foot to the other, itching to have a further go at me, transparently resentful of the mayor's intervention. 'It's the only thing these punks understand,' he growled. 'I'll take my goddam nightstick to the bastard.'

Kezler looked down the ridge of his suntanned patrician nose. 'A nightstick will never take the place of intelligence, Chief Gebhardt.' The eyes he turned to me were friendly. 'What is he charged with?'

'Nothing yet.' Gebhardt was uneasy. 'But he was just going to put his hands up about the narcotics trafficking.'

'He's not the man you want and you know it,' Kezler said crisply. 'Have you spoken to the D.A.'s office?'

'There ain't anything to speak to him about. Leave us to get on with the job, Mayor, and there will be.'

Kezler spoke to me. 'Do you want to tell Chief Gebhardt anything, Mr Tallis?'

I shook my head. 'There's nothing to tell.'

He made a small sound of satisfaction. 'So I thought. What about the dead girl?' he asked Gebhardt.

Gebhardt shrugged his meaty shoulders. 'A bit more checkin' and I guess he'll be near enough clean on that. But not on the narcotics.'

Kezler's lips compressed. 'You've ridden that horse too hard, Chief. If you're not charging him . . .?'

'I ain't charging him but he stays in on suspicion. There are things to be gone into.'

'As mayor, you force me to do something about protecting Mr Tallis's interests.'

A shadow of doubt moved in Gebhardt's eyes. 'Keep it legal,' he said heavily. 'You only run the city, not own it.'

Kezler sucked in his cheeks and for a moment lost his cool composure. Then he spoke to me. 'The Fourth Amendment to the Constitution protects you from the consequences of any so-called confession made under duress.'

I stared straight at Gebhardt and smiled. 'I can't think of any reason why I should need its protection.'

'Put him down,' Gebhardt ordered Sowerby. He sat, his face wooden, patently dismissing us.

Kezler gave me his politician's smile as he left the office. 'You know where I am, Mr Tallis. All you have to do is to ask.'

When he had gone, I said to Gebhardt, 'What sort of a point were you trying to make?'

His drab eyes measured me up and down as he stripped the band from a fresh cigar. 'I warned you, buster,' he growled, 'that something nasty could happen. Now it is.'

On the way to the cell block with Sowerby, we passed the ground-floor entrance hall. Waiting there, idly reading a wall notice about Fish and Game Laws, was a man with a small, neat beard. Although the glimpse I had of him was only momentary, it was enough. If he wasn't O'Brien, the similarity had me fooled.

The booking area resembled an aquarium with its sea-green walls and tubs of tropical foliage. Sowerby dictated the charge to a uniformed station sergeant who sat on a high stool at a desk. A gaoler stood watchful at his side, rattling a ring of keys.

I was entered in the book as one Roger Tallis, suspected of being concerned with others in the inter-state trans-shipment of a statutory narcotic; to wit, heroin. It was a wide enough definition to hold me legally in custody for the night.

With the departure of Sowerby, I was searched by the sergeant and my property entered on the sheet. I signed it and said, 'I'd like to make a telephone call.'

He looked sourly at the money he had already accounted for on his list. 'You are authorized to make one free call to a number within the city limits. Anywhere else, you pay.'

'I want to speak to San Francisco.'

He sighed and nodded at the hooded wall telephone. 'Use that.'

My mind retrieved the number Charles had given me from next to that of the flaxen Brünnhilde and I dialled it. A male voice answered, 'San Francisco 015-27801.'

'My name is Roger Tallis,' I said, 'and I'm a friend of Charles's from London.'

There was a moment's silence and I heard him switch over to tape. 'Swell,' the voice said guardedly. 'Can I help you?'

'It's why I'm calling.'

'We've been waiting. You want assistance?'

'Yes. I'm in custody at Shiloh City on suspicion of smuggling narcotics.'

He didn't sound surprised. 'We would know this.'

'You would?'

'We have a friend looking after you.'

'Oh,' I said feebly. Good old devious Charles. Everything organized and everybody but me in the picture about what was happening. I lowered my voice. 'I'm speaking on a police line.'

'I understand. I am in contact with your friend. Is there a message?'

I was silent for a minute. 'Yes. Sphex has flown Phoenix-wards in an enemy Pontiac. A brown sedan.' I quoted the licence plate to him. 'She's riding the wrong horse. The original mare is stabled safely near here. Waiting for a hostile contact. Does that make sense?'

'Sort of. It will to your friend. You want me to notify Charles?'

'Give him my love and tell him I've been stung by Sphex *and* a scorpion.'

'O.K. You want out from the tank? Bail or something?'

'I'll leave it to my friend. Let things ride for the moment. I'll yell when it hurts.' I replaced the handset and returned to the sergeant, feeling twice as tall and wanting to shake somebody's hand.

He tossed over my lighter and cigarettes. 'Make yourself comfortable,' he said without irony.

The cell faced the booking area, separated from it by a heavy grille of inch-thick steel bars. I sat on a mattress covering the metal bunk, leaning against a wall.

The evening crawled lizard-like and I yawned my boredom. I had worked things out to my satisfaction. Hitherto, I had been playing a sort of murderous game of chess in the darkness of my ignorance. Now I could at least distinguish between the black and white pieces. Which wasn't to be equated with winning.

Accompanying my coffee and square of rubber cheese, was a *Shiloh City Globe*. It had SHILOH CITY POLICE DEPARTMENT stamped on each page in purple ink.

At eleven o'clock the lights were dimmed to an orange glow and I slept. Most of the night I dreamed about Ingrid.

15

The gaoler who shook me awake was one I hadn't seen before. He brought me a small silverfoil tray with segmented compartments. There were cornflakes, a fried sausage and an egg, slices of bread and butter and a pool of jam that looked like tomato soup. Two waxed-paper cartons contained coffee and hot milk. The knife, fork and spoon were of white plastic.

When I had finished this breakfast, I was escorted to an alcove where I was allowed a supervised wash and the loan of my battery-operated shaver.

Almost immediately afterwards, Sowerby came to the cell block accompanied by a small plump man whose pink face was too self-complacent. He wore a black homburg hat and carried a briefcase.

'This is Counsellor Bannerman,' Sowerby said, iron-faced. 'You are being sprung.' The prospect was sackcloth and ashes to him.

'I'm glad,' I said to the lawyer, shaking the hand held out to me. I was careful not to ask for whom he was acting. Sufficient it was I could get away from the smell of disinfectant and rubber mattresses.

We signed papers and Bannerman handed over a bond for ten thousand dollars. Then I was given back my property and money, less the cost of the previous evening's telephone call. The State and I were even.

Sowerby spoke only words which were necessary. When we left, he said to Bannerman, 'Where will he be, Counsellor? I might want to see him again.'

'I don't know, Lieutenant,' he replied unhelpfully. 'It isn't a condition of his bailment he should give an address.'

I was one with Sowerby in not liking the little lawyer. His suit was too expensive-looking for him to be an honest man. 'I'll keep in touch,' I assured Sowerby. 'I shan't be leaving Shiloh.'

Outside, standing arrogantly in a no-parking zone, the door of Bannerman's enormous shiny black car was being held open for us by a negro chauffeur. The expression on his face suggested my bail might have paid his salary for a month. But only just.

The sun was beginning to warm the streets as we ticked along and the short drive was pleasant after the confines of my cell. 'Where are we going, Mr Bannerman?' I asked the small man. He sat next to me on the crimson nylon wool of the rear seat, his shoes barely touching the deep pile of the carpeting. A plate-glass screen segregated us from the chauffeur.

'To my office.' He snapped open a flap door near his knees and displayed a glittering phalanx of crystal decanters and glasses. 'A drink? To wash the taste of municipal coffee out of your mouth?'

I shook my head. 'I'd rather know who went bail for me.'

'Ah, yes.' He poured gin in a glass and drank it neat. He didn't get his pink complexion from exposure to the sun. 'A friend. But can I defer on that until I get further instructions?'

The shining car slid gently to a halt in the shadow of a lofty skyscraper of steel and glass. Blue sky and small gobbets of white cloud were reflected in its uppermost windows. The chauffeur opened the door, ignoring again the no-parking signs.

Once inside the vast circular concourse of palms and inquiry desks, I followed Bannerman across to the lifts. The suite of offices occupying the whole of the fourteenth floor was discreetly signposted 'Bannerman and Associates, Attorneys and Counsellors-at-Law.'

His own office accommodation was a suite within a suite. The simplest, least pretentious, object in its studied opulence was a framed certificate saying that James Q. Bannerman was a member of the Shiloh City Bar Association. Like Chief Gebhardt, he had American flags crossed behind his desk. It was an office from which State loans were floated and fiscal appropriations planned.

He ushered me into an inner room. 'Would you be kind enough to wait in here, Mr Tallis,' he said. 'I won't keep you long.'

As with the rest of his suite, it comprised an ostentation of gleaming wood panelling, black-leather furniture and large screened panoramic windows. I sat in an oversoft armchair and smoked English cigarettes displayed in a silver box on a small table. I read casually from *The New Yorker* and *Harper's*

Bazaar.

When Bannerman returned an hour later, he brought Kezler with him. The mayor was carefully groomed in a light-grey suit, his gold cufflinks and tie-pin reflecting the bright sun streaming through the slats of the venetian blinds.

He shook hands with me, enclosing our clasped fists with his other in an excess of welcome. 'I'm so glad,' he said. 'You had no more trouble?'

'No.' I released my hand. 'I'm surprised, Mr Kezler. You were under no obligation.'

'Consider it my pleasure.' He turned to Bannerman. 'I won't keep you from your writs and litigations, Counsellor.' He put his arm around the plump shoulders and squeezed them. 'Mr Tallis and I want to put the world right.'

When we were alone, he walked to one of the windows, his face solemn. He adjusted the slats of the blind. 'Come here, Mr Tallis,' he said.

I stood by his side. He smelled discreetly of toilet lotions and mouth wash. Very, very expensive ones. Far below us, the street was clogged with tiny moving vehicles. Knots of pedestrians flowed along the footpaths and over the street at crossing points. The tall buildings of the business section of Shiloh threw hard shadows across the canyons of their own making. No sounds came through the double-glazed windows.

'A prosperous, hard-working city is a wonderful thing,' he said portentously. 'And as chief executive officer of Shiloh I am a proud man. A proud man, Mr Tallis.'

'It's a responsibility,' I answered ambiguously.

'Yes, it is.' He seized on to that one very fast. 'It's about that I wish to speak.'

He left the window and walked over to a blondwood cabinet. 'I'm going to spoil myself with a weak whisky. Will you join me?' While he was pouring the drinks, he said, 'I'm also a selfish man, Mr Tallis, when it comes to serving the city. Undertaking your release was part of it.'

Handing me the glass of whisky, he smiled away any idea I might have had of taking his admission of selfishness literally. 'I want your help. Can I call you Roger?'

'Of course,' I said politely. I sat on the arm of the chair, still feeling battered by circumstances.

He talked striding to and fro, gesticulating with his free hand, shining his teeth at me. 'I am acutely conscious of my responsibilities as mayor, Mr Tall . . . Roger. One of those responsibilities is the administration of the Police Department. It's not the only one, of course. Health and Sanitation, too. Much the same thing,' he smiled wryly, 'but we'll stay with the Police Department. You wouldn't have to be too bright to cotton on that Chief Gebhardt and I don't see eye to eye over certain matters.'

'You mean over me?'

'You come into it. Not to put too fine a point on it, Chief Gebhardt isn't bursting any gut getting to the nub of this narcotics business.' He frowned anxiously. 'I can trust you, Roger?'

'If you mean, will I go running to him; telling him what you said . . . ?' I put a touch of frost on the words.

'I knew I could.' His eyes exuded bonhomie like warm treacle. 'Gebhardt's a good cop'—his expression was telling me he was no such thing—'but not very bright.' He held an admonitory palm up to me. 'I'm not saying he's corrupt, mixed up with the rackets, unable to put the pressure on his department to get serious crime cleaned up. You understand?'

'Yes,' I said doubtfully. 'More or less.'

'Good.' He bent, putting a hand on my knee. He was a top-liner for squeezing people. 'I want you to trust me, Roger. I'm not a crime-buster—I wouldn't know how to begin—but I'm determined to get to the bottom of what's going on. Now, Gebhardt believes you are criminally concerned.'

He went to the cabinet and poured himself another whisky. It didn't look very weak to me. He held the bottle up in interrogation but I shook my head.

'Now *I* don't,' he emphasized. 'Which is why I bailed you out. But—forgive me—I *do* think you are involved.' When I didn't say anything, he added, 'Innocently, I am sure, but involved.' He waited.

I swirled the dregs of the whisky in my glass and considered. I had been dodging the issue for too long. It was a time for letting my hair down. Well, some of it. 'I'm involved,' I admitted, 'and, as you say, innocently. Not knowing who to turn to for fear of being arrested and charged.' I drank the whisky and held the glass out to him. 'Perhaps I will after all.'

When he had replenished it, he sat opposite me. 'Tell me about it, Roger,' he said. 'Let's see what we can do to clear the mess up.'

'It's a stupid story, Mayor,' I began, lighting up one of Bannerman's cigarettes. 'You'll think me pretty wet around the ears when you've heard it. I met this woman, Mrs Hansson, in Spain two or three weeks ago. We got to know each other very well indeed. It finished up by my inviting her to come to the States with me. You know my firm is in association with Gribble Real Estate Incorporated of Phoenix?'

'Yes.'

I looked uncomfortable. 'I thought of it as just one of those affairs. Two people. No ties either end. Same needs, same tastes. Then, when I was flying her from L.A. I dropped her bloody camera overboard. I was taking a photograph of Gribble's ranch,' I explained, 'and the thing slipped out of my hands. She put on such a tragic act about what I'd done that I put the helicopter down in the desert and looked for it then and there. *That* wasn't any good. So, without telling her, I went back on my own and had another look.'

I drew deeply on my cigarette, thinking my words out carefully. Even the protection afforded by Charles might not be sufficient to cover the havoc I had wrought. My experience of authority told me that, with hindsight, it rarely understood the need for that which had been done without it. So I trimmed my activities to what I considered to be an acceptable level.

'I found it. The case had sprung open and I saw little plastic bags of powder inside. I didn't have to be very intelligent to know there's no profit in smuggling anything in powder form but narcotics. So,' I said, 'I took the bags and left the camera there.'

Kezler raised his eyebrows. 'Oh? Why?'

'Because my having the camera would equate me with having the narcotics.'

'Why not go to the police with it?'

'I'm sorry about that. But you understand ... I thought a lot of Ingrid. Mrs Hansson.'

He nodded, pursing his lips. 'I understand, of course I do. But, legally, morally, you made yourself an accomplice.'

'Which is why I was so unforthcoming with Chief Gebhardt.'

'What did you do with the powder?'

'I hid it.'

'And nobody else knows?'

'Nobody.'

'Please go on, Roger.'

'Then Sheriff Seamark called on me. You know him?'

'A fine law officer. He covers Caliente County.' He shook his head sorrowfully. 'He and Gebhardt don't hit it off.'

'The sheriff saw me land the helicopter so I had to tell him I'd dropped the camera.' I frowned. 'That put the cat among the pigeons.'

'It did?'

'He searched and found it. Thought he was doing Ingrid a good turn.'

'Ah, yes. So then Mrs Hansson knew the packets had been taken?'

'No. She was missing by then.'

'I see. This was when the girl had gotten herself killed in your room?'

'Yes. First of all though, two men held me up at gunpoint in the hotel. Then they released me. During that time, Ingrid was taken away from the ranch.'

He wrinkled his forehead at me. 'It's getting quite melodramatic, Roger.'

'It's true, nevertheless,' I said shortly. 'When I got back to the ranch she was missing. Then she telephoned me saying she was at the hotel. I knew she wasn't because I could hear gaming-machines in the background. The hotel doesn't have them.'

'But you went?'

'Yes. There was nothing else I could do. That's when I found the girl in my bed. You know the details of that?'

'Gebhardt kept me in the picture. The ballistics proved a second gun was used and a man was seen climbing down the escape.'

'At the time it worried me. Sowerby was so opportunely there, I knew I'd been framed. I ran for it.'

'And you haven't seen Mrs Hansson since?' He was watching me closely. For all his disarming bonhomie, he wasn't an all-out, one-hundred per cent supporter of Roger Tallis.

'Oh, yes. I traced her to a place called Paul's Bar.'

'That was clever of you, Roger.' He rose, took my glass from the arm of the chair and refilled the two at the cabinet. Then he dropped ice in them. Over his shoulder, he said, 'How did you do that?'

'I checked on different gaming-clubs. Then I saw a brown Pontiac parked outside Paul's Bar. It was the same car in which the two strong-arm men had driven to my hotel.'

He handed me my whisky. 'You ought to have Chief Gebhardt's job,' he said. 'That was an inspired bit of detection.'

'Luck,' I replied. 'I guessed she was in trouble, so I went in after her. I bought myself a pair of overalls and a hair lacquer aerosol. It was easy, really,' I said modestly.

'You had trouble?'

'Nobody was permanently damaged. I used the aerosol instead of a gun.'

'You told Mrs Hansson about the narcotics then?'

'I didn't get the opportunity. She wasn't in a talkative mood anyway. Not very grateful I'd lifted her from Paul's Bar, in fact.' I paused. 'I took her up to Painted Rock. Sheriff Seamark'd told me—quite fortuitously—about a hunting lodge up there. To be fair, he didn't know I was dodging the Police Department at that time. No sooner had we got there than I was stung by a scorpion.' I laughed deprecatingly. 'It doesn't sound much, I know, but it laid me out for an hour or so. When I came to, she was gone.'

Kezler eyes were hard. 'Gone? Where?'

'I don't know,' I said helplessly. 'Certainly she didn't go in my car. I thought I saw other tyre tracks but I couldn't be sure. The ground was stony.'

'You were in the lodge?'

'No. When I was stung, I staggered into the brush like a sick cat. I didn't know what I was doing. Afterwards, I drove the car back towards Shiloh, looking for Ingrid. That's when I ran off the road and got myself arrested.'

'Um,' he mused. 'I can't pretend I understand it all but I do appreciate your frankness. Now,' he said briskly, 'to the matter of the powder.'

'Yes?' I was wary now.

'You don't actually *know* it to be a narcotic?'

'Now you mention it, I don't. I assumed it was . . .'

'Then the first thing is to have it tested and checked.' He smiled. 'Fortunately, I'm in a position to have the Public Analyst from the Health Department get to work on it . . .'

'I'm sorry,' I interrupted. 'I haven't handed it over yet.'

His eyes were momentarily angry. 'But you are going to?'

'Yes. To a duly constituted police authority.'

'And, as mayor, I'm not one?' He was teetering on the brink of losing his wool.

'I'm sorry. No.'

'Not Chief Gebhardt, I hope?' He was daring me.

'No. I thought the Federal Bureau of Narcotics.'

He wasn't wildly enthusiastic. 'You know an agent?'

'I thought you might.'

'You want me to make the arrangements?'

'I don't want to trouble you—or involve you. Tell me where their nearest Field Office is and I'll telephone.'

He stroked his fingers round his beautifully shaved chin, beginning to look happier. 'It's no trouble, Roger. Being an elected official, I'm not averse to occasional flattering publicity. It never does any harm.' He laughed. 'I'm showing you the worst side of the American political appointee.'

'I'll survive it,' I said. 'I shall be happy to leave it to you.'

'They have an office in Phoenix,' he said, 'and I'll go personally.' He noticed my look of surprise. 'Never telephone top secret material, Roger. It's a basic law of politics. Bugging is endemic in our cut-throat society. Where and when?' he asked.

I already had it worked out. 'I'll hand it over at the ranch,' I said, 'at ten o'clock tonight. There'll be nobody else there.'

'And you'll give evidence about its recovery?'

'Of course. I shan't be any trouble. I'm glad to be rid of the whole thing.'

'You can identify the two men who held you up at the hotel?'

'It would be a pleasure.' Poor Mendoza and Luigi. So it would have been for them.

'Good. What are you doing for the rest of the day?'

'Collecting my car from the airport, eating the best lunch I can buy and catching up on my sleep. I haven't fully recovered from the scorpion yet.'

'I have a personal assistant who'd be glad to show you round, Roger. To look after you.' He grinned as if embarrassed. 'She's young and personable and has no tag on her.'

I laughed. 'Don't fret about me, Mr Kezler. I'll keep out of trouble and turn up with the stuff.'

16

It took time and some unblushing misstatements of fact to explain to the hire company manager how I'd come to write off a perfectly good Chrysler station wagon. Admiring his healthy cynicism, I then took a cab to the heliport to recover the Chevrolet I left there after being picked up by Gost.

Its blue enamel skin was blistering to the touch in the late morning heat and yellowish from blown dust. Braving the oven-hot interior, I recovered my sunglasses from the parcels ledge and hooked them on my nose.

I was waiting impatiently for the heat to leak out through the open doors when Sowerby came quietly up from behind me. Not unfriendly, his face possessed the sandy stare of a calculating ferret. He wore his chocolate suit and narrow-brimmed hat with a cool disregard for the temperature.

He nodded and gave me a brief smile. 'Going somewhere?'

'If I am, it'll be on my own.' I didn't feel companionable.

He was impervious to discouragement. 'I thought you and me could talk about things.'

'Without your holding my arms?'

He was distinctly uncomfortable. 'No ill-feelings,' he said. 'Nobody was very serious. The boss was horsing about.'

'Talking of your boss,' I said, 'does he know you are trying to get matey with me?'

He ignored this. Away from Gebhardt, he was a different man; more sure of himself.

I said, 'Either he doesn't trust you or you don't trust him.'

'Stop needling me,' he said mildly. 'I've got a mean temper.'

'Was Gebhardt trying to impress Kezler with that pseudo rough stuff?'

'If he was, he had a good reason for doing it.' He cleared his throat. 'Kezler bailed you, didn't he?'

'He did?' I kept my face expressionless. A good policeman can read his answers in the unconscious tightening of jaw muscles, in the flicker of eyelids. And Sowerby was good.

'It's right, then?'

'Even if it was, I don't think he'd want me to say so.' I waited a few moments while a turbine-engined helicopter roared its intolerable noise over our heads and whipped up clouds of choking grit. I continued, 'I was offered a personal guide and chaperon by my benefactor.'

He scowled. 'So?'

'I turned her down.' I thought Kezler might have sicked Sowerby on to me, not trusting my integrity. If he had, there was nothing in the detective's demeanour to confirm it.

'I don't know what you're yakking about,' he growled.

'Neither do I,' I said. 'It was but a passing thought.'

The leather of the upholstery had cooled sufficiently for me to enter the car. I slammed the doors shut and pumped fuel into the cylinders with the accelerator pedal. When the engine started, I said, 'I'm hungry. If you've anything to say, it had better be now.'

He leaned on the door. 'The guard at the gate reported he passed you through in this Chevvy the night before last. After midnight,' he said with immense satisfaction.

'Yes?' I was glad my eyes were shielded by the sunglasses and I fiddled with the choke button.

'He says you had a passenger.'

I looked up astonished. 'He did?'

'Yes. A man with white-ish hair. He was sitting in the rear seat.'

'He was kidding you,' I said, not too confidently. 'He never left his office.' A cold climate had settled in my stomach. My lips felt numb.

'You feel we've something to talk about?'

'Not really,' I replied, 'but if you think we have, you'd better get in. I'm still hungry and still proposing to eat at the Blue Stetson.'

'Sure,' he said, 'I'll join you.'

I put the car into gear and trundled her towards the exit gate. When we were outside, he turned and reached an arm over to the rear seat, rubbing a squeaking finger on the leather. 'I took a swab of a stain from here,' he observed. 'The lab called it blood. Group O.' He watched me intently.

'It's a hired car. Anybody could have bled in it.' Now I knew how he had placed Gost so accurately in the rear seat. He was guessing.

'Oh, yes,' he agreed. 'It's my nasty suspicious mind.' He

bared the steel watch on his wrist. 'If we hurried, we could make Painted Rock and back before lunch. A late lunch.'

'Why should we do that?'

'I wanted to show you something interesting.' He narrowed his sandy-lashed eyes. 'I wouldn't pass it up if I were you.'

'You aren't hoping to make me?'

'Of course not. I'm advising you.'

'After lunch,' I said firmly. 'Then we'll go in my helicopter. It's out at Mohawk Creek and I have to collect it anyway.'

He settled in his seat as I took the concrete slip-road to the city centre and the tyres began to hum. He tipped his hat until its brim rested on the bridge of his nose and he whistled soundlessly. His self-satisfaction didn't cheer me at all.

On Third Avenue, I pulled up outside the Post Office. 'I've a telephone call to make,' I said. He badly wanted to know to whom but couldn't think of a good enough reason to be pushing about it.

I chose a booth from which I could watch him and dialled San Francisco 015–27801. 'The man from Charlie's Bar here,' I said. 'I'm bailed.'

'Good for you,' the voice said laconically.

'Was the message delivered?'

'Yes.'

'Any news of Sphex?'

'Her car was found in Phoenix. Our agent reports no soya flour in it. That's all.'

'I'm handing over the real stuff tonight. Ten o'clock at El Rancho Madrito.'

'This is for your friend?'

'Without fail. I want company. In case I walk on a banana skin.'

'I'll pass it.'

When I rang off, I dialled the sheriff's office. I had asked him to find Ingrid for me and to check on Mendoza and Luigi. That events had overtaken me and the information was now pointless did not alter the fact I was obliged to him. He seemed too nice an old boy to ignore.

A young male voice told me that Sheriff Seamark was out in his territory—he made it sound like the Dakota Badlands—and would I leave my name. I did, saying I would call again.

Temporarily detached from interrogating me into an unguarded admission and with his nosebag on, Sowerby was interesting company. Surprisingly, he shared my interest in music and we talked Stravinsky and Shostokovich and agreed what an enviable old satyr Debussy had been.

When I mentioned contemporary women, he hid behind the ugly blotch on his cheek and I had to tread carefully. It was similar to being with a man who stuttered; the impulse to stutter oneself trembling on uncontrollable lips. In his case, my eyes always sought their way back to the disfigurement on his face.

I found him to be that most dangerous of all policemen: the dedicated, wifeless man with little else to do but pursue his ambition. A man to whom every criminal was a personal *bête noire*.

When I offered to pay for his meal, he said, 'No. When I arrest you I shall do so without strings.'

I admired him for that. 'And the charge?' I asked.

'You've knocked somebody off, Tallis,' he said affably. 'All I have to do is to find out *who*.'

I drained my wine, then refilled both glasses. 'You've been in the sun without a hat,' I derided him. Nevertheless, I remained uneasy. Ferrets hang on until something gives. Usually something vital like an artery.

It was nearly three before I let his growing impatience nag me into leaving the restaurant. The helicopter hadn't been stolen or pillaged and rested relatively cool in the shade of the cottonwood clump.

Strapping Sowerby in the passenger seat, I asked, 'You've been up before?'

'Only with a real pilot,' he said.

'If you feel sick—and I hope you do,' I said unkindly, 'stick your head out of the window and open your mouth.'

The rotor-blades turned slowly as I thumbed the button. Then the engine caught, banging out puffs of brown smoke a couple of times, the blades whistling as they accelerated through the hot, lifeless air. After I had finished the take-off drill, I lifted her up into the brassy sky like a blue and white skylark. At a thousand feet, I pirouetted her round on the rotors, aiming for the drift of light green foliage on the flank of

Painted Rock.

Hovering above the hunting lodge, I adjusted the controls to counteract the warm wind upthrusting from the side of the mountain. I was glad to see Sowerby's fingers were gripping the sides of his seat. I dropped the aircraft suddenly, causing him to jerk in startled fright. Then I held her, settling the undercarriage gently in the creosote bushes skirting the copse of aspens.

Sowerby scowled at me and jumped out. The door was already unlocked and I followed him into the lodge. 'You've been here before?' I said unnecessarily.

Inside, I saw the signs of a specialized, professional police search. A yellow crayon ring had been drawn on the door frame. The carpeting had been turned back and there were two similar markings on the floorboards near the spot Ingrid had lain. Each yellow circle enclosed a splintered bullet hole, the results of Mendoza's despairing shots.

Sowerby put his toe against one. 'Three bullet holes,' he drawled. 'Quite a party. You had a woman here.' He wasn't asking; he was saying.

'Yes,' I agreed, looking around. 'It's that sort of a place.'

'Mrs Hansson?'

'Yes.' I offered him a cigarette. He shook his head.

'You said you hadn't seen her after you left the hotel.'

'Gebhardt was so upset over my sexual *mores* at our first interview, I didn't want to add to his unhappiness.'

'You could buy yourself trouble telling lies.'

'*And* telling the truth.'

He bent and flung aside further carpeting. 'I took scrapings this morning. There were traces of blood in the cracks.'

'It could be anything. A jack rabbit; a mountain lion. Have you had it identified?'

'No,' he admitted. 'Our serologist's away today. But,' he said confidently, 'it'll be human all right, don't you worry.' He narrowed his eyes at me. 'You seem to move around in a sprinkling of bullet holes and spilt blood.'

'You've shown me all this. I can't explain—I don't have to explain—any of it.'

He gave it to me then; his saved-up *coup de main.* 'Where's Mrs Hansson? Eh?' He watched me closely. Seeking, I supposed, the sudden pallor of fear, the starting of sweat on the upper lip. 'What have you done with *her*?'

I hadn't expected this. He clearly suspected—and logically so—that I had killed Ingrid. 'She left in her car before I did.' Sweat trickled down the backs of my thighs.

'Her car?'

'Yes,' I said, irritable at being on the defensive. 'A big brown Pontiac. I don't know the number.'

'You asked her up here?'

'No. She asked me. And was already here when I came. She also obtained the use of the lodge.'

'From?'

'I don't know. It wouldn't have been nice to ask.'

'She's around here,' he said stubbornly, 'and I'm going to search until I find her.'

'Not in my time, you're not. I've seen what you've had to show and it means nothing. Now I want to go.'

'One more thing,' he pressed. He led the way out and through the shading aspens, halting below the cataract. 'It's a long way down that hole,' he said, 'but not too far for a man on a rope.'

A bronze lizard squatted on the hot rock at the hole's entrance, chewing patiently at a struggling beetle almost as big as itself.

'I'll take your word for it,' I said as disinterestedly as I could. He scared me with his efficiency. I couldn't afford to be arrested on suspicion of murdering Ingrid: waiting for Mendoza and Luigi to be found and hauled up by some eager speliologist. With no Ingrid to support me, I hadn't the best of answers to account for my bullets being in their bodies.

Sowerby touched the baking rock with his finger, frightening the lizard into gulping its beetle whole and darting away in panic. 'Scuff marks,' he said. 'Fresh ones.'

There are some policemen who can, by their sheer tenacity, transmute a suspect's blood to water and set it thundering through his dilated veins. Sowerby was such a one.

'I'm sorry,' I said. 'You seem to be trying to make a point I'm just not getting.' *Oh, Lord,* I thought, *but how I do get the point.*

'There'll be a team of experts up here later to turn the place over; to tear it apart.' He was deadly serious, dedicating intelligence and energy to exploiting his intuition and judgement.

'Isn't this Sheriff Seamark's territory?' I asked. 'And doesn't yours end at the city limits? Aren't you, in fact, sticking your nose in his business?'

'Murder is everybody's business.' Although he said it with confidence, I could sense I'd touched an exposed nerve. He hadn't yet cleared with the County authorities and the sheriff wasn't going to like it when he knew.

'Are you coming back with me?' I said shortly. 'Or are you walking?' I turned and made my way back to the helicopter, neither looking to see if he followed nor waiting for an answer.

He strapped himself in, not liking to concede the initiative to me. 'You're beginning to crack, fella,' he said with what must have been misguided optimism.

'I want to call in at the ranch-house,' I said. 'I need a change of clothing.'

The racketing of the engine shut off further conversation until I bounced the undercarriage on the crab grass lawn of the ranch in a hurricane of lashing palm fronds.

I kept the rotor turning and shouted at him, 'You coming in with me? I might crack at any moment!'

He unsnapped his lap belt and climbed out, not wanting me away from his sight if he could do something about it. He was becoming an embarrassing incubus.

I trimmed the controls to idling and fiddled in the First Aid Box before following. Unlocking and opening the door, I preceded him. What happened then was so quick there was no time for realization to enter his consciousness before the hissing spray of gas, aimed from only a foot or so, stunned and blinded him.

He whirled away from me, choking and falling to the floor, the heel of one palm pushing into his screwed-up eyes. His other hand snatched the gun from inside his jacket and he measured six unsighted shots in a wide arc. I was already face down on the carpet as glass tinkled from a holed window. Then he groaned, releasing the empty gun from nerveless fingers.

I stood and looked down at him. He was a policeman any department would be proud to own. He never stopped fighting, never compromised.

His handcuffs were in his hip-pocket and I clasped them around one wrist. I put my hands under his armpits and dragged him unresistingly out of the room and down wooden steps to the furnace cellar. He groaned once or twice as his heels banged on the steps but nothing more. I snapped the free handcuff to a stout iron pipe. He was still eyeless and snoring and gargling in his throat when I brought him down an uncorked bottle of wine and some opened tins of Newt's special fodder. I then secured the door on him, leaving the key in the lock.

After I had changed, I took off and landed the helicopter in Mohawk Creek. I dropped the backs of the seats and opened the windows. There was enough room on the makeshift bed for me to lie down and watch the fairweather cumuli sailing overhead.

Two hours later I awoke, transferred to the waiting Chevrolet and pointed its big bonnet in the direction of Shiloh City.

17

It was nine o'clock when I left the booming darkness of the air-conditioned cinema where I had killed time until the coming of night. The Chevrolet was an anonymous lump in rows of other anonymous lumps stacked in the airfield-sized car park.

I watched the car for a few minutes; looking for the silent, patient shadow that would be a police stake-out. When I was satisfied, I went to it. Before driving out, I took a screwdriver from the toolkit holdall and unscrewed the chromium rims and ruby lenses from the tail light nacelles. From their hollow interiors I untaped the polythene packets and transferred them to my pockets.

At the first drugstore I encountered, I used its telephone to call the Police Department, adopting my terrible version of a mid-Western accent to disguise my Englishness. 'I wanna speak to Lieutenant Sowerby,' I demanded. 'This is a friend of his. Joe Simmonds.'

There was a waiting period of muffled inquiry and the clicking of terminals. 'He isn't in, Mr Simmonds,' I was finally told. 'Would you leave a message?' One could gauge the importance of Sowerby in the Department by the respect accorded to his supposed friend.

I said, 'No thanks,' and closed down. It wasn't a very satisfactory check but the best I could do without going back to the ranch and seeing for myself.

A large paper-white disc of a moon kept station with me as I drove along the broad freeway out of the city. I pulled up in the livid green glow of blazing neons that told twenty miles of uncaring desert that here was sold 'Cut Rate Drugs & Liquor'.

I hunched on a wooden bar stool and drank bourbon whiskey, ignoring the truck-drivers and salesmen and the used-looking women they had with them. My thinking in the cinema had given birth to a conclusion that there was nothing for it now but to let events overtake me.

Without being consciously narcissistic, I examined myself in the mirror at the back of the bar. The cigarette in my mouth contrasted its whiteness against the sun-darkened skin of my face. The bruising was now yellow and fading into the tan. The fierce light of the desert had bleached my hair to the colour of tow. I wore a dark grey suit with a salmon-pink shirt and a maroon tie. Dressed for the kill, I thought wryly. I should be in black. The pistol was pressing awkwardly into my waist, reminding me how much I disliked all it stood for. I had had a sickening of guns.

I felt very alone and a little sorry for myself. Tonight was the culmination of my blundering interference and involvement with the affairs of the Syndicate. When I saw the bartender observing my quizzing myself in his mirror, I grinned self-consciously and ordered another whiskey. 'It's all right,' I said. 'I was wondering if a skin-graft would help.'

I had monitored my rear view mirrors on the way out without seeing anything to suggest Kezler or anyone else was having me followed. None of the occupants of the bar looked as if they cared for anything more important than alcohol and fornication.

Leaving the place, I surprised the bartender by giving him a five dollar tip. I felt I needed to propitiate the gods of good luck and fortune in any way I could.

Passing over the Gila River on the Phoenix road, I swung left to Painted Rock. The desert floor stretched silver and black before me as I drove slowly in third gear, the warm night wind blowing the smell of sage in through the open windows. Occasionally, a flying beetle cracked itself to death on the windscreen. When I left the freeway for the dirt road leading to the ranch, I saw Painted Rock rising in the background, a massive pyramid blotting out much of the metallic sky.

With nearly half-a-mile of road still to negotiate before reaching the ranch, the beams of my headlights pinned on to a long gleaming car with a seven-pointed star blazoned on its door. It was parked sideways on to my approach and blocked the road. I stamped hard on the brake pedal and sat there, my fists clenched on the steering-wheel rim, my pulse thumping in my ears.

Sheriff Seamark moved out into the moonlight from the cactus bordering the road. His thumbs were hooked in a polished gunbelt, his legs apart. His pale grey eyes were steady on me, the whites glinting in the black shadow cast by the brim of his hat.

He walked towards me, quietly like a grey cat. 'Well, son?' he said. 'I guess I've got to be all official this time.'

I swallowed, conscious of the heroin in my pockets, but said nothing.

'You were going to the ranch?' So close to me, I saw his khaki drill was crisp and neatly creased from recent pressing, the brim of his hat stiff.

'Yes.'

'Sorry, son. Keep your hands on the wheel nice and steady like.' He opened the door on my side of the car and pushed it back on its hinges. A gun was in his hand and pointed straight at me. He leaned forward, his pale eyes never leaving mine, patting my body with his free hand. He removed my pistol and pushed it behind his belt. When he found the packets, he said, 'Aagh!' with satisfaction, puffing out his moustache.

'Switch on the roof light, son,' he ordered. 'Very careful, so I don't misunderstand you.' Using the glow of the tiny bulb, he examined the packets and then put them in his breast pockets. There was a slight tremble in his hands.

'I was going to hand them over to a Federal Agent,' I said. 'A Narcotics Agent.'

He shook his head, his expression sad. 'I'm sorry, son. There never was any Agent.'

In the quiet that followed, I saw things in sharp focus: the silent, gliding moon and the small clouds dappling the sky; the spidery cacti with their uplifted whiskered arms throwing an inky-black latticework of shadows. I saw, too, the sheriff's glittering eyes above the bony nose and Edwardian moustache.

'I never thought there was,' I said at last. 'I laid it on for Kezler to produce the right man. The city Paymaster in person.'

He thinned his lips behind the moustache. 'Out,' he said, 'and do it slowly.'

All around me were the stealthy sounds of things hunting and being hunted. A coyote howled at the moon somewhere near Painted Rock. It sounded the same coyote I heard the night I buried Gost and I didn't like it. When I was standing outside the car, I said, 'What now? Are you going to shoot me in the back?'

'Don't irritate me, son.'

'And do you irritate because you aren't so smart, Sheriff?' I prodded at his vanity. There was only so much future for me as I could squeeze from time by talking. And being listened to. 'You didn't fool me. I took safeguards before I came here tonight. I've a colleague, a friend . . .'

'Not *here* you haven't, son. Nor over at the ranch either. I've been staking it out since sundown. Nobody—nothing— moves on the desert but I know it.'

'There's always before sundown, Sheriff. Just ask yourself; would I walk wide-eyed into a trap like this?'

He gave me a thin smile. 'Conversely, son, would I? So maybe, maybe not. But none of it won't help you. The first sign of anybody hornin' in and I'll drop you. Killed resisting arrest, it'll be. Then I fire your pistol afterwards. Who's to prove which was popped off first? Tell me,' he said. 'How come you think you were so smart?'

'Mrs Hansson for a start. When I left her at the ranch she was scared. She wouldn't have opened the door or left peaceably with anybody she didn't know or trust. You were the only one she'd met since our arrival.'

'That isn't much. You're guessing, son.'

'I am. I'm also guessing a lot of other things. How you knew my name and the number of my helicopter. Good, penetrating work for a county sheriff who doesn't have any "in" with the Police Department. I'll guess you got both from Mrs Hansson. And talking of the Police Department. An honest sheriff doesn't work against it like you did. He might not co-operate, but he doesn't fight it. Covering up for a killing; aiding some-one you knew, or guessed, to be a fugitive.'

'Go on, son.' His eyes were chips of obsidian.

'Your two gangster friends, Mendoza and Zacchio. How would they know I was at the lodge if you hadn't told them? Who else in Shiloh knew but you? Then the delivery of that letter and the search of the ranch-house. Sowerby just isn't the type. He lives by the rule book.' I lifted my hands, palm outwards. 'Can I smoke?'

'One of mine.' He used his spare hand to dig out his case, juggling to light a cigarette and tossing it at my feet. He thumbed back the firing pin of his gun. It cocked with a well-oiled click. 'Careful does it,' he warned me. 'Don't be brave. I wouldn't miss at this range.'

The muzzle followed my head down as I stooped and picked up the cigarette. It stayed on me until I had straightened. The smoke I blew out was silver floss in the moonlight. 'You planted that pathetic little drug addict on me and tipped off Sowerby,' I said. 'At first I thought he was in on it.' I let him see the dislike in my face. 'He couldn't be. It needs the kind of dirty unscrupulousness he wouldn't have.'

'I didn't know she was going to be killed, son.' He really wanted me to believe that.

'Perhaps not, but it's something I'll never forgive you for.'

His finger was bone-white on the trigger. He nearly pulled it but he wanted to know more.

I continued. 'You knew the man who shot her was Mrs Hansson's husband. *That* needed a special kind of knowledge, Sheriff. The kind you could only get from me or Mrs Hansson. You wanted me locked up, of course?'

'You were becoming a nuisance, son. I had to find the camera.'

'So you found it.'

He wagged his head sorrowfully. 'You got me in bad. We weren't even sure of Mrs Hansson after that.'

' "We" being you and Kezler, I suppose?'

He didn't answer that.

'You tried to shoot me on Painted Rock?'

'Yes. Things were piling up. Mendoza and Zacchio hadn't done their job. I decided to cut our losses.' He lowered his eyebrows. 'Just between you and me, son, what did you do with them?'

'I didn't do anything. I thought they went off with Mrs Hansson after the scorpion business. Kezler told you of that?'

He nodded. 'But I ain't so gullible.' The muzzle of the gun dropped to my chest for the killing shot. 'Who are you, son?'

The coyote was howling again and I swallowed, my mouth dry. Against the fact of the aimed gun with its chambered bullet waiting quietly for the firing pin, Charlie's Bar seemed suddenly a far-away, pitiful masquerade of bungling amateurs. I had left the main beams of the Chevrolet on as a guide, but the thickness of brush and cacti and the brightness of the moon militated against their being seen. Moths were using them to dance in and that was probably all the use they were. If Seamark was right and we *were* alone in the desert, I was seconds from being dead. His eyes were too steady, his manner too competent, not to be able to kill me before I could do more than flinch.

He repeated softly, 'Who are you, son? A snitch? A cop on the make?'

'You'll know when they drop that gas pellet under your nose in the death chamber,' I said. 'I've written it all down . . .'

The gun had dropped its muzzle slightly and now he brought it up again. 'Just a minute,' I said desperately. 'You remember at the ranch? When I was grinding coffee? Well, I also ground up some sugar. That's what you've got in your pockets.'

His eyes flickered his dismay. He pulled out one of the little bags and tore off a corner with his teeth. He moved to the bonnet of the Chevrolet and dribbled a few grains on its surface. His gun remained fixed on me. Putting the bag back, he moistened the pad of his small finger and dabbed it in the powder. Then he licked the grains, tasting cautiously, spitting them out hastily and smacking his lips. 'I reckon that was a lie, son. Now I've got to kill you. I'm sorry, but I've got orders.'

I dropped the cigarette butt, tensing my mind and muscles for a despairing leap at him. He was only ten feet away but I would need more than luck. 'You're not even your own man,' I sneered. 'Just Kezler's tame jackal.'

I thought he was going to shoot me then and there but he still hesitated. His teeth were showing in a baleful glare. 'I can hit you in the belly where it'll hurt, son, so don't rile me.' He tapped his fingernail on his breast pocket. 'Who else do you reckon knows?'

'Gebhardt,' I said, 'He'll nail you. He doesn't think much of you at any time.' I could sense he was reluctant to shoot me; that he was screwing up his resolution to do so.

He spat once more, a small glistening globule that buried itself in the silver dust. 'You're lyin' again,' he said. 'He tried mighty hard to grill it out of you, but didn't. There isn't anything Gebhardt can do to help you.'

A dark shape moved behind him and my heart leapt in an agony of hope. In the confusing complex of moonlight and shadows, I could distinguish the dim white points of a shirt collar and the paleness of cheeks and forehead. There seemed to be no chin.

I released my breath and called out. 'Is that the good ol' United States cavalry galloping to the rescue?'

'It sure is, partner,' the shape answered in a broad and phoney Texas drawl. There was a sharp click of a thumbed-back firing pin. 'All ready to come a-shootin'.'

The sheriff's jawbone muscles twitched and he hunched his shoulders. His face slowly went grey, his breath rasping in a tightened throat.

'The friend I was talking about, Sheriff,' I said gently. 'Mister O'Brien.'

'Agent O'Brien,' the voice corrected me, 'of the Federal Bureau of Narcotics. With a gun in his hand,' it warned, with no trace of a southern accent. 'Drop it, Seamark, and do it smartly.'

The sheriff's eyes never left mine but he spoke to the man behind him. 'No. You'll have to kill me.'

'I will,' O'Brien promised grimly. There was a finality in the words that chilled me.

'I'm the Sheriff of Caliente County makin' a lawful arrest . . .'

'You are a murderous thug and a disgrace to the badge you wear,' O'Brien said frostily. He was another such as Sowerby: no forgiveness, not much understanding and living in a landscape implacably coloured black and white. You were either a bastard or a saint. 'If you move, I'll shoot your backbone out.'

'What about it, son?' Seamark asked me. 'What if I take you with me? You that caused all this ruckus.'

'It isn't in you, Sheriff,' I said. 'You were taking too long making up your mind about it.'

'Don't bank on it,' he said.

'You told me yesterday about a female getting her tits caught up in a wringer. Why don't *you* give a bit,' I urged. I was feeling sorry for him.

'You know what's at the end of it, son? Thirty years in a stinkin', rotten State Prison with scum I've helped put there. They'd bury me alive in the exercise yard inside a month.'

One of O'Brien's shoes moved a pebble. 'No nearer,'

Seamark warned over his shoulder. He still hadn't looked round. To me, he said, 'Move away, son.' He jerked the nose of the gun.

I backed away to the rear of the Chevrolet. I felt suffocatingly, horribly apprehensive as a man might in watching the preliminaries to an execution. I could almost smell the blood in the warm night air, the crawling in my spine telling me I could still be Jack-in-the-middle.

O'Brien's body remained in the shadows but moonlight struck on his hand and on the .38 Police Positive he held in it.

The sheriff's weapon was a long-barrelled .45, capable of knocking a heavy man off his feet. He spoke at last to O'Brien. 'Let me turn round and we'll shoot it out, man to man.' He was acting out Wyatt Earp, going back eighty years to Dodge City. I was glad he hadn't made the offer to me. I would have been fool enough to have taken it.

'Drop your gun,' O'Brien snapped.

When the sheriff whipped round, it was with the smooth speed of a striking rattlesnake. Yet, O'Brien's were the faster reflexes. His bullet hit Seamark in the rib-cage before the big .45 exploded aimlessly, the slug hitting sploshy green slivers from the cactus above O'Brien's head.

The sheriff, on his back, his staring eyes slowly closing, was dead. Lying there, he reminded me poignantly of my own dead father. There had been something between us. Perhaps it was that. Ironically, the bullet had penetrated his breast pocket. The spilled white powder mixed with the blood seeping through.

O'Brien walked out into the light. He was replacing the expended bullet in the chamber. 'This isn't the ranch,' he said without preamble. 'You made me walk miles in this goddamned wilderness.'

'He jumped me. He was a shrewd old bird.' I lit a cigarette with shaking hands, hoping O'Brien wouldn't notice. 'You saw my lights?'

'Yeah.' He scratched his beard with a thumbnail. He didn't act as if he'd just killed a man. Perhaps he did it every other night and indifference came with practice. 'Like they say, I only just made it.'

'You heard enough?'

'Enough to want to have a go at Kezler straight away.'

'We'd better get back to the ranch first,' I said. 'There's a certain Lieutenant Sowerby handcuffed to a boiler pipe and locked in a cellar. No doubt getting madder by the hour.'

18

Two hours after a city ambulance had collected Seamark's body, my hand was being shaken by Chief Gebhardt in his office. He was anxiously concerned I should believe in his good will; pushing cigars and a whisky bottle at me as evidence of it.

Even the Dobermann Pinscher had been instructed not to growl at me.

Sowerby and O'Brien sat with us. The lieutenant, watery-eyed, had one wrist skinned and raw from his efforts to slip the handcuff.

'I'm sorry,' Gebhardt was saying, 'about the hamming I did: the pushing around I gave you.' Now solidly on my side, he seemed less physically gross, his drab eyes warmer. He still smelled of sweat and cigar smoke. 'When you were first brought in, I took you for one of Kezler's runners. So I reacted as you'd guess I would. Then O'Brien comes here and tells me you are working undercover and the brightest white there is. Then I've got to treat you like a punk so's you'll fall ass-over-tit in Kezler's direction.' He smiled toothily round his cigar. 'And I did. I should've been in the movies.'

'Yes,' I agreed, 'a Wallace Beery type. You did a good job of convincing me. Until I read the teletype in your basket, that is. The one that *didn't* say I should be deported for illegal entry.'

He looked crestfallen. 'You read it? A pity. I thought it was a bit of quick thinking on my part. I wanted to screw you into the right mood for Kezler. He was the guy I wanted. I had to make him believe you might start talking to me. You cottoned on he was mighty anxious to get you away? To shut you up?'

'He overdid it. Like the sheriff. Nobody loves you that much without they want something out of it. That's when I began to slot things into place. I reckoned if he was bent you must, as a corollary, be honest. Only then did it start to make sense.' I kept my face wooden. 'The only one who wouldn't fit in was Sowerby. He kept on chasing me into the ground.'

Gebhardt cleared his throat. 'The trouble was—still is—the Department is infiltrated by the Syndicate.' He was avoiding

Sowerby's hard stare. 'I didn't know who was the Mayor's bag-carrier and who wasn't.'

'You could have trusted me, Chief,' Sowerby said shortly, a dull red flush creeping up from behind his shirt collar.

'I could have,' Gebhardt admitted. 'On the other hand, it could have been an unjustified risk with men's lives at stake. Accepting you weren't the bagman—which I know now you aren't—still don't make a secret shared worth half as much as one you keep under your vest. If Kezler even suspected I was gunning for him, I'd have been out on my ass on some fix or another. Tallis here,' he waved his cigar at me, 'could've got himself knocked off.' He shook his head. 'No, I reckon I played it the right way.'

He grimaced at his dour lieutenant. 'Poor Sowerby's flipping his lid, naturally. He had you lined up for the death chamber in the State Pen.' He dug his toe in the Dobermann Pinscher's ribs and guffawed. 'It's like taking a steak away from Judy here.'

'I'm sorry about the gas, Sowerby,' I said civilly, 'but I had to get you off my back. No ill effects?'

He managed a tight, ferrety smile. 'It's O.K. fella,' he said. 'I enjoyed the wine.'

I wasn't off his hook yet. I could only hope Mendoza and Luigi had drifted to the bottom of a deep, impenetrable subterranean sea. True, neither of the two policemen seemed overly concerned about any tidying up of the facts. Gost had not been mentioned at all. I hoped they were not just being polite.

'What about Kezler?' I asked.

Gebhardt said, 'The son-of-a-bitch has to come. Sowerby and O'Brien'll pull him in tonight.' He hefted a big silver watch from a pocket and read the time. 'Seamark's in the morgue with his big toes tied together. Nobody has to bother to tell Kezler he's dead. Let him sweat on his return with the junk for another hour. It can't do him anything but harm. Pull one brick out of a wall and sometimes the house falls down.'

'And behind Kezler?'

He pulled irritably at his bottom lip. 'One thing at a time. There's a Kezler, a Seamark, in every goddamned State. Perhaps in every city. I'm only concerned with the baby on my own porch.'

I looked at Sowerby. 'Are you happy I didn't murder Mrs Hansson?'

O'Brien intervened. 'Are *you* happy, period,' he said to me.

'She got away?' I cleared a suddenly dry throat.

'She was lifted at Phoenix.' He was needling me by being cryptic.

Apprehension was a leaden weight in my chest. 'At least Sowerby now knows I didn't kill her.'

'It's just as well you didn't,' he said dryly. 'She works for the B.D.A.C.' His liver-brown eyes watched me closely. I didn't think he liked Englishmen; certain he didn't like me.

'The *what*!' I was stunned at the unexpectedness of his bombshell and reacted slowly.

'The Bureau of Drug Abuse Control. It's a department of the Food and Drug Administration.'

There was a silence in which the Dobermann Pinscher's stomach could be heard working on her last meal. Then I flared angrily. 'Christ! I could have got her killed! Where's the liaison? Why didn't you tell me?'

His beard bristled. 'Because I didn't know,' he snapped. 'Not until today.' He pulled himself together. 'The B.D.A.C. recruited her in Sweden. Not us. Her marriage had all but folded and she found—in addition to his womanizing—her husband was in the narcotics business. She wasn't too difficult to sign up after that. The Gothenburg Narcotics Squad knew all about Gost and together they pulled the rug out from under him by feeding in rumours to the Syndicate. The simplest, easiest one was that he had been spotted as a runner by the authorities and tabbed for an early grab. The Syndicate didn't want to know him after that. Anyway, by substituting his wife, it dropped into the trap. After she'd penetrated, she acted completely under the control of B.D.A.C. She did a couple of minor trips; both arranged to be successful, of course. This last was her big one. Designed to catch New York's biggest Paymaster.' He was sarcastic. 'Why should they know of the Federal Bureau of Narcotics? Or, for that matter, your outfit either. So, nobody told anybody anything.'

'I feel bad about it,' I growled, pouring myself a gluttonous measure of whisky. My hands were shaking again. 'I said some unforgivable things.'

'Don't get yourself in a lather,' he said offhandedly. 'She knew what she was doing. If you snarled things up for her, you did so in the line of duty. She was after the Syndicate too,' he reminded me. 'You just got in each other's way.'

'She wanted to go to New York.'

O'Brien was patient with me. 'Sure,' he said, 'but it didn't really matter that you bollixed it up. Like Chief Gebhardt says, there's a Syndicate member under every stone you look at. When she landed up in L.A. she telephoned the New York Syndicate contact and was passed on to Seamark. All she had to do was to hand the stuff over.'

'She failed,' I pointed out. 'Largely because of me. It isn't likely to help her with her own office. Not turning up with bags of sugar instead of heroin. And with nothing but bruises to show for it.' I swore bitterly. 'I made her look a fool.'

'She's being pulled out, yes. But not finished. They can't expect a hit every time. Especially not when its loused up by a limey plant she doesn't know about.'

I regarded him thoughtfully, wondering whether I'd ever be able to rationalize myself into hitting him smack in his beard and deciding I wouldn't. I said, 'She knows about me?'

'Yes. I thought it best. She was concerned for your safety.'

'Can I see her?'

'She's taking off for San Francisco from Sky Harbor on the noon flight tomorrow. I don't suppose anybody could stop you even if they wanted to.'

On the way out, he came with me, his politeness overriding his dislike. 'Tell me one thing,' I said. 'Why give me the chop in L.A.?'

He looked at my neck as if he'd like another go. 'That was embarrassing,' he said. 'I was with an agent who wouldn't know Charlie's Bar from a horse's ass. You were on the point of snarling me up as well. Just for keeping tabs on you. It was lucky you didn't, mack. That sheriff would sure have planted you in the desert without my having been there to back you up.'

Which was probably true. I would leave Shiloh now with O'Brien setting his sights on a doomed Kezler. And Sowerby, when Gebhardt let him, gnawing away at the connection between the blood on the seat of the Chevrolet, the bullet holes in the lodge and the convenient fissure beneath the cataract. When he found it, I hoped to be eight-thousand miles away in an easterly direction and unfindable.

Rain clouds were boiling up from behind the mountains and obscuring the moon and stars as I drove back to the ranch. Ghostly balls of tumbleweed bounded through the cacti and cottonwoods in the rising wind, leaping the road through the beams of my headlamps.

I was miserable with a belly uncomfortably full of whisky and chicken sandwiches. When I wasn't worrying over Ingrid, I was thinking of Sheriff Seamark and regretting he had to be such a nice, fatherly rascal.

I wasn't drunk: only just wishing I was.

*

I watched Ingrid sitting in the Sky Harbor passenger concourse for some minutes before approaching her. She wore a peacock-blue dress with a floppy hat shielding her pale bruised face. She smoked a cigarette in her long holder, as alone among the milling passengers as she had been in the Malaga hotel. She was withdrawn and deep in a Swedish blackness of the spirit, an unread book on her lap.

Above us, heavy rain drummed on the curved roof. Aircraft, taxiing outside on the puddled concrete strips, gleamed like wet fish in the lancing water.

When I stood before her she looked up at me, her holder between stiff fingers, her eyes wide with surprise. 'Roger!' she exclaimed and stood, the book falling to the ground. She gave me a tentative smile.

'I'm so sorry, Ingrid,' I said. We had started our association with my apologizing. 'I rather mucked things up for you.'

'Yes,' she said, waiting.

We stood in an enclosing, muffling glass bowl of mutual awareness. The babble of tongues and booming of loudspeaker announcements were muted. The howling screams of jets taking off came from the other side of the universe.

I wanted to touch her face gently with my fingers and make her happy. But I knew, starkly, that the gulf dividing us was real and unbridgeable. We were no longer each acting a part, secure in the illusion of the deception we wove around our emotions. What we each had now was a consciousness of ourselves as we really were. And neither of us liked it very much. Abruptly, instead of failed lover and mistress, we were brother and sister; fellow conspirators and guilty protagonists in an incestuous union.

'Your face? It's all right?' I asked. 'No bones broken?'

She touched her cheekbone with a gloved fingertip. 'It is all right. You are better from the scorpion?'

'Yes. I think the scorpion died though.' That was no good. It was joking at a funeral. 'Is there anything I can do?'

'No,' she said. 'It will be all right.'

I couldn't even say, '*What I said . . . what happened . . . I meant.*' I didn't know whether I had meant it or not. We had both lived and acted out our lies. Which was the real 'us'? Although I still saw in her the pride of a Coptic priestess, I saw also the final abject defeatism in her last hours at the lodge. And between us, as solid as a sheet of plate-glass, lay the bloody shadow of her dead husband.

'I came to say "goodbye".' It was out of me at last.

She put her hand in mine, her eyes sad and melancholy. 'Goodbye, Roger.'

We stood a long time in baffled silence until she released her fingers and I walked out of the concourse, not looking back. I trudged in the pouring rain until my clothing was dark and my hair stuck spikily to my forehead. When I knew her plane had gone, I returned to my car and left the airport.

*

I flew back over the Palamos Plain through the towering aerial canyons of clouds, the shadow of my helicopter a tiny dancing midge in the patches of yellow sunshine on the desert beneath.

Skimming the surface of the Gila River, I opened the window and dropped my pistol and spare shells into it. The firearm held for me all the grisliness of a blood-stained knife and I was glad to be rid of it.

Two hours after reaching Los Angeles and booking in at the Biltmore Hotel I had bathed, shaved and changed into a formal suit. The need to forget Ingrid was paramount. Without dining, I crossed the street to the salon employing the surly ex-pug bartender. He was still there, looking as if in the meantime he had lost a couple of fights and several hundreds of dollars.

Although it was early evening, the bar was crowded. I ordered a whisky and what the bartender reluctantly identified as a Blood-on-the-Rocks and occupied a small vacant table.

I had replenished my glass twice when she came in, the diamonds glittering below her ears and still very, very edible indeed. When she saw me in the crush and noted the tall glass of raspberry syrup and mint shrubbery I had on the table, she came across to me.

She was clean and pink and wholesome and so much more of a catharsis than alcohol and tranquillizers. She wouldn't want me to fall in love with her and there was no danger that I would.

As with using guns, I'd had a bellyful of falling in love.